Advance Praise for *The Audrey Hepburn Estate*

"A complex family tale of love and deception. Brenda Janowitz always delivers delightfully complicated stories that leave me with tears in my eyes and hope in my heart!"

—KRISTIN HARMEL, *New York Times* **bestselling author of** *The Book of Lost Names*

"Janowitz adeptly crafts a tale that is sentimental yet enigmatic, and readers will find themselves engrossed by this absolute treat of a book."

—PAM JENOFF, *New York Times* **bestselling author of** *Code Name Sapphire*

"Brenda Janowitz strikes again! Fast-paced, emotional, and unputdownable."

—LISA BARR, *New York Times* **bestselling author of** *Woman on Fire*

"*The Audrey Hepburn Estate* is as charming and elegant as Miss Hepburn herself and, also like Audrey, hides a huge heart."

—JENNA BLUM, *New York Times* **bestselling author of** *The Lost Family*

Praise for *The Grace Kelly Dress*

"Exactly the type of book I love: charming, smart, and brimming with heart."

—EMILY GIFFIN, #1 *New York Times* **bestselling author of** *All We Ever Wanted*

"A charming, heartfelt novel. Fast paced and entertaining from beginning to end."

—KRISTIN HANNAH, #1 *New York Times* **bestselling author of** *The Nightingale*

"A poignant and delicious novel about how family can lovingly reinvent itself."

—LAURA DAVE, #1 *New York Times* **bestselling author of** *The Last Thing He Told Me*

Also by Brenda Janowitz

The Liz Taylor Ring
The Grace Kelly Dress
The Dinner Party
Recipe for a Happy Life
The Lonely Hearts Club
Jack with a Twist
Scot on the Rocks

The
AUDREY HEPBURN ESTATE

A NOVEL

BRENDA JANOWITZ

GRAYDON
HOUSE

GRAYDON
HOUSE®

ISBN-13: 978-1-525-81148-7

The Audrey Hepburn Estate

Graydon House
22 Adelaide St. West, 41st Floor
Toronto, Ontario M5H 4E3, Canada
www.GraydonHouseBooks.com
www.BookClubbish.com

Printed in U.S.A.

To Doug, Ben and Davey. You are my home.

The

AUDREY
HEPBURN
ESTATE

"To plant a garden is to believe in tomorrow."

—Audrey Hepburn

PART ONE:
FOUNDATION

1

Now

They say lots of things about going home. Home is where the heart is. There's no place like home.

You can never go home again.

But Emma Jansen was, in fact, going home again. Well, not home, exactly, because the place she grew up wasn't really hers, never really belonged to her.

Still, she had lived there. She had lived there and loved there and had a life there. And that meant something to her.

The train slid into the station at Glen Cove three minutes late. Every time she walked off the train at the Glen Cove station, she imagined herself as Audrey Hepburn, in that scene from *Sabrina*. She would simply walk to the curb and the dashing David Larrabee would drive up, as if on cue, in his Nash Healey Spider.

Was that why she hadn't taken one of the catering vans out to Long Island? An attempt to live out the plot of one of her favorite childhood movies? She'd watched and rewatched

Sabrina so many times with her father as a kid that she had practically every line, every scene memorized. Sabrina may have been a chef, like Emma was now, but Sabrina Fairchild certainly did not drive around in a catering van like Emma Jansen usually did.

Emma walked to the cab stand. No David Larrabee in sight. She adjusted her tote bag on her shoulder as she got in line for a taxi. Moments later, she was in the back of a cab, windows down.

"First time in Glen Cove?" the driver asked when she told him the address.

"No, I grew up here," she said, forcing a smile as she looked out the open window.

In the city, thirty-two-year-old Emma usually took the subway. She hated when cabdrivers tried to make conversation. She never knew what to say. She chastised herself for not ordering a rideshare. At least with the press of a button she could request a quiet ride.

It wasn't that Emma was unkind. She simply wasn't good at small talk. Emma usually jumped right to the big talk.

"In that case, welcome home," the cabdriver said, his smile as wide as the length of Long Island.

Emma didn't know how to respond.

The longer they drove through Glen Cove, the larger the houses became. When they drove up to the address Emma had given him, it looked like an abandoned parcel, not the formerly grand estate it once was: Rolling Hill. A huge construction gate circled the property, with a small opening off the main road.

"This it?" the cabdriver asked. A tiny sign on the gate read, Sales Center, with an arrow directing cars to drive through.

"Yes," Emma said, staring out the window up the long,

sweeping driveway. Even in its disarray, she'd know this place anywhere. "That's it."

As they pulled up the drive, Emma felt as if she were in a dream. The sort of dream where you know exactly where you are, but everything is different somehow. The property seemed smaller than she'd remembered. Was that because now, as an adult, she was bigger herself? Or had her mind made things grander in her memory, made every pathway wider, made every structure more imposing?

The estate was in shambles. The grass was brown, dried-up, all over. The bricks on the main driveway were falling apart, breaking away at the edges in some spots, completely missing in others. Gone were the beautiful rows of boxwood shrubs, lined up neatly with nary a leaf out of place, that Linwood would tend to with care. He would spend hours each day meticulously cutting back the greenery, making sure the garden looked polished, manicured. But now there were no flowers in sight, no hydrangea bushes or peonies. Things that made the estate look alive, happy. Lived-in.

It looked abandoned. Which was what it was, really. When the family left, it had been bought by a real estate developer who'd planned to flip the house and the property. But then the recession hit, and there were no buyers for the house and its surrounding eight acres. It soon went into foreclosure and sat empty for years. As the estate deteriorated, it became harder and harder to sell, because even though the property had value, it was a fixer-upper. The amount of money it would take to get the estate back to its former glory seemed infinite. No other developer would touch it.

Until now.

The cab drove past the main house. Emma squinted—surely that wasn't it. The house she knew was stately, and stood proudly among the tall pine trees. One of the pines had fallen over and had taken permanent residence in the left wing of the house, in what used to be the formal living room. The rest of the house hadn't fared much better: the Juliet balconies on the front windows were in various stages of disrepair, and there were broken windows throughout the first floor. The grand lighting fixture that used to hang under the porte co-chere was missing, and Emma noticed some faint spray paint marks across the front door.

The house wasn't her house anymore. It had been damaged and vandalized. It wasn't cared for, loved, like in its heyday. Emma felt it in the pit of her belly. Coming back had been a mistake.

"Up here?" the cabdriver asked, stopping at a clearing with a lonely construction trailer standing in the middle. A few luxury cars—one Mercedes and two BMWs—were parked in front. There was a small sign next to the door marked Sales Center.

"Thank you," Emma said, and paid the driver.

She stepped out of the cab and took a deep breath. Whenever she'd come home, the smell of the pine trees would always calm Emma down. She'd forgotten that, the way the pine trees greeted you. The smell of the place was such a huge part of her memory. Walking into the kitchen, the warm perfume of roasted garlic, fresh rosemary, and bread baking in the oven. Every spring, the faint smell of the lilacs, which would tell her that summer was coming. When the lilacs bloomed, they'd sleep with the windows open, the lovely scent seeping into her dreams, making them sweet. Even the back shed, which housed the bikes, had a particular aroma. Dirt and sweat and nectar. It smelled like an adventure to come.

But Emma didn't smell anything wonderful like that as she walked toward the Sales Center. It smelled like construction, which she supposed made sense, since the estate was now a construction site, but the notes of wood being torn down, dust lingering in the air, and gasoline from the massive construction vehicles didn't soothe her the way the pines used to. It only brought on an allergy attack.

"Are you here for the tour?" a kind voice asked. A woman opened the door to the trailer as Emma approached, sneezing.

Emma tried to say yes as she crossed the threshold, but another sneeze escaped. "Excuse me," Emma said.

"Looks like you could use one of these," the woman said, offering Emma a napkin and a bottle of water. The water had a printed label, dark gray with the word *Hepburn* in white block letters.

"Thank you," Emma said. She took a sip of water and then turned the water bottle over in her hands, examining the label.

"The presentation's about to begin," the woman said with a wide smile as she walked into the Sales Center. Emma followed her lead.

The inside of the trailer didn't match the outside. From the outside, it looked worn down, beaten up. But inside was another story entirely. Decked out in rich carpeting overlaid with thick rugs, and tasteful wallpaper and crown molding, it didn't feel like you were inside a trailer. It was bigger, too. Emma would later find out that it was actually two construction trailers combined to create the elegant Sales Center she was standing in.

Emma followed the woman to the center of the trailer, where they had a graceful living room set up. A chocolate-brown leather couch, distressed in all the right places so as to denote "lived-in." Two oversize rattan armchairs, with cushions in the same fabric as the pillows on the couch. A large tufted ottoman made of a rich brown velvet, with an enormous rattan tray placed just so. A dark red rug was laid down on the floor to delineate the space. And it worked. Emma truly felt as if she were in someone's warm living room, and not in a construction trailer. The attention to detail was impressive—small vases filled with flowers were scattered about, a coffee and tea station had been set up toward the back, and the tiny windows all had big window treatments, giving the illusion that they were larger.

The couches and chairs were already filled with people, so Emma stood behind the oversize leather couch.

A man walked out from the back of the trailer. When he saw her, he smiled. "Well, I'll be."

Emma directed her eyes down toward the plush rug, suddenly embarrassed. She wished she'd checked her appearance before walking in. She was probably disheveled from the train ride, from the allergy attack. And here he stood, looking expensive in his custom-made sport coat and designer jeans. His look now was so different from the way she remembered him as a child—messy, always with filthy knees from playing in the dirt. It was different from the last time she'd seen him, a mere seven years ago.

She wondered what he thought when he looked at her.

"I'd like to welcome you all to Hepburn," he said, throwing his arms out wide. It wasn't only his appearance that was more polished, Emma thought. It was his whole manner. It was soft, silky smooth. "What we're building here is a new community, one we hope you'll want to be a part of."

The woman who'd greeted Emma at the door now passed around glossy brochures.

"Hepburn is so called because you are standing on a piece of history. And I don't say that just because it's where I grew up." He paused for laughter. Most of the people laughed. Everyone, in fact, except for Emma. She narrowed her eyes, examined every square inch of his face. "This estate, throughout my childhood, was lovingly known as the Audrey Hepburn Estate."

"They filmed *Sabrina* here, didn't they?" a woman seated on the brown leather couch asked. "I knew it looked familiar!"

"Good eye," he said, flashing a warm smile. Emma looked down at his hands: no wedding ring. "This estate was the inspiration for the Billy Wilder picture, *Sabrina*. Originally built in 1899, neighbors took to calling it the Audrey Hepburn Estate soon after the release of the film."

Wrong, Emma thought. That was wrong, and he knew it. She didn't know what to tackle first—the snooty way he was calling a movie a *picture* as if he were a Hollywood executive, circa 1950, or the fact that he was perpetrating a lie. But that lie, she supposed, was the reason all this was happening. He was tearing down the estate and creating an entire new world in its place. A world filled with very small, very expensive condos. A luxury apartment building and a bunch of town houses. He justified the price with this story that the estate was the inspiration for the Audrey Hepburn film *Sabrina*. He was leaning into it—the brochure had photographs of the indoor tennis court, and the caption referenced the scene in the movie where Audrey Hepburn waits for William Holden, only to be surprised by the appearance of Humphrey Bogart instead. Hell, he was calling the place Hepburn.

Truth was, they called it the Audrey Hepburn Estate because it shared an address with the Larrabee estate in the movie. Dosoris Lane. Sometimes the owners said that the estate was supposed to have been used in the film, but ultimately wasn't because of studio red tape, and sometimes they said that the property had merely been the *inspiration* for the Larrabee estate in the film.

Even though they filmed parts of the movie in Glen Cove (hello, Glen Cove train station!), the place where Emma grew up was not one of them. Hill Grove, the home of George Lewis in Beverly Hills, was used for filming.

But none of this really mattered, because now he was tearing it all down.

Emma had needed to see it one more time.

"Will we get a tour of the main house?" Emma asked, casually flipping through the brochure. The pictures of the main house weren't real—it took a minute to figure out, but they were computer-generated images from old photographs. Emma marveled at how true to life they looked. She looked away for a moment, trying to picture the real house in her mind's eye.

"We hadn't planned to do that," he replied with a wide smile. "It's fallen into disrepair, and we wouldn't want anyone to get hurt."

"Or is it," Emma challenged, "because you wouldn't want anyone to know that it's haunted?"

The guests on the couch all gasped, but he didn't even flinch. He laughed a deep, throaty laugh, very unlike the many belly laughs they'd shared as kids. This was a grownup man's laugh, not a child's. This was a rich person's laugh. This was a patronizing laugh. "The house is not haunted. Simply another bit of old folklore about the estate. We can't go in because, among other things, an enormous pine tree is in the middle of the living room. And a family of squirrels have made themselves quite at home inside."

"So this has nothing to do with the summer the chef died?" Emma said. "Who haunts the house to this day?"

A woman sitting on the couch squealed with delight. "Is that true?" she asked, her eyes searching.

"It's not true," he said, rubbing his eye carefully with his pointer finger. He rearranged his face into a broad smile. "Of course that's not true."

"The house is haunted," Emma said, staring him down. "You know it, and I know it."

"Oh, did you grow up here, too?" the woman on the couch asked. She had swiveled her body around and now had all of her focus on Emma. "Are you a van der Wraak?"

"No," Emma said, adjusting her shoulders so that she stood up straight. "My mother was the maid."

2

Then

Age five

They were raised like siblings. Emma and Henry. Henry and
Emma.

They were inseparable. Best friends. Two peas in a pod.
Not equals, because Henry was the grandson of the owners
of the house and Emma was the daughter of the woman who
worked there, but they wouldn't be able to see these differ-
ences until they were older. Until the world pointed them out.

They were the only children in a house filled with adults.
There were the van der Wraaks, of course, Felix and Agnes,
and then there was an entire staff that tended to them. A
driver, and a chef, and a gardener, and a groundskeeper, and
a house manager. There were nannies and tutors for the kids.
And security. There was a team of five, charged with the
safety of the family and the grounds. Emma's parents, Mila
and Hans, were the maid and the butler.

Felix and Agnes van der Wraak: born and raised in Holland,
came to America after the war. They arrived with only a few

pennies in their pockets, but quickly remedied that. Felix was an art dealer, and worked with the most priceless of pieces. There was only one rule that Emma and Henry needed to obey in this house full of adults, and that was to keep away from Felix's study, where he would temporarily store Rembrandts and van Goghs and Vermeers and Renoirs and Klimts.

Mila was known for her wide smile that could brighten anyone's day, even clients of Mr. van der Wraak, who came to the house angry that their art hadn't appreciated in the way that it should have. Thirty-one years junior to Emma's father, Mila was beautiful, even in her unflattering uniform.

Emma marveled at the way her father took such pride in his job. Hans Jansen could make carrying a tray with high tea to Agnes van der Wraak and her high society friends seem like an art. Agnes and her friends were charmed in equal measure by Hans's handsome face and the care with which he handled his daily duties. His suits were always perfectly pressed, his shoes always neatly shined. He looked like a soldier in his butler's uniform, and when she would come home after kindergarten each day, he would offer her a salute. Emma always offered Hans a salute in return, just like he'd taught her. Hans had been a Resistance fighter in another life, at age fourteen during World War II. Before Emma was born. Before Emma's mother was even born. Back when he lived in Holland.

"One day," he would tell her, "we will be as rich as the van der Wraaks. You'll see. But for now, your mother and I will work here, save our pennies, and bide our time. Before you know it, we'll be buying a house that's even grander than this one. We will have what we deserve."

Emma lived with her parents in the apartment over the garage. Even though they didn't live in the main house, Hans tended to it as dutifully as if it were his own. He made sure every doorknob was polished. He carefully monitored the humidity levels in the house to make sure the wood trim and moldings didn't dry out in the winter. In the ways that mattered, Emma believed, the house belonged to her father more than it belonged to Felix and Agnes. He was the one who loved the house, who cared for it. He was the one who made it a home.

Each night before bed, Emma's father would sit in the rocking chair in the corner and tell her a bedtime story. Every night, a new story. There was always a princess, and she was always being hidden away. Something would happen, and everyone would realize that the little girl they'd ignored was truly special. Destined for something great. The details changed nightly, but every story had the same ending: our princess, pure of heart and soul, finally realizing her destiny.

Henry's parents died in a car accident when he was only three years old, and he'd been living with his grandparents since then. Emma didn't think that Mr. van der Wraak would ever sit in Henry's room and tell him a bedtime story. He was always running out of the house at odd hours, rushing around, as if his life depended on it. He took his artwork and his career entirely too seriously. His grandson less so. Even though Emma was jealous of the wealth that Henry's family had, she never envied him his grandparents. Henry may have had the house and the money, but Emma had the love.

Age six

They called it the Audrey Hepburn Estate. At age six, Emma had no idea who Audrey Hepburn was, or why it was important to give Rolling Hill some other name, but on her first day of the first grade, the other students all asked if she lived there. Even the teachers were whispering about it. Emma was the girl who lived at the Audrey Hepburn Estate.

"Who's Audrey Hepburn?" she asked her father when she came home from school that day. They were sitting in the kitchen, eating freshly made biscuits that Fleur, the van der Wraaks' chef, had made especially for them. Fleur and Emma's father were close friends. Both from the Netherlands, both the same age, and both with a sweet tooth that demanded treats every afternoon. Fleur always saw to it that Hans and Emma had a proper tea after school, when Hans would take a quick break from his work. They would regale Emma with stories of their childhood, tales of how they ate bread made from tulip bulbs to survive the famine.

"A very famous actress, back from my time, before you were born," Hans told her. "Why do you ask?"

"Everyone at school seemed to know who Henry and I were," she said. "They said that we lived at the Audrey Hepburn Estate."

Her father laughed. Emma loved her father's laugh. It was deep and rich, and he always held his stomach when he laughed out loud. "You live at Rolling Hill."

"Then why did they keep calling it that?"

"There was a famous movie called *Sabrina*, and an actress named Audrey Hepburn starred in it," he explained. "In the movie, Sabrina's father was the chauffeur for a very wealthy family called the Larrabees. Sabrina lived with her father over the garage, just like you do. The estate was in Glen Cove, and there were rumors that the movie was filmed right here, at Rolling Hill."

"They filmed a movie here?" Emma's eyes widened in excitement.

"Well, no," her father said, taking a measured sip of his tea. "They began filming in Glen Cove, but the breezes coming off the water ruined every shot. They ultimately filmed the movie in Los Angeles."

"Then why does everyone think that Rolling Hill is the Audrey Hepburn Estate?"

"For a while about eight years back, right when your mother and I came here, Mr. and Mrs. van der Wraak were thinking of selling the estate. They hired a real estate agent, and that real estate agent mistakenly thought that Rolling Hill was a stand-in for the Larrabee estate in the film, since they share an address. Mr. van der Wraak never corrected him—he thought that using the name of the film while advertising the property might help bring in buyers—and then the name stuck. People started calling it the Audrey Hepburn Estate."

"But that's not true."

"Well, it was a misunderstanding."

"Mr. van der Wraak lied," Emma said, furrowing her brow. "He is a liar."

"It's not quite that black-and-white, sweetheart," Hans said. "It was a silly misunderstanding."

"It was a lie," Emma said, shaking her head. "Lying is bad."

"Lying *is* bad," her father said. "That's true. But perhaps I'm not explaining it properly."

"If it's not the truth, then it's a lie," Emma said, reciting what she'd learned in kindergarten the year prior. Then, reasoning from there: "So, Mr. van der Wraak is a liar. He's a bad man."

"Mr. van der Wraak is a not a bad man," Hans said, laughter in his voice. "No person is all good or all bad, anyway. Things in the adult world are more complicated than you understand."

Emma *didn't* understand. If saying something that wasn't true was a lie, then Mr. van der Wraak was a liar. And if lying was bad, then Mr. van der Wraak was a bad man. Emma thought that maybe her father was the one who didn't understand.

"But none of that matters now," Hans said. "We're lucky

that the house wasn't sold and that your mother and I still have jobs here. Coming to America from another country is hard. We're lucky to have jobs that pay well. So don't go around calling Mr. van der Wraak a liar, all right, *mijn pure liefde?*"

Emma loved her father's pet name for her: my pure angel.

"Yes, Father," Emma said. She certainly wouldn't go around calling Mr. van der Wraak a liar, but she would still think it, in her heart of hearts. Her father always said that your thoughts were your own—if you kept them to yourself, no one would ever have to know.

"I have a good idea," Hans said. "Why don't you and I go rent a copy of *Sabrina* tonight and watch it together?"

"All right," Emma said, even though the idea of watching an old black-and-white movie didn't exactly appeal to her.

"You're going to love this movie," her father said. "And I promise you this: you're going to fall in love with Audrey Hepburn."

Age seven

Emma opened her sleepy eyes, and there it was: shiny, cherry red, with a little bell attached to the handlebars. It was exactly what Emma wanted for her seventh birthday. What she'd wished for, even when she hadn't said it out loud. For a moment, Emma wondered if they could afford such an extravagant present, but she quickly brushed the thought away. Why shouldn't she have a bright new bicycle? Henry had three bikes. When they went out to play after school, she usually borrowed one of his hand-me-downs. One that didn't quite fit properly, her legs always a bit too long for the frame he'd outgrown himself. But not anymore. Now she had her own bike, and she'd proudly ride on it beside Henry every day after school.

"Thank you!" Emma yelled, and jumped into her parents' waiting arms.

Her father lifted her up and placed her on the bike. "Let's get this sized for you."

Emma put her feet down onto the ground and found that she was able to perch her toes on the floor.

"It's a perfect fit, my sweet girl," her mother said, a wide smile on her lips. Mila set down the plate of fresh pancakes she'd just prepared for Emma—their birthday tradition, pancakes made from scratch served with homemade whipped cream on top. She walked over to her daughter and gave her a warm hug. "Happy birthday."

"Let's take it out for a spin," her father said.

Emma immediately jumped off the bike and ran into her room to get dressed for the day, completely forgetting about the pancakes. Minutes later, she and her father were on the path in front of the garage.

"Isn't Mommy coming?" Emma asked hopefully, even though she knew the answer before the words were fully out of her mouth. Her mother would not come and bike with them today.

"She had some things to do in the house," Hans said carefully. For months now, her mother had been distant toward her father. Always working in the main house with Mr. van der Wraak, always preoccupied. Emma couldn't remember the last time she'd seen her mother hug her father, or show him any affection.

But she wouldn't let that dull her excitement for the day. "Daddy, we need a bike for you!"

"You think your old dad can't keep up on foot?"

Emma laughed. "I know you can't." Emma was so fast on her bike that even Henry couldn't keep up, and he was a full four inches taller than she was. She sped off, kicking up dust in her wake. She pedaled faster, harder, wanting to show her father that the gift wasn't a waste of money. She wanted him to be proud of her, as proud of her as she was of him.

Emma heard the gentle beep of a horn behind her, and adjusted the mirror on her handlebars to see where the noise was coming from.

It was her father, driving behind her in a golf cart. Emma rang the silver bell, egging him on. Faster, faster. She laughed as she heard the golf cart behind her, catching up.

Emma pedaled as fast as she could across the estate. She knew exactly where she wanted to go—the hill toward the back of the property. She loved the view once you climbed to the top. It felt like a reward, something like what her father would have taught her: work hard, and reap the prize. Emma had to stand up and pedal harder, faster, in order to keep herself ahead of her father.

As an adult, Emma would look back on this memory and know the truth—she hadn't been outrunning her father, he'd been in a motorized vehicle, for God's sake!—but in the moment, she'd thought her seven-year-old legs capable of riding faster than a man in a golf cart.

Emma kept checking the mirror on her handlebars. Yes, she was still firmly in the lead, but not by much. She had to keep going. Emma willed her legs to go as fast as they could. She wanted to make her father proud by staying in the lead. By showing him that she took pride in the things that she did, just as much as he had.

At last, they made it to the top of the hill, and Emma's father applauded as he got off the golf cart. The birthday girl was, of course, the victor.

"Good job, *mijn pure liefde*," he said, and swept her into his arms for a bear hug.

"Thank you, Daddy," Emma said. "It was close."

"It certainly was," her father said. "Now, let's enjoy this view." He put his arms around Emma's shoulders, and together, they looked out at the water view in front of them.

"It's my favorite spot," Emma said.

"Mine, too," her father said. "The perfect place to celebrate your victory."

Emma had raced bikes hundreds of times with Henry after school. But winning a race had never been quite this sweet.

Age eight

Emma held her ear to the door as her mother huddled with Mr. and Mrs. van der Wraak in Mr. van der Wraak's office. She couldn't hear the entire conversation, she could only make out snippets: *accident, keep it quiet,* and: *what will you tell the girl?*

The door opened quickly, nearly swatting Emma in the shoulder. Her mother walked out, wearing an expression Emma had never seen before. It wasn't sadness, not sadness exactly, it was something else.

"Emma, I need to talk to you," she said, taking Emma's hand in her own and whisking them back to their apartment over the garage.

"I don't understand," Emma said a half hour later. Her mother had her arm around Emma's shoulders as she spoke, but Emma still could not process what she'd just told her. "He's not coming back?"

"He's not coming back, my sweet girl." Emma resented her mother's use of her pet name—my sweet girl—when she was delivering such awful news. Mila gave her daughter a hug and held her close. "The funeral will be next week."

Emma had never been to a funeral before. She didn't want to go. The funeral would mean that it was final. It would mean that her father was really dead. But that couldn't be true, could it? After all, she'd been with him the day prior. Emma didn't understand how someone could be with you one day, only to be gone the next.

It was an accident, her mother had explained. Her father had been playing cards with Mr. van der Wraak and his business associates. He'd had too much to drink, and instead of going back to their apartment, he'd found his way into the garage, where he turned on a car without remembering to open the garage door. Within minutes, he'd died of carbon monoxide poisoning. All while Emma and her mother were asleep upstairs with the windows open, inhaling the sweet scent of the lilacs, unbothered, unaware.

But an accident left Emma with nothing to hold on to, no one to get angry at, nothing to rail against. This was her mother's fault, she decided. If she hadn't been so cold to her father, he wouldn't have been out of the apartment that night. He would still be alive.

She was always leaving them alone. Always tending to Felix van der Wraak.

"I wish it had been you," Emma said under her breath.

Her mother turned to her, as if to say something, and then nodded and walked away.

Age nine

Emma barely spoke at all that year, still mourning her father. Her only solace was Henry, who would come to the apartment and drag her outside for some fresh air. They would bike, they would climb trees, and it was the only time she didn't think about how hollow her father's death had left her on the inside.

Having lost both of his parents suddenly, Henry understood her in a way that no one else could. He understood when she didn't speak for hours at a time. He understood when she broke down in tears, unprovoked. He understood that her father was the person she thought of every morning when she woke up and every evening before she went to bed, the person who ran through her dreams every night.

Her mother, Mila, spent more and more time in the main house with Mr. van der Wraak. People started to whisper.

Age ten

The kitchen was Emma's favorite room in the house. The smells, for one. The tastes. But it was so much more than that. Fleur, the chef, always had a special treat for her. When she'd make bread, she'd make Emma a small roll out of the dough so that Emma didn't have to wait until dinnertime for a taste. She'd save Emma the best leftovers to eat as after school snacks, and she always made sure to create a special lunch for Emma to bring with her each day, since she knew how much trouble Emma had with the girls at school.

Also, Fleur reminded Emma of her father.

It wasn't just because they were close friends. And it wasn't just because they both hailed from the Netherlands, had both survived the war. Fleur was meticulous, for one. And she had the same intensely serious countenance, which made the sweet and tender moments all the more delicious. Emma marveled at how orderly Fleur kept the kitchen—the pantry had cans and jars lined up like soldiers, labels out, not a thing out of place. Emma could sit for hours, watching Fleur cook and bake.

With her father gone, Emma's mother had to take on more of the household responsibilities, becoming less of a maid and more of a right hand to Mr. van der Wraak. Emma had lots of time to be alone. Too much time to be alone. So she spent it with her father's favorite person. Why be alone in her small apartment when she could be with Fleur in the professional-size kitchen?

Emma and Henry did their homework most afternoons at the kitchen table, sneaking bites of whatever delicacy Fleur would dream up for dinner. She favored Dutch classics, things she told the kids she'd grown up on—*erwtensoep*, a thick pea soup, *stamppot*, a mash of potatoes and other veggies, or *hachee*, a thick meat stew—but she'd learned how to cook American dishes as well. Pasta with butter sauce, nutty and sweet; chicken cutlets, flavorful and moist; a special mac 'n' cheese, made with three different types of cheese (the secret was the Gruyère). She even learned to use the outdoor grill, and she'd make the kids hot dogs on request, but mostly used it to make lamb chops on Thursday nights.

"Will you stir this while I prepare the rest of the sauce?" Fleur asked Emma.

Emma looked back at her as if she'd asked her to do calculus. Had she heard Fleur correctly? Henry was off in the music room, taking piano lessons, and Emma could hear the wrong notes floating into the kitchen.

"Come on, now. We can't let the base settle."

Emma got up from the kitchen table and walked to Fleur's side. She had never cooked before, had never even stood on Fleur's side of the kitchen island. The closest she'd ever gotten was when Fleur offered her a taste of something. Stirring a sauce? It seemed as complicated as reciting all fifty states and their capitals. She couldn't do either one.

"You take the wooden spoon and stir it around," Fleur said. "Be careful not to touch the side of the pot. It's hot."

Emma stood on her tippy-toes to stir without touching the side of the pot.

"That's it," Fleur said as she quickly chopped an onion. "You're a natural."

Emma couldn't help but smile. Getting praise from Fleur was like having the sun shine down on you. "Thank you."

"And here we go," Fleur said as she carefully slid the onions down from the cutting board. "Smell that."

Emma took a deep breath—the kitchen had filled up with the sweet aroma of the onions. "It smells good."

"The smell of onions makes me think of home," Fleur said with a smile. "Every recipe that my mother made began with onions."

"What's this?"

Emma turned toward the voice that came from the hallway. It was her mother, standing ramrod straight, eyes fixed on her. Emma felt her legs get shaky. She knew that the only thing that would make her mother angrier than she was at that moment would be if Emma didn't respond. She eked out: "I was just helping Fleur."

"You're supposed to be doing homework," her mother said, her face a stone. "Go back to the apartment and get your work done."

"It was only for a moment," Fleur said. "I can assure you that Emma was doing her schoolwork before I bothered her."

"Emma," her mother said, ignoring Fleur, "go to your room. I'll be back home shortly, and then we can take our dinner in the apartment together later."

Emma put her head down and walked to the kitchen table to scoop up her notebook and schoolbooks. She hoped her mother couldn't see how disappointed she was. Emma's favorite nights were when her mother got so caught up her in work with Mr. van der Wraak that they ended up eating in the dining room with the family. Henry would kick her leg under the table, and they'd sneak extra dinner rolls when the adults weren't paying attention. Fleur would always make sure they got extra-large portions of dessert.

"Bye, Fleur," Emma said as she walked out of the kitchen.

"Goodbye, *mijn lievje*," Fleur said. *My little dear.*

Emma let herself into the apartment over the garage. There was so much security at the estate that they never locked the front door. She set her books down on the kitchen table—this one much smaller than the one at the main house—and flipped open her notebook. She wondered how long it would take for her mother to wrap up work with Mr. van der Wraak. She wondered if Fleur would bring their dinner up herself or if she'd send someone else to do it. She wondered how things might have been different if her father were still alive.

Emma's mother came home around seven. She brought over their dinner herself, and they ate it silently.

"Henry asked if you could play after dinner," her mother said.

"Can I go?"

"If your schoolwork is finished."

Her face beaming: "It is."

Most of the time, Mila was so overprotective it hurt, but she must have understood that the freedom of running around outside, unattended, was something Emma needed. Craved. Emma cherished the nights Mila allowed her to go out with Henry after dinner. (Even though she knew that her mother had the groundskeeper, Linwood, secretly keep an eye on them.)

There was something so magical about the property after dark. The trees were all lit up by their very own little spotlights, giving the entire space an ethereal feel.

Emma knew exactly where she'd find Henry. Where she always found him: their favorite tree. The one-hundred-year-old Japanese maple that sat directly in front of the house, in the center of the circle on the driveway. Emma and Henry had both claimed ownership of the tree long ago, each one declaring it theirs. Henry loved the intricate shape of the tree, more beautiful than a painting, but Emma favored the fiery-red leaves that came out each year in the fall.

Linwood hated when Emma and Henry climbed the tree, shouting that it was a specimen-quality tree, and they could damage it, since it was over one hundred years old. But that was the other great part about it: its leaves were so full, if they climbed high enough, Linwood couldn't see them.

Emma had made it out to the tree before Henry. She decided to climb up high, and then surprise him when he got there. She'd jump down from the branch and scare him, and they'd have a good laugh. Once she perched herself on one of the high branches, Emma could hear sounds coming from the front of the house. She couldn't make out the words, but she knew the voice. It was Felix van der Wraak, yelling at Henry.

Mr. van der Wraak often yelled at Henry. Emma never saw Henry's grandfather treat him with any kindness, any warmth. Though his grandmother was an incredibly kind and warm person, his grandfather was an overly serious man who never smiled. He was tough on Henry, as if preparing him for some war to come.

She heard Henry scream *fine!* and then slam the front door behind him. Suddenly, her plan to jump down from the tree and scare Henry seemed silly. When Henry got to the tree, he sat down, with his back against the base of the trunk, and began to cry.

Emma didn't know what to do. She hadn't announced herself, and to do so now would embarrass Henry. But how could she let her friend sit there and cry alone?

"Are you all right?" Emma whispered from her perch up above.

Henry startled at the sound of her voice. "I didn't see you up there." Emma looked away as he roughly rubbed at his eyes, cleared his throat, and adjusted his voice so that it didn't sound like he'd been crying.

"I heard your grandfather yelling," she said softly. "I'm sorry."

"It was nothing," he said, and leaped up to reach the first branch.

That was the trick to climbing it—the first split, where you could easily put your foot to hoist yourself up, was high off the ground. You needed to hop up to grab it. But that was part of what Emma thought made their tree so special. Not just anyone could do it. And she noticed that when Henry had friends over, they never climbed this tree. This one was only for them.

In a minute, Henry was in the branch across from Emma. "Got you," he said, swatting her arm gently.

"I had a bad night, too," Emma said. "My mother wouldn't let us eat at the main house."

"I noticed," Henry said, putting his hand into his pocket. "I brought you something from the dinner table."

Emma looked at Henry's hand, expecting some delectable treat from Fleur's kitchen, but what Henry held in his hand was not a pastry. It was a knife.

"How do you eat it?" Emma joked.

"I thought that we could put our initials in the tree," Henry said, his eyes trained at the ground. It was as if he wasn't sure of himself, which confused Emma. Henry always seemed sure of himself. After all, if the heir to Rolling Hill wasn't completely confident all the time, what chance did she, the maid's daughter have?

"Linwood will kill us," Emma said.

"True," Henry said, nodding. "But I think we should do it anyway."

Without giving Emma a chance to respond, Henry started carving.

"Maybe we shouldn't." Emma glanced over her shoulder. "I don't want to get in trouble."

Henry looked up at her with a devilish smile. He'd already carved the *H* and was starting in on the *V*. Emma's heart raced. She didn't know what to think. On the one hand, at least Henry didn't feel sad anymore. But on the other, she didn't want to face the wrath of Linwood when he discovered what they'd done.

"There," Henry said, showing off his handiwork. "Do you want to do yours now?"

"You did a good job on yours," Emma said carefully. "Can you do mine?"

Henry didn't respond; he merely got back to work. Emma reasoned that Linwood couldn't get too mad at Henry, at least not as mad as he'd be at Emma. Henry's grandparents owned the estate, employed Linwood. This Japanese maple belonged to them, so Mr. and Mrs. van der Wraak's grandson could do what he wanted with it.

"Ta-da," Henry said, fanning his hands out so that Emma could admire his handiwork.

Emma almost fell out of the tree when she saw what Henry had done. He hadn't just carved their initials into the tree. He'd connected them.

$$H.V. + E.J.$$

Emma couldn't help but think the "+" meant something. "So," he asked, "what do you think?"

"I love it," she said, feeling her face grow warm. Then, quietly: "Thank you."

"Well, it's *our* tree," Henry said matter-of-factly. "Now, for the next one hundred years, everyone will know it."

3

Now

"It's good to see you," he said, after the tour was over and the guests had emptied out of the trailer. He squinted, as if he couldn't quite trust what he was seeing with his own eyes.

"I can't believe you're doing this." Emma hadn't meant to say that—she'd meant to make small talk, start things nicely. But Emma wasn't good at things like that, things that came so easily to other people.

"Isn't it good to see me, too?" He smiled broadly at Emma. He still had a beautiful smile. He still had a beautiful face. Emma searched his features for the boy she once knew, but all traces of that kid were long gone. He dressed differently, too. His button-down shirt had his initials monogrammed onto the cuff.

When Emma didn't respond, he said: "Okay, so...*not* good to see me."

"Isn't there some way to save the house?" Emma asked. She put one leg behind the other, as if to hide the old Converse sneakers she'd thrown on that morning.

"You didn't come here to see me," he said, his face falling, filled with the realization of why Emma had come. "You came because of the house."

"You knew I would come to see the house."

"Right. And no, there's no way to save the house. It's too old, it's no longer structurally intact."

"I'm sure it could be saved…"

"The cost to rejuvenate the house isn't worth it. I'd never make my money back."

"Why are you doing this?" Emma asked, narrowing her eyes. She found that looking directly into his eyes was like staring directly into the sun. "Are you doing it to hurt him?"

He regarded her. "No, I'm not doing it to hurt him. I haven't seen him in years. He has nothing to do with my life. I never even really think of him at all. I'm doing this for myself. For my company. I can't believe, after all these years, you'd think that."

"There must be some way—"

"There's no way," he said harshly, cutting off Emma's sentence. He shook his head. "You know, when you walked through the door, I was excited to see you. I thought you were here to see me, because you wanted to see me. I thought you'd be proud of me. Proud of what I've become. But you're just here for him, aren't you? After all this time, after everything, it's still all about him."

"I'm not here for him." Suddenly, it felt like he was standing too close.

"Why do you even care about the house?" he asked. He waited to speak again until Emma turned her head up, allowed her eyes to meet his. His deep brown eyes bore into hers. "I don't recall you having such a happy childhood here. Why would you want to save it?"

"It was our home," Emma said. "Don't you feel anything when you come back here?"

He regarded her. "I feel nothing."

"Well, it was my home," Emma said, pointing at her chest as the words left her mouth. She felt her voice break. Then, quietly she added: "And my father's home."

"Your parents *worked* there. It was not your home."

"It still belonged to me," Emma said, her voice barely a whisper.

"It did not belong to you," he said. "It *never* belonged to you. How could you even think that?"

"I—"

"Emma, this was not your home," he said, not unkindly. "And how you could fondly remember living here is completely beyond me. The property was up for sale, so my company bought it, and now we're going to make something of it. It's going to be beautiful, and lots of families are going to get to enjoy it. If you don't like it, I guess you can leave."

"Well, then, I guess I will."

"Goodbye, Emma."

"Goodbye, Leo."

4

Then

Age eleven

When they were at school, Emma and Henry never spoke. Even though their afternoons and weekends were filled with each other, at school, they pretended that they didn't know each other. After all, Henry was the prince of Rolling Hill, and Emma only lived on the estate because her mother ran the house. Once the maid, the house manager they now called her. Mr. van der Wraak said that he couldn't live without Emma's mother. Mrs. van der Wraak said that without her, her life would be mush. They called Emma and her mother *family*, an integral part of theirs. But does family live over the garage? No, that was the help.

It was an unspoken rule that every day after school, they would meet at the shed. It didn't matter what had happened at school that day (and a lot could happen in a school day). Once they got home, back to Rolling Hill, all of that was washed away, as if it never happened.

But it had happened.

This day had been particularly difficult for Emma. All morning, she'd overheard the girls calling her *MD*. Emma was thrilled to finally have a nickname. Perhaps now, after years of desperately trying to fit in, she really did. Emma assumed that the moniker referred to the fact that she wanted to be a doctor when she grew up, and she felt pleased when she heard it being bandied about in class.

When she set her lunch tray down at the last seat at the table, Brittany Wakefield said, "What's up, MD?"

Emma's face lit up. It wasn't often that the Queen Bee deigned to speak to her. "Hi, Brittany," she replied, her voice full of nervous energy. Emma heard the other girls at the table laugh. Unsure of what they were laughing about, she joined in.

"Hey, MD, wanna trade me your sandwich?" Ashley Small, Brittany's second-in-command, asked.

"Sure," Emma said, even though she didn't want to trade. That day, Fleur had made her favorite—roast turkey with a thin layer of brie on a thick, crusty nine-grain bread that she'd baked fresh that morning, before dawn. Emma relinquished the sandwich with a smile and took Ashley's sandwich in return, a sad peanut butter and jelly on plain white bread. When she took the sandwich out of the plastic bag, it felt damp. Fleur always packed Emma's lunches in butcher's paper for freshness.

Emma forced a smile onto her face as she ate. Sure, she hadn't been happy about giving up the sandwich, but nothing filled her with more glee than being accepted by the popular girls. She would gladly trade her wonderful lunch for Ashley's sad sandwich every day, if it meant social acceptance.

"Brit, what's up?" Henry said as he walked toward the table with his friends, situated right next to where the girls sat.

"Hey," Brittany said back, as if she didn't care. But Emma listened to the gossip—she knew that Brit had a crush on

Henry van der Wraak. Every girl at the school had a crush on Henry van der Wraak, herself included.

Henry did not acknowledge Emma, sitting at the end of Brittany's table.

"Keep yourself," her mother always cautioned her. "Never forget who you are, my sweet girl."

But Emma had known Henry her whole life—she'd grown up at Rolling Hill. In many ways, she felt it was more hers than his. Henry was her best friend, her constant playmate, her most trusted confidant. Emma understood why they couldn't speak at school, and she respected it.

Leo L'Unico did not yet understand the rules. He had moved to Rolling Hill from Italy a few weeks prior with his father, the new driver for the van der Wraaks, and he couldn't see the delicate social order that existed at school. He seemed to think that he could sit anywhere at lunch, could talk to anyone he pleased.

Emma had overheard her mother talking about Leo's father, Enzo—he was a race car driver, badly injured in his last race. He could no longer race competitively, so he'd come to the United States for a fresh start for his son. Although they were divorced, Leo's mother, Sofia, had come, too, and got a job as an Italian teacher at the middle school two towns over. Even though she wouldn't be working for the van der Wraaks, Felix had given Sofia the studio apartment in the staff quarters next to Enzo's, since it was understood that the job of driver meant being on call at all hours of the night. (This arrangement would ensure that Leo would have an adult to take care of him, no matter what time of the day or night Enzo was needed.) Sofia looked like a movie star, with thick black hair and deep, dark eyes. Enzo walked with a slight limp, imperceptible if you weren't looking for it, and he had the same dark eyes, only his turned down at the edges.

"This seat taken?" Leo asked Emma, not waiting for a response as he pushed his hip into hers to make room.

"It *is* taken, actually," Emma said, and shimmied her body over to push him off the bench. Emma knew that Leo was not well-liked at school, and she couldn't risk being too friendly with him. She couldn't let his social currency bring her down. Hers was low enough as it was.

"There's room for your boyfriend, MD," Brittany said, smiling sweetly in Emma's direction. When Emma didn't respond, Brittany stared her down. More forcefully: "Let him stay."

"He's not my boyfriend," Emma said quietly.

"Can I talk to you?" Leo whispered to Emma.

"Oh, how cute," Ashley said. "Look at MD getting all cozy with her boyfriend!" The girls all laughed in unison.

"He's not my boyfriend," Emma said, louder this time. She felt her cheeks flush, which made the girls laugh even harder. Then, facing Leo: "Please leave. You are not wanted here."

Leo stood and looked down at Emma. "*You* are not wanted here, either."

Through gritted teeth: "You're embarrassing me."

Quietly: "You're embarrassing yourself. Don't you know why they call you MD?"

"Because I'm going to be a doctor," Emma whispered back angrily. "Now, please go."

"MD doesn't stand for *medical doctor*," he said, leaning down closer. He whispered into her ear: "It stands for *maid's daughter*."

After school, it was as if anything that had happened that day was washed away. Like the chalk off a blackboard. It was as if Emma hadn't spent the rest of the school day holed up in the third floor bathroom, crying. It was as if Henry hadn't witnessed Leo and Emma's confrontation, as if the whole school hadn't heard. It was as if Emma didn't hate Leo for what he'd told her, as if she didn't hate Henry more for not having had the guts to do it himself.

Emma needed the day to be over. It wasn't like she could tell her mother about what went on with the girls at school—she'd call the school and make things even more miserable for her. The first time Brittany had bullied her, Emma made the mistake of telling her mother. Brittany and her friends had all gotten called to the principal's office, which only made things worse for Emma the next day.

Emma heard the shed door open. But it wasn't who she was hoping to see.

"I'm sorry about today," Leo said.

Emma shook her head. Yet another rule Leo didn't understand—you didn't talk about school once you were at home.

"I shouldn't have said that in the cafeteria," he said, coming closer. "I should have told you privately."

"Should we bike?"

"Listen to me," Leo said, grabbing Emma's arm. Emma brushed it away and walked over to her cherry-red bike, which she had outgrown but still used. Leo quickly followed suit, walking over to his bike, a speed bike painted black, and pulled it off the rack. Quietly, he said: "Why don't you like me?"

Emma didn't look up from her bike. "I like you just fine."

"You ignore me at school, and when I try to help you, it… it just goes all wrong. You know I was telling you that to help you, right?"

"I don't want to talk about it."

"They were trying to humiliate you," Leo said. "It made me so angry. I couldn't let you sit there without knowing."

"Well, now I know," Emma said. "And can't you see how happy I am now?" She lifted her head.

"They were calling you *the maid's daughter*," Leo said, louder. "First of all, there's nothing wrong with being a maid. That fake Brittany bitch's father was indicted for insider trading. Now *that's* something to be embarrassed about."

"You don't understand anything about school."

"Your mother isn't even the maid here!" Leo said, his arms flying around. "She's the house manager. She runs this entire estate! Without her, the whole thing would fall apart inside of a month!"

"When my mother first came here, she was the maid," Emma said quietly. "I'm not embarrassed about it, but it's the truth. It's only after years and years of working for the van der Wraaks that she was promoted so many times."

"Oh," Leo said. His face twisted into an expression Emma couldn't quite decipher. Then, regaining his composure: "But that's the point, isn't it? They're making fun of your mother, and she's this incredible woman who worked her way up from—"

"Can we please not talk about my mother?"

"Sorry," Leo said. Then, under his breath: "I just want you to like me."

"I do."

"No, you don't," Leo said, turning to face Emma. "Not the way you like him. I want you to like me the way you like him."

Emma felt her face flush, and busied herself with her shoe-laces. She always changed into her mother's old Converse sneakers to go bike riding.

The barn door opened, and Henry walked in. He looked from Emma to Leo. "Am I interrupting something?"

"Nope," Emma said, and jumped onto her bike and was out of the barn in one fluid motion.

Minutes later, she could feel Henry and Leo biking behind

her. Emma wished that Leo had not come that day. She was ignoring the rules that she herself had made—she had not let the day go. She couldn't. She couldn't pretend that things were okay now that they were at home. Things were not okay. Her body was still tingling with the embarrassment, the humiliation she'd experienced at school. It felt like she was covered in it, like it was stuck to her body.

Emma couldn't help it; she was still mad at Leo.

Emma biked harder, faster. Leo called out for her to slow down, to wait up, but Emma couldn't stop.

She was angry at Leo for trying to sit with her at lunch today, for putting the magnifying glass firmly on her. She was mad at him for refusing to understand the unspoken rules at school, the social order. And though she couldn't admit this part to Leo or even to herself, she was mad at him for telling the truth.

Henry shouted out that they should head past the stables, where they'd created a dirt path in the grass, alongside the pond. It was a beautiful ride that Emma and Henry had forged for years when they were younger and took at least three times a week. Serene, easy. But that wasn't what Emma wanted. That wasn't where Emma wanted to go.

Henry called for her to turn left, but she turned right. Up the hill at the back of the property. The place she always went when she was upset. The place that made her think of her father. Her legs burned as they made their way up the steep climb.

"If we're doing the hill, we should circle back for elbow pads and knee pads," Henry called out to Emma. "The way down can be rough."

"I'm not scared," Emma yelled back over her shoulder. Years prior, her father had asked Linwood to pave this stretch, since he knew how much Emma loved to ride to the top. He'd thought it would be safer to bike up and down the hill if it was paved. If there was a clear path.

Usually, they stopped at the top to admire the view. From the top of the hill, you could see the bay. The water view was what made the property so valuable, so special. Emma loved it up here. Things were always clearer at the top of the hill. Calmer.

But Emma didn't want to be calm. Emma didn't want to think at all. She turned her bike quickly, too quickly, and sent herself barreling down the hill. Henry called out as she went, cautioning her to ride her brake. But Emma didn't listen. Seconds later, the sound of Henry's voice was replaced by the wind, sharp in her hair, cool on her face. For a minute, she wondered what would happen if she closed her eyes. If she let herself give in completely to this sensation of rushing down the hill without a safety net.

So she did.

It felt like freedom, like she was flying. The thoughts that filled her mind floated away, replaced by the sensation of the air blowing past, and the thrill of how fast she was going. Emma didn't pump the brakes, she didn't make an attempt to slow down. She wanted to go faster, harder.

Then, the rock.

By the time Emma realized what was happening, it was already too late. Later, she'd discover that it was only a tiny bit of pavement, probably kicked up from the last time the snowplows came through the previous winter. If only she'd been one centimeter to the left, she would have missed it completely. But she was going too fast to swerve.

Anyway, her eyes were closed at the time.

Her front tire hit the rock, in the exact wrong spot, right on the edge, and it sent her bike soaring through the air, this time for real. It happened so quickly, she couldn't react, couldn't get herself upright, and the bike landed with a thud, her right knee making contact onto the paved pathway first. From there, the rest of the bike slammed into the blacktop, and she slid along the path, burning the skin on her legs, her arms, her shoulders.

By the time Henry and Leo ran down to see if she was okay, Emma was numb with shock.

"Don't move," Henry said. He gently leaned over her. "Did you hit your head?"

"No," Emma said, still dazed, her voice barely a whisper.

"Stay right there," Henry said. "Stay still. Leo, go get help."

Henry held her hand as they waited for Emma's mother. He rode in the car with her to the hospital as she cried, and told her that everything would be all right, even though her mother's face told a different story.

Emma had fractured her leg in two places and broken her wrist. Even though she was in massive pain, secretly she was thrilled. She stayed home from school for a month.

5

Now

Emma rushed out of the Sales Center. Coming back had been a mistake. She should never have come back to Rolling Hill.

She couldn't believe Leo had kicked her out of the construction trailer. He *had* kicked her out, hadn't he? She wouldn't have thought Leo capable of something like that—he prided himself on being European, on being gracious and well-mannered—but then again, she didn't really know him anymore. Maybe he wasn't that person now. He used to be her best friend. But she hadn't spoken to him in seven years, ever since that night. The fight that changed everything. The fight that ended their friendship.

Emma pulled out her phone to open a rideshare app. There certainly wasn't a taxi stand out here like there had been at the train station. She walked around in circles, trying to get service on her phone, and found herself at the tree. Her tree. The Japanese maple that Linwood lovingly tended to for years.

The place where Henry had carved their initials, binding them together for the rest of their lives.

Without thinking, Emma jumped up to climb the tree, but found that her legs didn't work in quite the same way as they had as a kid. She missed the spot where her foot was supposed to land, and fell to the ground, ending up on her back instead.

"Are you all right?" someone asked.

"Well, this is embarrassing," Emma said as she tried to sit up. The woman put out a hand and helped Emma get back on her feet.

It wasn't one of the women who'd been in the trailer earlier. She didn't look Long-Island-expensive like those women had. This woman seemed different, harder. Her hands were rough, not manicured. She wore her hair back in a ponytail, not blown out and glossy. And her face was devoid of makeup, Botox, or fillers.

"I didn't see you in the trailer earlier," Emma said.

"Oh, I was there," she said, glancing over her shoulder. "You must not have noticed."

Emma could have just agreed—*I must not have noticed*—but Emma never did what was easy. Anyway, her interest was piqued. "You weren't there," she said. "I would have seen you."

"Okay, busted," the woman said, laughing, putting one finger up to her lips, as if to say *shhh*.

"Who are you?"

"Oh, sorry," she said, putting her hand out for Emma to shake. "I'm Stella Knight. The reason you didn't see me in the trailer is because I was inside the house."

"You went inside?"

She put one finger to her lips again. "Don't tell, but yes, I was inside. I was taking photographs."

"Of what?"

"I'm from the Glen Cove Historical Society, and we're try-ing to get Rolling Hill registered for historical status before Leo and his people can tear it down. We'll be filing an in-junction soon. The photographs will prove that there's his-torical value to this home. The house is incredible, even in its current state. Some of the millwork and marble work date back to 1899. I found a chandelier that looks original, and the crystal doorknobs do, too."

"Wow, that's great," Emma said. "That's actually why I came here today. I had to see it one more time. I don't want Leo to tear it down, either."

"A fellow history lover," Stella said, smiling for the first time.

"How can I help?"

Stella gave her a flyer—there was a meeting at the Glen Cove Historical Society with Rolling Hill on the agenda in two weeks. The edges of Emma's lips curled. This was her chance. She'd wanted to see Rolling Hill one more time, but this was even better. She could help save Rolling Hill. Stop Leo from tearing it down.

"I'll be there," Emma said.

"I didn't catch your name."

"I'm Emma Jansen," she said. "And it's not so much that I love history—I mean, I do love history, of course history is important and preserving landmarks and all that—but, I have a more personal reason. I grew up here."

"I wasn't aware that Felix and Agnes van der Wraak had a granddaughter?" She looked up in the air, as if trying to re-member something.

"They didn't," Emma said. "My mother worked for them. We were staff. We lived above the garage out back."

"Well, then, you must know my aunt," Stella said, clapping

her hands together. "I'm not sure if the timing would have lined up, but she was Mr. van der Wraak's personal chef for about fifteen years. Her name was Fleur."

6

Then

Age twelve

Something had changed that summer. Everything had changed that summer.

Summers were for lazy days, biking and swimming with Henry and Leo. They would roam the property, completely carefree. No school, not the social order that existed there, not the homework they had to complete each night before meeting up together to hang out.

But this summer, things were different. Everything seemed charged. Electric. Henry had magically transformed, seemingly overnight. Where his body once was short and soft, now it was tall and lean. Emma's eyes couldn't help lingering on every square inch of it when they went swimming in the pool.

The feeling was reciprocated. Emma could feel Henry's eyes on her own body, too. She'd turn around quickly, only to find him chatting with Leo, but she'd felt it. Something was happening.

Fourth of July weekend always meant a big barbecue

thrown by Mr. and Mrs. van der Wraak for all the staff who
worked on the property. A party tent was set up in the backyard, on what the staff referred to as the "grand lawn." Beyond the grand lawn was a massive rectangular swimming
pool, and right past that was a cabana. To call it a cabana was
a bit of a misnomer. It had its own kitchen and living room,
along with a bedroom upstairs, two bathrooms, and an outdoor shower around back. It was decorated just as stylishly as
the main house, and a humongous Chagall hung on the back
wall of the living room. Most of the art in the main house
would come and go, Mr. van der Wraak often buying pieces
as casually as a normal person would a gallon of milk. But
the Chagall never moved. It stayed right where it had been,
always. Emma wondered if it was disrespectful to have the
work of such an important artist relegated to the pool house,
but no one ever mentioned it.

The best part of the barbecue was that unlike at every
other van der Wraak party, none of the staff had to work.
This party was different. This party was only for them. Emma
could feel her mother's mood lightening each spring as they
approached the Fourth. Even Fleur didn't have to work—the
van der Wraaks brought in a caterer who handled everything,
including the setup, bringing out rented tables and chairs, and
the cleanup, breaking down the whole party, afterward. Once
everyone was full and sated on a feast of anything and everything you could imaginably put on a grill—hot dogs, hamburgers, skirt steaks, fresh corn, avocado, watermelon, clams,
peaches—they'd all bring blankets up the hill to watch the
fireworks that Mr. and Mrs. van der Wraak would commis-
sion each year.

The morning of the barbecue, Leo complained of a stom-
achache, and spent the day indoors. Alone for the first time
all summer, Henry and Emma lingered in the pool that day,

playing games that gave them excuses to touch: tag, Marco Polo, a race where Henry would "accidentally" bump into Emma over and over again. When they got out of the pool, Henry held Emma's towel out for her and wrapped it around her cold body. He rubbed his hands along her arms, under the guise of "warming her up." Emma showed him the goose bumps on her arms, proof that she was still freezing cold, so that he wouldn't stop. They spent the rest of the day coming up with excuses to crash into each other, pretending they each wanted to climb the same branch of the tree, leaving them in tight proximity to one another at the top.

As they walked back to the house to get ready for the barbecue, Henry bumped his hip into Emma's. She swatted his shoulder, as if to tell him to stop. And then, he did something he'd never done before—he walked her back to her apartment over the garage.

"I think I know the way," she said, once it was clear he wasn't going into the main house.

"I just want to make sure you get home safe."

"Through the dangerous streets of Rolling Hill?" Emma laughed at her own joke, and Henry smiled in return.

When she took her shower, her thoughts were filled with him.

An hour later, she walked with her mother out of the apartment for the barbecue. Henry was waiting for them at the bottom of the steps.

"Where is your grandmother?" Emma's mother asked.

"Um," Henry began, "I don't know. I was waiting for Emma."

"You should find your grandparents." And with that, Emma's mother had made it clear: Henry was dismissed. He looked at Emma hopefully, but she looked down at her feet.

She could not stand up to her mother. He shouldn't have expected her to.

Emma ate her dinner seated firmly next to Mila. Henry sat with his grandparents, a world away.

"I should make a plate and bring it up to Leo," Emma said to her mother.

"His mother is up at the apartment taking care of him," Mila said. Emma glanced over to where Leo's father sat, at a far-off table, flirting with one of Henry's tutors. He held her hand in his own, and brushed his fingers across her palm, as if he were reading her fortune. Emma's mother's eyes followed Emma's line of sight. "Anyway, you can't eat barbecue with an upset stomach. I'm sure his mother prepared him some chicken soup and plain toast. I'll go get us some grilled peaches."

Once her mother left, Emma got up to use the bathroom. Their apartment was closer, but Emma decided to walk to the cabana instead. Emma loved having an excuse to look at the Chagall. Most of the art that Mr. van der Wraak brought home, Emma didn't understand. But the Chagall was easily understandable to Emma, with a bride and groom at its center. As a little girl, she'd thought that she and Henry were the bride and groom in the painting.

The Chagall made her feel something. Something she couldn't quite articulate that she felt deep in her belly—the various symbols that floated in the background, the dramatic use of color and light. Each time she stood before it, she discovered something new. Some detail in the work that she hadn't noticed before. She was in awe at the painting's ability to constantly surprise her.

Emma walked slowly past the pool, thinking about how Henry had held her towel out for her. That meant something, didn't it? Had she imagined it all day? The way things felt different?

The sliding pocket doors to the cabana had been left open, and Emma took a moment to admire how beautiful it was— the elegant living room with that stunning Chagall on the back wall. She walked in and made her way to the bathroom. As she studied her reflection in the mirror as she washed her hands, she silently chastised herself for not putting on makeup. Some of the girls at school were doing it; Brittany and her crew had been doing it all year. Maybe if she wore some eyeliner and a bit of lip gloss, she would look more grown-up. Prettier.

"Are you here?"

Emma would know the voice anywhere. It was Henry. He'd come to find her.

"Yeah," she said as she slipped out of the bathroom and made her way to the living room. "Did I miss dessert? Is it time for the fireworks?"

"No," Henry said, biting his lip. "I wanted to see you."

Emma didn't know what to say. She'd seen him all day. They'd sat one table apart at dinner. But she knew she shouldn't say any of that. After all, she'd wanted to see him, too.

"I'm right here," Emma said, and Henry inched closer to where she stood, in front of the painting.

"I had a really good day today," he said.

"Me, too." Emma stood still as Henry inched closer once again. And then again.

"It was cool how it was just us two, you know?" He reached out and took her hand.

"Yeah."

"I was thinking…"

"Yeah?"

"Um…"

They were so close that their bodies almost touched. Emma could feel the heat coming off Henry's frame.

Henry put his other hand gently on Emma's cheek. She could feel her face light on fire. "I really want to kiss you."

"Okay." As soon as she said the word, Henry pressed his lips to hers. Soft and sweet, exactly like she'd imagined. He drew her closer, so close that their bodies touched. His kiss went deeper, and Emma felt every nerve in her body ignite. She inhaled his fresh scent: lavender and sage, and a hint of something else. Nutmeg, perhaps?

It was her first kiss.

Emma didn't know how long they stood there kissing—it felt like time was moving at a different pace, like she was living in another dimension. All she could remember was that when they finally broke apart, she looked over to the entrance of the cabana, where her mother stood, staring.

"You are not to see that boy," her mother said later that night as they got ready for bed.

"It was my first kiss," Emma murmured, her head bowed.

"My sweet girl," Mila said, her voice soft. "You will have many first kisses in your life. Some will be the right boy, some will not. I beg of you, find another boy."

"But I love him."

"You love him because he's like a brother to you," her mother said. "You are not *in love*."

Emma had wanted to say more, she'd wanted to tell her mother that she was wrong, that what she and Henry shared was the real thing. But none of that mattered. Because Emma would later learn that Henry's grandfather had told him the exact same thing that exact same night.

The next day, Leo would be feeling better, and they'd go back to being a threesome. As if the kiss had never happened. As if it had merely been a dream.

Age thirteen

It was a snow day.

The perfect sort of snow day—one where there was enough snow to cancel school because the roads hadn't been cleared overnight, but not enough snow to make it dangerous. And certainly not enough snow that Emma couldn't make her way to the main house to hang out with Henry all day.

Emma put on her snow boots (and, at her mother's insistence, a snowsuit that barely fit anymore, in case they decided to play outside, she shouldn't catch pneumonia) and made her way to the back door of the main house. Linwood had already cleared the path from the garage, as if he knew that she'd be heading over before even she had. As she reached the door, she saw that Leo had had the same idea. He, too, was making his way to the back door, but he was not decked out in winter wear like Emma was. He wore his usual sneakers and jeans, as if he'd already known that Linwood would clear the path from the staff quarters to the house for him. Assumed it.

Emma's face flushed when she thought about what she was wearing. She looked foolish and juvenile. She needed to get the snowsuit off before Henry could see her.

"Are we venturing out into the snow?" Leo asked. "I could go back to the staff quarters and see if anyone's got snow boots in my size."

"No. It was my mother," Emma said as Leo held the back door for her. "Don't ask."

The housekeeper had put down towels by the back door, and Leo quickly slipped off his sneakers so that he wouldn't get the wood floors wet. Emma shimmied out of her snowsuit quickly, uneasily, and tried to make herself look presentable for Henry.

It wasn't because of the kiss the previous summer. It was one kiss, and it could never happen again. Both Mila and Mr. van der Wraak had made sure of it. Emma and Henry had never even mentioned the kiss after that night.

But still, Emma wanted to look her best in front of Henry, always. Perhaps a kiss might be in her future once again, despite the fact that it was forbidden.

Once Emma had peeled off the snowsuit (and the housekeeper had taken it to hang in the laundry room, keeping it warm and dry), she and Leo headed into the kitchen, where Henry sat waiting for them.

"Did you eat?" Fleur asked. Fleur always asked if they had eaten, no matter what time of day they showed up in her kitchen. Emma nodded, but Leo said that he had not. Fleur set out a platter of freshly made corn muffins, along with a jar of homemade raspberry jam.

"What should we do today?" Henry asked. "I was thinking we could sled down the hill?"

"Emma is definitely dressed for it," Leo said, his mouth full of food. Emma kicked his leg under the table.

Henry checked under the table to see what Emma was wearing, what Leo was referring to, and Emma quickly crossed her legs to appear more ladylike. She'd been sitting with her legs splayed wide apart, and she didn't think that lounging about like one of the guys was the way to get Henry to kiss her again.

"What about hide-and-seek?" Emma suggested. Splitting up as a group, hiding in snug, dark nooks of the house...*that* was the way to get kissed.

"Aren't we too old for hide-and-seek?" Leo asked, applying a generous amount of raspberry jam to his corn muffin before popping it into his mouth.

"You're it!" Henry said to Leo, and grabbed Emma's hand. They jumped up from the table and ran out of the kitchen.

"Count to thirty!" Henry called out after them. And then, to Emma: "Where should we hide?"

Emma couldn't help but smile. Her plan was working out even better than she'd expected. She thought that she'd hide in a closet and let Henry find her, leading to the perfect setup for a secret kiss, but this was even better. She'd get uninterrupted alone time in an enclosed space with Henry. Who knew how long it would take Leo to find them?

It didn't take long. The moment after they sneaked into the upstairs linen closet, their shoulders pressed against each other as they sat on the floor, Leo threw open the door and said: "Gotcha. Henry, you're it."

Then, it was Leo's turn to grab Emma's hand and rush off as they left Henry on the second floor, counting out loud.

"Where are we going?" Emma whispered as Leo led her down the back staircase. Leo's hand was warm and soft. He smelled like the corn muffins he'd just eaten for breakfast. Fresh and sweet and delicious.

Leo put his finger over his mouth—*shhh!*—and led her behind the butler's pantry. He ran his hands along the molding, searching for something. Emma wondered why they were wasting their time like this, staring at a wall, when Henry was almost done counting to thirty. But then, Leo pressed a button, and suddenly, as if by magic, the wall released itself, revealing it to be not simply a wall, but a secret door.

"Oh, my God," Emma said as she stared at the door. How many times had she been in the butler's pantry without knowing that this secret door existed?

"Come on," Leo whispered, "before Henry finds us."

"How did you know this was here?" Emma whispered back as Leo ushered her inside and carefully shut the door behind them. With the door closed, the room was pitch-black. Leo reached up and turned on the light. Emma almost pointed out that if the light was on, it would be easier for Henry to find them, but then she didn't want to be alone with Leo in the dark, so she held her tongue.

"Pretty cool, huh?" Leo said. "This house is full of secret doors and closets and hallways. You didn't know?"

"I had no idea," Emma said, her eyes searching the space. The room seemed to be filled with old china, all in plastic cases. It was largely covered in dust. Leo blew on one of the bags, and dust went flying everywhere. Emma sneezed.

"Shhh!"

"Well, then, stop blowing dust everywhere!" Emma sneezed again.

"Look at how beautiful this is," Leo said as he opened the case. He turned the dish over and examined the watermark. "I wonder how old this is."

"Put it back," Emma said. "We're not even supposed to be in here."

Leo didn't respond. Emma turned to look at him, and noticed that his face had gone pale. He stood motionless, holding on to another plate.

"Put it back," Emma said, more firmly this time, taking the plate from Leo's hands. And that's when she saw it. The thing that had made Leo's face lose all color, the thing that made his hands go cold.

The plate looked like any other piece of china—an ivory-colored bone china dinner plate with a gold border. Elegant, delicate, beautiful. But there was something different about this plate. Something that made Emma freeze in place, too.

A Nazi insignia. Right there in the center of the plate. Emma didn't even know what she was seeing at first. Surely it was something else.

"What is this?" Emma said under her breath.

"I think you know what it is." Leo's eyes searched Emma's.

"It can't be."

"But it is. We're both staring right at it."

"Maybe it's not. The swastika is used in other cultures, you know," Emma said.

"That's not what we're looking at, Emma," Leo said carefully.

"Isn't it used in one of the Indian religions?"

"Yes," Leo said, his voice measured.

"But that's not this?"

"That's not this," Leo said. "And I think you know that."

"Maybe Mr. van der Wraak is storing this for a client," Emma said, her words coming out rushed, a jumble. "He might not even know that it's here."

Leo furrowed his brow. "Or maybe Felix is a Nazi."

Emma gasped. "He's not a *Nazi*. He's an *art dealer*. Maybe these are for a client."

"Only a Nazi would collect Nazi memorabilia. So either they're his, and he's a Nazi, or they are for a client, and he works for Nazis. I'm not really sure which one is worse."

7

Then

Age fourteen

Emma was surprised to find that she actually enjoyed Leo's company. They were both obsessed with the vintage clothing store in town, watching double features at the mall, and Model UN, which met every Wednesday after school. And they were both obsessed with discovering the truth about Henry's grandfather. Was he secretly a Nazi, hiding out in America?

They spent all of their free time in the school library, researching Nazis and the German occupation of the Netherlands, where Felix was from. In social studies, they'd studied World War II, but they didn't know much about what happened to the citizens of Holland during the war.

They didn't invite Henry to come with them, for obvious reasons, but that didn't matter. As they entered the ninth grade, Henry made the varsity lacrosse team, the only freshman his year to have done so, so there wasn't much opportunity to hang out together after school, anyway.

"I cut this out of today's paper for you two," the librarian said to Emma one day after school. Emma wasn't aware the librarian had been tracking what she and Leo had been doing each day. They usually started each afternoon in the library with their cover story—that Emma was tutoring Leo for English class—before diving into their research. Of course, like all cover stories, it was partially true. Leo needed the help. Though his spoken English was perfect, his essays always needed a once-over, since their teacher this year was a stickler for grammar. Emma loved helping Leo with his essays. His arguments were so incredibly smart and well-thought-out. He always captured something in the classwork that Emma, herself, had missed.

"Thank you," Emma said carefully to the librarian as they settled into their usual table.

"'Nazi-stolen artwork returned to a Jewish family,'" Emma said, reading the headline out loud.

"It was a Vermeer," Leo said, pointing at the photograph of the stolen painting. He looked at Emma. "I've seen Vermeers at the house."

"Me too," Emma said. "I think." Emma closed her eyes for a moment, struggling to remember which ones were the Vermeers. When they were little, Henry would brag about the various paintings that were in his grandfather's office, and they'd sneak in to look at them. But Emma hadn't been in Felix's office in years.

"Dutch painter," Leo said. "Famous for domestic interior scenes of middle-class life."

Emma squinted, trying to recall.

"Girl with a Pearl Earring?" Leo asked.

"Hmm?"

"That's one of the pieces he's known for," Leo said. "Also *The Girl with the Wine Glass.*"

"Lots of girls with things," Emma said, lost in thought as

she tried to conjure the image of a Vermeer. Then, turning to face Leo: "How do you know so much about art?"

"I'm Italian," Leo said with a gleam in his eye. Emma quickly looked away; this was Leo flirting. He bumped his knee into hers, and she swiveled her legs in the other direction. "What can I say? We love beautiful things."

Emma put her head back down into the article. Right then, the librarian came over with a book. "I thought you two might be interested in this book on Vermeer, too." She set the book down, and Leo opened it.

"This could be how Felix made all of his money," Leo said, flipping through the pages of the Vermeer book. "He could be dealing in these stolen paintings and artwork."

"The article says that the Nazis also stole silver and china, books. All sorts of cultural objects. We should make an inventory of what's in the hidden closet behind the butler's pantry."

"Maybe we should report him," Leo said.

Emma felt her breath catch in her throat. "We couldn't do that."

"Why not?" Leo asked, slamming the Vermeer book closed. Emma startled at the loud sound; it reverberated through the library. After muttering a few *sorry*s to the people around them, Leo whispered: "Is it because you're in love with Henry?"

"I'm not in love with Henry," Emma said, shaking her head, but she knew her voice betrayed her. She sounded like she was lying to him, she could tell. And she was, wasn't she? There had been one constant through her entire life: she was in love with Henry van der Wraak. "Anyway, Henry is not his grandfather. And more importantly, I shouldn't have to remind you that both my mother and your father work for Felix and Agnes."

"So?"

"Reporting Felix would upend their lives."

Leo shrugged.

"Our lives."

Leo shook his head.

"And have you considered the ramifications of accusing Felix, only to find out that we were wrong?"

"My father is not raising me to be a coward," Leo said. "He always says that we need to stand up for what's right."

Leo's words struck her in the heart. She couldn't help but think of her own father. If he were still alive, she could go to him with this information. Ask him what to do. He was a brave man, a hero, and he would have swept in and saved the day. If he were still alive, he would make sure that justice had been served. But all of that felt too personal to share with Leo. Instead, she stuck with what she knew: "I'm not a coward," Emma said.

"I know that," Leo said, opening the book back up and leafing through its pages. "Well, then, we should at least tell Henry the truth. He should know that his grandfather is a monster. He deserves to know."

"We can't tell Henry," Emma said, as if it were the most obvious thing in the world.

"Why not?" Leo closed the book—more quietly this time— and looked directly at Emma. His eyes challenged hers.

"We just can't," Emma said. "It would devastate him. Anyway, the plates are really the only proof we have that links Felix to the Nazis. And he's an art dealer, so the plates can be easily explained away. They could belong to a client, or a client brought them to him to sell, and he refused. Being in possession of one stack of plates isn't proof of anything. We shouldn't accuse him of being a Nazi—an actual living, breathing embodiment of pure evil—until we have more proof."

"All right," Leo said. "But how do you suggest we find out more?"

"We photograph and catalog the artwork that is in Felix's office."

Leo raised his eyebrows and couldn't help but letting a smile take over his face. "Are you suggesting what I think you're suggesting? We break in to Felix's office?"

"We don't have to break in," Emma said, shrugging her shoulders. "My mother has a key."

Age fifteen

"I forgot my wallet," Henry said, patting down his pockets, and rushed back into the house.

Leo rolled his eyes for Emma's benefit. She laughed quietly. Even though Emma was glad to have Henry hanging out with them that night for the first time in months, lacrosse practice winding down at the end of the school year, she couldn't deny it. She and Leo were now a closed set of two, and Henry didn't fit in with them quite as seamlessly as he used to. Emma and Leo had grown so close over the past year. Constantly sneaking off to break into Felix's office had helped them to form a bond. They'd cataloged countless pieces of artwork coming in and going out, and even though they'd never once found any additional illicit evidence, they didn't stop. Anytime Emma asked Leo if they should move on and accept defeat, he'd say that they were doing important work. They couldn't stop if they'd wanted to.

"Rich guy forgetting his wallet," Leo said, tilting his head toward the house.

"You forget your wallet all the time," Emma reminded him. "I paid for the last three movies we went to!"

Leo considered this. "But I'm not a rich guy, so it's an adorable quirk when a poor guy like me does it."

Emma laughed. "I'm going to have to double down on

house chores for my mom to make enough money to keep hanging out with you."

"You really do need to keep me in the lifestyle to which I've become accustomed. I expect double features on Sunday afternoons. With an extra large tub of popcorn."

"Noted," Emma said, smiling brightly. "Soda, too?"

"I think we both know the answer to that."

Leo winked at her, but Emma ignored it. She was staring at the front door.

"How long does it take to find a wallet?"

"Maybe it's harder to find because it's filled with so much money." Leo made an exaggerated gesture, as if showing the wallet weighing him down, and then dropping to the ground.

"Wouldn't the opposite be true?"

Leo offered a sheepish smile. Emma examined the curl of his lip. "Look, all my jokes can't be winners."

"This is the beauty of living in an apartment," Emma said. "When I lose something, I only have two rooms to check."

"Race you to the tree," Leo said. Before he could finish his sentence, Emma had already taken off toward the Japanese maple. The tree that she'd once thought tied her to Henry.

She jumped up to the first break—the trick for getting started—and flew up to one of the highest branches. Leo was close behind, but tried to gain footing on the tree without realizing that he needed to hop up to where the branches separated.

"Nope," Emma said from her perch up above. "That's not gonna work."

"A little help?"

"What would be the fun in that?" Emma's finger ran over the branch where Henry had carved their initials all those years ago. It seemed like a lifetime away, those lazy nights with Henry.

Leo figured out what he'd been doing wrong, swung his leg to the right spot, and hoisted himself up. He stood on the branch, bringing himself to his full height, and found himself face-to-face with Emma.

Emma hadn't realized quite how tall Leo had gotten. Or that the branch that she once thought was so high up wasn't quite as high as it had seemed when she was younger.

"Well, hello," Leo said, his face mere inches from Emma's.

"Hello back." Emma didn't get any closer to Leo, but she certainly didn't pull away. She had no idea what was about to happen, and the thought thrilled her.

Leo leaned closer. Emma held her breath; he was about to kiss her. She wondered what his lips would feel like—would they be soft, like Henry's? Would he put his hand on her cheek as they kissed, like Henry had done, drawing her in? Would their bodies touch, so close that Emma wouldn't be able to tell where she ended and Leo began?

A sudden commotion broke her from her reverie. Emma almost fell off the branch she was perched upon as she reacted to the noise. Yelling. She could almost make out yelling. Leo threw his arms around her body so that she wouldn't fall backward off the tree. Emma instinctively put her arms around his shoulders. She told herself it was merely to hang on, so as not to fall. But she'd wanted to get closer to Leo. Of course she had.

Leo pointed up, and Emma followed his finger. The noise was coming from the roof, it seemed. Emma furrowed her brow—*what's going on?*—and Leo shrugged in response—*no idea.*

Emma kept her gaze turned upward, following the sound of the yelling, of things crashing and rattling around up above. And then, through the branches of the tree, she saw a figure walk out onto the widow's walk.

As kids, Emma and Henry were never allowed to go up to the widow's walk, expressly forbidden by Mila. Accessible only through the attic, it was a small rooftop platform, bound by a small wood fence. To get up top, you had to pull down the ladder and climb up through a trapdoor. Henry had once told her that it was called a widow's walk because young wives would use them to watch for their husbands to return from sea, and not all of the seamen would return, turning their wives into widows. But her mother had offered a more logical explanation—it served as a safety protocol when the house was built in 1899. Since the chimney was integrated into the platform, its actual function was to aid in putting out chimney fires. Either way, it was one part of the house that Emma didn't mind never having seen up close.

Another figure came out onto the widow's walk. Felix.

"What's Felix doing up there with Fleur?" Leo asked, pointing upward.

Emma hadn't realized that the other person up there was Fleur. "Is that thing safe?" Emma asked Leo.

Felix and Fleur continued to yell at each other. Felix seemed to be trying to lure Fleur back into the house, but she refused to follow. He grabbed hold of her arm, and a struggle ensued.

"Fleur!" Emma called out, but she was too far away. Fleur couldn't hear. She turned to Leo: "We have to go help her."

Fleur screamed. She scratched Felix's face, and he used both arms to restrain her. Emma could barely believe her eyes—clearly, Fleur was running away from Felix. He'd chased her to the attic, and she'd tried to escape through the trapdoor, only to realize that once she was up on the widow's walk, she was stuck.

"Let's go," Leo said, and put out an arm to help Emma get down. Not willing to wait, she jumped down from the tree. The next thing she saw was Fleur, falling from the widow's walk. It happened so quickly, like an acorn falling off a tree. You couldn't be sure it had happened, but you saw the proof on the ground.

Emma gasped as she saw her beloved Fleur crash onto the driveway below to her death. Leo caught Emma from behind and spun her to him.

"I've got you," Leo said, smoothing her hair as her chest heaved with sobs. "Everything's going to be okay."

Emma couldn't respond. One minute, she'd seen Fleur on the widow's walk with Felix. The next, she saw Fleur on the driveway, dead. She soon found that she was unable to speak entirely. It would be hours before she could speak again. Before she could come to terms with what had just happened. Before she could connect the two things she'd seen. Before she could admit to herself the truth: that Felix van der Wraak had killed Fleur.

8

Now

"Your aunt was Fleur?"

"Yes," Stella said. "Did you know her?"

A million memories flooded Emma's mind. Did she know her? Of course she knew her. But it was so much more than that. Emma had loved her. Loved her deeply. Fleur's death affected her still.

"Yes," Emma said, overcome with sadness. The irony of standing so close to the spot where she'd fallen to her death. "I knew her."

"Hey," Stella said, bringing her back to the present. "Do you like cheese fries with gravy?"

"Excuse me?"

"I'd love to keep talking to you," Stella said. "Wanna go to the diner and split some cheese fries with gravy?"

Ten minutes later, they were seated in a booth at the Glen Cove Diner, two cups of decaf and a large order of cheese fries spread out on the table. It was a Long Island staple—no matter what town you were in, there was always a diner, and no matter what diner it was, they always had amazing french fries, covered in mozzarella, with a huge dish of gravy on the side.

"So, your mother was Mila," Stella said, dipping a french fry in gravy. "Felix's assistant."

"She wasn't his assistant," Emma corrected her. She took a sip of her coffee. "She was his maid, and then later, after my father died, she became more of a house manager."

"Where's your mother now?"

"She died, too," Emma said. "Eight years ago."

Stella stretched her hand across the table and took Emma's in her own. "I'm sorry for your loss."

Emma looked down at her hand. Usually, she hated it when strangers touched her, but there was something so familiar about Stella. "Thank you," she replied.

"I don't know what it's like to lose a mother," Stella said. "But I lost my father when I was a little girl, so I sort of know how you feel."

Emma didn't respond.

"Have I said something wrong?"

"I lost my father when I was a kid, too," Emma said.

"I knew I felt a connection with you," Stella said, nodding. "What was he like?"

"He used to tell me stories each night. Each one ended the same way—that I was a princess, pure of heart and soul." Images of her father flooded her mind. Then, remembering herself, she straightened her back and laughed. "That must sound so silly to you."

"It doesn't sound silly at all," Stella said. "My father told me such stories, too. Tell me more."

"He took such pride in his work, you know? I carry that with me, and try to treat my work with the same reverence."

"What do you do?"

"I'm a chef," Emma said. "I own a catering company."

"You're a chef?" Stella said, surprised.

"Why, don't I look like one?" Emma said, smiling. "I can show you the burn marks on my arms from a life spent in the kitchen, if you want."

"No," Stella said, shaking her head. "I didn't mean anything by it."

"Tell me about your dad."

"He was so great," Stella said. "He was really involved in our community. Believed in community activism. Taught me to be the same way."

"Is that how you got involved with the Glen Cove Historical Society?"

"Yeah," Stella said, staring off through the window. "But this one is so personal to me. I want to save Rolling Hill for my aunt."

"I want to save it, too," Emma said. "I get it."

"I'm not sure you get it quite yet," Stella said, squinting at Emma. "But I'm glad that you're invested, too."

"What do you mean? My father and I both lived here, just like Fleur. It was our home. That's why I want to save it."

Stella's hands were balled into fists, and she carefully unfurled them as she spoke. "I want to save it because it's evidence in my aunt's death. Once it's gone, there will be nothing to implicate Felix van der Wraak. And I want him to pay."

"It was tragic," Emma said, trying to choose her words carefully, "and at first, I assumed that Felix had done it, too. But there was a full investigation at the time. It was ruled an accident."

"No."

"No, you didn't know that?" Emma asked. "Or, no, you don't think it was an accident?"

"I think she was murdered."

Emma's words came out slowly: "I saw the whole thing, and I gave testimony in the investigation. I believe it was an accident."

Stella tilted her head, as if remembering something. "I read your statement to the police. You're underage witness number two."

"I gave a statement to the police, yes," Emma said, nodding. "I told them exactly what I saw."

"Well, you're wrong."

"I was there. You weren't," Emma said as softly as she could. "I know that you're upset about your aunt. I am, too. I loved her. But what makes you think that I'm wrong?"

"Because underage witness number one said that she was pushed."

9

Now

Emma took a deep breath. What a relief to be back at work. Work was her happy place. She loved being her own boss, at the helm of a company that she'd created from nothing.

La Vie en Rose, she'd called it. After spending four years at a restaurant in downtown Manhattan, following her training at the Culinary Institute of America, she'd been ready to go out on her own. She started a catering company out of her apartment, and within five years, she'd grown her small company into a large one.

Emma had started college premed, a biology major. She'd wanted to be a doctor as a little girl, but as her coursework piled up, she realized that she enjoyed cooking for her apartment-mates after class much more than she enjoyed her lab work. By senior year, she found herself applying to culinary schools rather than medical schools, and was thrilled when she got into her first choice, CIA.

At La Vie en Rose, Emma built a team that felt like family.

She'd started out hiring people who graduated from CIA, like she did. Highbrow, and highly trained. She'd envisioned her company as an annex to the French restaurant where she'd cut her teeth, but then soon found that the true gems came from the unlikeliest of backgrounds: a failed model, a former tattoo artist, and an ex-con. Her very own island of misfit toys. Somehow, they all fit with each other.

She told anyone who asked that she'd named it La Vie en Rose because of her background in French cuisine, as a nod to her favorite French song. But that wasn't the whole truth. She'd named it La Vie en Rose because of the song's importance in the movie *Sabrina*. The film always made Emma think of her father, the many nights she would ask him to watch it with her on repeat. The name was an homage to the movie. An homage to her father.

"You didn't want to name it after yourself?" Emma looked up and saw Leo at her door. "Don't most people name these things after themselves, like Emma's Edibles? Oh, wait...that would be something else..."

Emma's assistant followed closely behind, apologizing furiously for the fact that Leo wouldn't wait in the showroom, like she'd asked him to.

"We're old friends," Leo told Emma's assistant, his wide smile as warm as it was dazzling. "You wouldn't want to keep two old friends from each other, now, would you?" Emma's assistant laughed nervously, and looked to Emma for confirmation.

"It's fine, Kaitlin," Emma said, noticing how flushed her assistant's cheeks had become. At first she'd figured Kaitlin was embarrassed to have let Leo past her gatekeeping, but then Emma wondered if perhaps she had been taken with his charm. The faint Italian accent his voice still had around the edges did have a certain sexiness to it.

Emma motioned to a chair for Leo to sit down. "So, you tracked me down. Is this because I told you that I don't want you to build Hepburn?"

"No," Leo said, a devilish smile playing on his lips. "I'm here because I want to hire you."

"Oh, really?" Emma said. "What for, exactly?" For a split second, she wondered if he was going to ask her to cater his wedding. "Are you and Alison—"

"No," Leo said, shaking his head. "We're not together anymore."

"I'm sorry to hear that," Emma said. She felt the edges of her mouth lift, and then remembered herself. They were two old friends catching up, nothing more. "So, then, this would be for?"

"A big, fancy party," Leo said. "The kind that the van der Wraaks used to throw."

"A big, fancy party..." Emma trailed off, the words falling from her lips slowly. Surely he was not asking her to cater an event at Hepburn.

"At Hepburn, of course," he said.

Emma felt her face getting hot. "I don't think that's a good idea."

"Not a good idea to cater a black-tie party with over two hundred people? Are you afraid it will be a bunch of teenagers trying to sneak glasses of champagne, the way we used to do?"

"No," Emma said, resisting the temptation to smile at the memory. "I don't support what you're doing out there. I'm not going to cater some party and pretend that I'm okay with it."

"You always did care too much about what people think," Leo said. He tapped his foot against the base of her desk.

"Why did you really come here?" Emma asked carefully.

"Because I'm having a big grand opening party, and I want

you to cater it. I heard you were the best. Is my information mistaken?"

"No, it's not," Emma said, even though that wasn't what she meant. When she asked why he came there, she wasn't asking why he came to her office that day. She was asking why he was back in New York. On Long Island. She sat up a little straighter in her chair. "I'm the best. Top of my class at CIA, if you recall."

"You're also a spy in your spare time?"

"Culinary Institute of America," Emma said, rolling her eyes. Leo had made this joke before, countless times. "It's a big deal."

"You were always a big deal to me," Leo said quietly. "I thought you knew that."

"Look, let's not waste each other's time," Emma said. "You know I'm not going to cater this grand opening, and I bet you don't actually want me to, anyway."

"Why do you say that?"

"Too much has happened between us," Emma said. "We're not even going to talk about the fact that we haven't spoken in seven years?"

"We can talk about that, if you'd like." Leo tilted his head to the side, waiting.

"I think it's best if you leave."

"Well, I wouldn't want to be anywhere I'm not wanted." Leo stood, then paused. "But before I go, could you answer one thing for me?"

"What's that?"

"After all this time, after the way we grew up," he asked, "why would you become the help?"

"I beg your pardon," Emma said. Leo stood tall at the edge of her desk, making Emma feel small where she sat. She straightened her back once again. "I am not the help. Not that there would be anything wrong with it if I was. But I'm a business owner, same as you."

"True," Leo said, rubbing his chin. "But you're also the help. You *cater* to your clients. It's in the name of the field itself."

"And you don't cater to yours?" Emma rose from her desk chair to face him. But it was no use—his six-foot-two frame still towered over her, standing at barely five foot four.

"Sure, I guess," he said, laughing under his breath.

Emma didn't respond.

"I must have misunderstood, then," Leo said, and walked toward the door. "Emma?"

"Yeah?"

"When you change your mind, give me a call."

He walked out of the room without saying another word. Emma stood still for a moment, waiting for him to return. When he didn't, she took a deep breath, pulled out her phone, and scrolled through it randomly. He had such nerve to track her down and come to her office. To call her the *help*. Why was he still able to get under her skin after all this time?

She had left that part of her life behind. It was so far away that it felt like another lifetime. She certainly didn't need him coming back into her life and stirring things up.

But then Emma realized: he hadn't come into her life out of nowhere. She'd invited him back in. All because she hadn't been able to resist going back to the house.

There was something about that house, the estate. She didn't know why, but she knew that she had to save it. Could it be because of her father, who she still missed with the same ferocity as the day he died? Or was it Fleur, who'd stepped in as a role model when her father was gone? Or was it because of her own mother, unknowable to her until the end? Was she still trying to figure out her own mother? Was the house the key to that?

She walked to her office door and called out to her assistant. "By any chance, did Leo leave his business card?"

10

Then

Age sixteen

It was ruled an accident. An unfortunate accident. Felix van der Wraak explained it all to the police: he and Fleur had argued over some antiquities gone missing in the house. She denied stealing them. She fled to the attic, and then the widow's walk, where they'd continued to fight. Realizing how dangerous it was, Felix had tried to talk her back down, tried to get Fleur back inside. And when she wouldn't go back into the house, he tried to *force* her inside. Unfortunately, in the ensuing fight, Fleur lost her footing and fell to her death.

Felix's explanation made Emma question everything she'd seen. After all, she and Leo hadn't heard what the fighting was about—they were too far away for that. And from their perch in the tree, they hadn't had a clear view of the widow's walk. Since they'd been climbing down from the tree at the exact moment when Fleur fell, they hadn't actually seen how it happened.

Emma and Leo would meet up late at night in the cabana, going over what they'd witnessed.

"Maybe it *was* an accident," Emma said as they sat in the living room in the dark, so that no one would be able to see them. Linwood did his rounds of the property at eleven, and they didn't want to be questioned about why they were there.

"You and I both know that it was not."

"How can you be sure of that?" Emma asked, opening a can of soda that she'd swiped from the kitchen. "Why are you so sure of Felix's guilt?"

"Because he's a Nazi," Leo said. "The man is obviously pure evil."

Hanging out in the pool house was a new thing for Emma and Leo, neither one of them a rule breaker by nature, though Leo was certainly the more daring of the two. But they couldn't bear to be in the main house after what had happened to Fleur. In the days right after the accident, they'd tried to sneak in to examine the attic, but didn't make it past the staircase. Emma screamed when she walked through a cobweb, and Leo had gotten his foot stuck in a wood slat on the steps that had somehow rotted but had never been repaired.

They became convinced that the house was haunted. Emma could swear that she heard Fleur's voice when she walked into the kitchen. And Leo reported seeing things move on their own, like a set of candlesticks that fell off the grand piano in the living room, untouched.

They'd gone down to explore the basement.

"Do you feel that?" Emma said, sidling up to Leo for protection. She reached for his hand and held on tightly.

"Feel what?" Leo asked as he looked down at their hands.

"It's like a breeze or something," Emma said. "Are we near a window?"

"We're underground," Leo said, nervous laughter punctuating his words. "So, no windows."

Right then, Leo jumped.

"You felt it," Emma said. A statement, not a question.

Leo kept his face calm, but his voice betrayed him: "Let's get out of here!"

They were still gasping for air as they collapsed on the floor of the cabana, having run up a flight of steps, through the main house, and across the backyard to get there. Both splayed out on the floor, Emma felt the tips of Leo's fingers touch hers.

"You know what we need?" Leo asked Emma, bolting upright. "We need answers."

"And how, exactly, will we get those?" Emma turned over onto her side, her breath still shallow.

"We need to speak directly to Fleur."

"Sure," Emma said. "Pass me the phone."

Leo laughed. "I have another idea."

The next day after school, they rode their bikes into town to buy a Ouija board at the local toy store. The shop owner put it into a black plastic bag, not the usual white one with the logo of the store on it, and told them forebodingly: "Be very careful with this."

After everyone went to sleep that night, they met up to try it out.

"What's with the candles?" Leo said.

Emma had found a bag filled with tea lights and was positioning them all around the room, lighting them one by one. "I think we're supposed to make it welcoming for the spirits."

"I think you're going to burn the pool house down to the ground."

"It's going to work," Emma said. "I've seen this on TV a million times. Trust me."

The tea lights gave the cabana an ethereal glow; it felt like they were doing something sacred. Something important.

"How do these things work?" Leo asked.

"First, you put the board on the floor," Emma said. The board was made of a thick wood, with the words *yes* and *no* printed on the top corners. Next to the word *yes*, there was a sun, and next to the word *no*, there was a moon. The entire alphabet was printed on the bottom, along with the word *Goodbye* underneath.

Leo placed the board down onto the floor.

"I think you put this plastic thingy down onto the board," Emma said, holding said plastic thingy up in the air for Leo's inspection.

Leo held a tea light up to the instructions. Then he went about setting the board up. "The plastic thingy is called a planchette."

"I don't think anyone calls it that. Put it down."

Leo did as he was told.

"Then, we summon the spirits and it moves, giving us our answers."

"Okay," Leo said. He let his fingers lightly rest on the plastic planchette, and Emma followed suit.

Their fingers touched, and it gave off a spark.

"Oh," Emma said, drawing her fingers to her lips. She blew on them.

"Static electricity," Leo said. "From the rug, I guess."

He motioned to the planchette, and Emma brought her fingers back down.

"We summon the spirit of Fleur Bekkers," Leo announced loudly.

Emma studied the room. Surely if Fleur's spirit had entered the pool house, she would know. She'd sense it.

"Do you see anything moving?" Emma asked, still scanning their surroundings.

Leo shook his head.

"Fleur Bekkers," Leo said loudly and dramatically, "did Felix van der Wraak murder you?"

Then, a strong breeze entered the pool house, and all of the tea lights went out.

Emma screamed, and jumped into Leo's lap. Leo held her tightly as Emma burrowed her face in his chest. She felt safe and secure, wrapped in Leo's arms. With her eyes closed, her other senses felt heightened. She could hear Leo's heart beating. Fast, just like hers.

"It worked," Emma whispered into his shirt. "She's here!"

Leo tapped her shoulder, her cue to open her eyes.

"It is after eleven at night," Linwood said, standing in the doorway of the cabana, his voice firm. "You two should be in your beds, asleep."

Emma slowly got off Leo's lap and sat back down on the ground. "You scared us to death, Linwood."

"What on God's green earth are you two doing out here at this hour?" Linwood asked. "I have half a mind to call your mothers."

"Please don't call Leo's mother," Emma said, quickly covering. There was no sense in both of them getting in trouble. "It was my idea. It's my fault, not Leo's."

"And what is this?" Linwood asked. He shone his flashlight onto the ground, illuminating the Ouija board.

"We were trying to contact Fleur," Emma explained.

Immediately, Linwood's face softened. "Oh, kids. Don't you know that all of that stuff isn't real?"

Emma and Leo knew, intellectually, that Ouija boards weren't real and that houses weren't haunted. But try telling that to their hearts, still fluttering outside of their chests.

11

Now

"Aren't you going to let me in?" Emma asked Leo three days later. They stood side by side, in front of the main house at Rolling Hill, right beyond the porte cochere, with its missing light fixture and the faint mark of spray paint across the door.

Emma had called him back ten minutes after he'd left her office. Of course she had. She couldn't let it go—the house. Her memories. This idea that she would save it all from destruction.

"That's why you called me, isn't it?" Leo regarded Emma. "You didn't want to see me, and you certainly didn't want to cater my party. You only wanted to get inside the house one more time."

"No. Of course not."

"Liar."

"Okay, fine," Emma said. "Yes. I wanted to get into the house one more time. I needed to see it again. I need to prove to you that you shouldn't tear it down. Full disclosure, I'm planning to work with the Glen Cove Historical Society."

Leo laughed.

"What's so funny?"

"This house is not going to qualify for historical status," Leo said. "Don't you think I did my research before buying the property?"

Emma puzzled over this. "Did you know Fleur had a niece? I met her, and she's working with the Glen Cove Historical Society, too."

"Fleur had a niece? Strange that we wouldn't have met her."

Emma shrugged. "Well, I've met her now, and she's really invested in saving this place, too. She thinks it's evidence in her aunt's death."

Leo furrowed his brow. "It's not. There was a full police investigation at the time. And anyway, it's not like they can get better evidence *now*. The house is falling apart."

"Maybe it is," Emma said, her eyes trained on the house. "I think it's only fair that I be honest with you about my intentions."

"Intentions noted."

"When you meet Fleur's niece, Stella, you may change your mind about the house."

"I look forward to meeting her when the two of you chain yourselves to the front door," Leo said, laughter in his eyes. "But does this mean that you're *not* planning to cater my grand opening?"

Emma did the math—from what Leo had told her, the grand opening wouldn't be happening for six to nine months. She could play along and pretend to cater Leo's grand opening. When the Glen Cove Historical Society halted construction on the project, she'd gladly give Leo his deposit back. "Yes."

"Yes meaning no? Or yes meaning yes?"

"I'll cater your party. *If* it ever happens."

"It's going to happen." Leo smiled widely at her.

"We'll see. So, are you going to let me in?" Emma pointed toward the front door by way of explanation. "Being inside the house might give me some ideas."

"The party's not going to be *inside* the house, though," Leo said. "I'm going to do it outside, tented. The way the van der Wraaks used to do those barbecues."

Emma smiled at the memory of the Fourth of July barbecues. Her mother used to be so happy on those days—having the day off work, being the one catered to, as opposed to what she regularly did, which was cater to everyone else. Emma had so many wonderful memories wrapped up in the Fourth of July because of those barbecues. Especially her first kiss with Henry.

She spent her adult years trying to recreate the memory. And the feeling. Each summer, she'd throw her own Fourth of July party on the rooftop of her downtown Manhattan building. Her friends would haul up a portable barbecue, and they'd spend the day cooking hot dogs and hamburgers. She'd try to make her party a small-scale version of what the van der Wraaks used to do, grilling things you wouldn't usually grill: avocados, watermelon, clams, and of course, those peaches that melted in your mouth when you bit down into them. Each year, she'd try to get the peaches the exact way she remembered them from her childhood. They were never as good.

"How are you going to get your guests to the backyard if you don't take them through the house?" she asked.

"Oh, I'm not doing it in the backyard," Leo said matter-of-factly. He laughed. "I'm doing it out here. In the front."

Emma looked around at the front entryway to the main house. She supposed the driveway did have enough room for a big tent, but it didn't seem right. That wasn't the way they did things at Rolling Hill. Parties were in the ballroom or in a tent out back. But then, she realized, he didn't want to do things the way they'd always been done. That was why he was tearing the house down.

"What about the tree?" Emma said. She tried to keep her voice nonchalant.

Leo saw right through her. He raised his eyebrows. "What about the tree?"

"Are you tearing it down?" she asked. When Leo didn't answer, she immediately filled the air with more words: "I mean, Linwood would roll over in his grave. It's a one-hundred-year-old Japanese maple. A specimen tree. It's very valuable."

"So, in addition to being a chef and a spy, you're also an arborist?"

"No," Emma said. "I... I mean...that tree means something."

"We almost kissed in that tree," Leo said, his eyes meeting hers. "Once upon a time."

"Right," Emma said, the word falling slowly from her mouth.

"But that's not what you meant, our kiss," Leo said, his voice soft. "You meant that Henry carved your initials in it."

"I don't know what I mean," Emma said, running her foot along the brick driveway where they stood. Then, her words a jumble: "You'll have to tell the tent company that you also need a wood floor. Your customers will appreciate the beauty of the brick driveway, but they're not going to like it after a few cocktails if they're wearing high heels."

Leo regarded her, pointed at the driveway. "There will be one massive tent set up for the party here. And yes, there will be a wood floor. Don't worry, it won't affect your precious tree. I was thinking the catering tent could be set up back there?" He gestured toward the side of the house. It was a bit far from the tent where the party would be held, but Emma could make it work.

"Closer is better," she said. "But it's doable, if that's our only option."

"Or you could set up inside the house and hope that it doesn't cave in on your staff." He smiled widely at her, daring her not to laugh.

"Yeah, well, I have really good insurance."

They both laughed. Emma took a deep breath—it seemed like the tension was diffusing. She loved this about Leo, the way they could always make each other laugh. A memory came to the surface: the week after a bad breakup. Her, barely able to move, draped across the couch in Leo's apartment. Leo, doing impressions of her ex, shaking her from her funk and making her laugh for the first time in days.

"So, you're really not going to let me inside the house?" she asked.

"Why do you want to go back in so badly?" he said. "Did you stash something there before you left for college or something?"

Emma laughed. "I just really want to see it again."

"It's too dangerous," Leo said. "The house is a mess. I wouldn't want you to get hurt."

"You don't have to protect me," Emma said. "I'm a big girl now."

"It's your funeral," he said, and made his way to the front door.

Emma didn't need to be told twice.

The bones were still there. The house wasn't the house anymore, but you could still see vestiges of its former glory.

It felt surreal to be back inside, like a dream you could hardly remember upon waking. She'd lived a life there, but it was no longer hers. It never really had been in the first place.

Leo held the door for her, and Emma entered the house. A

film of dust covered the floor, and as they walked, it kicked up. Emma sneezed. And then she sneezed again.

Leo picked up a mask from the safety station and held it out for her. "It's what the drywall guys use. Keeps the dust out of your nose and mouth."

Emma put hers on. She looked around the entryway—as a child, it had felt so large to her. But now, seeing it as an adult, she realized that it wasn't nearly as massive as she'd remembered it. Some of her clients out in the Hamptons had entryways this large. But the millwork was impeccable. It wasn't something you saw in that new construction out east, this attention to detail. Every piece of wood in that entryway had been carved by hand, with care. The banister of the staircase to her left was a work of art. She looked up—the entryway was two stories high—and reminded herself of how this part of the house always made her feel so tiny.

Her eyes traveled to the double doors that led to the formal dining room. When she saw the crystal doorknobs, she couldn't help but think of Stella's remark about how some of the doorknobs dated back to 1899. Emma wondered how valuable they would be, and if Leo planned to sell any parts of the house. When he tore the house to the ground, would Leo salvage the crystal doorknobs? Emma recalled the way her father had always kept a cloth in his pocket, how he'd give the doorknobs a shine as he walked by.

"Those doorknobs," she said, pointing. "They're real crystal."

"They are," Leo said. "But they're not worth as much as you'd think."

"So, you're not going to save them?"

"Would you like one?" Leo carefully removed the doorknob from the door. He held it out.

"No, thank you." Emma was struck by the gesture and

smiled. But then the smile left her face when she realized how easily something that she thought had been solid could be taken apart.

"I insist."

Emma let Leo give her the doorknob. "Well, thank you."

"You're very welcome. Now, look, we can't really go past the staircase into the living room," Leo explained, "because that's where the tree fell into the house. But we can check out the ballroom, if you'd like."

"I'd like to see the kitchen, please," she said. As she passed the living room, she saw that there was still furniture, covered in drop cloths.

"They didn't take anything when they left," Leo said, as if reading her mind. "Could you imagine moving out of a place like this and leaving things behind?"

Emma shook her head, and made her way into the kitchen. She tried to take a deep breath in, to see if the kitchen still smelled the way it used to, but the mask didn't allow it. She took off her mask. Nothing. Anyway, it had been seventeen years since Fleur had been in this kitchen. Another chef had taken her place, even. And then another chef after that. There were no traces of Fleur that remained.

"Check this out," Leo said, removing his mask, too. He pressed a button in the hallway. A buzzer sounded in the kitchen.

"What is that?" Emma said, trying to pretend that the loud noise hadn't startled her.

"A vestige of when the house was originally built in 1899. Back in the Gilded Age, they would have these dramatic dinner parties. The servants would buzz this thing when guests had finished eating each course. The buzz would alert the kitchen staff that it was time to get out the next part of the meal."

"How did we not know that was there?" Emma asked, moving out into the hallway to examine the buzzer. The French restaurant, *La Ferme*, where she'd trained, had had a similar system in place—it was how the owner, Pierre, created the perfect flow of service that the restaurant was known for. Still, she was surprised to see it at Rolling Hill. Surprised to discover something about it that she didn't know, after all these years.

"I have no idea," Leo said. "Turns out, there were *lots* of things we didn't know. My team discovered them all. Press the right panel on that wall."

Emma did as she was told, and the door released itself, revealing a narrow hallway. "Well, I'm not walking through that. So creepy!"

Leo laughed. "It's a secret passageway to the back of the house. Leads you to the staff quarters quickly. Quicker than walking through the house."

"I'll take your word for it," Emma said. "We thought the house was haunted *before* we found stuff like this."

"Still think it is?" Leo asked.

Emma closed her eyes to listen to the silence. It was in moments like this, back then, that she could swear she still heard Fleur's voice. "I don't hear anything."

"The van der Wraaks moving out must have exorcised the house of its demons," Leo said, walking over to where Emma stood.

"Maybe we should call the Long Island Medium to be sure."

Leo laughed. "There's all sorts of secret cabinets where you can stash stuff."

"Let me guess," Emma said, "for the servants."

"Bingo. There's actually one right behind you," Leo said, reaching his arm past Emma's head. As he pushed the panel to open up the hidden cabinet, he took a step toward Emma.

She was suddenly very aware of his breath, sweet on her face, and his body, his knees brushing against hers.

"Oh," she said, not moving from where she stood. Emma closed her eyes.

"What are you doing?" he said.

Emma opened her eyes with a start. "I thought you were going to kiss me."

"Why would you think that?" Leo said, making no move to get farther away from Emma.

Emma felt her face flush, mortified. "Um, I..."

"Is it because I gave you a doorknob?" Leo asked, laughing. "Just because a man gives a woman a doorknob, it doesn't mean that you can have your way with him."

"I'm sorry," Emma said, flustered. "I thought we were having a moment or something."

Leo held her stare. "Look, even if we kiss, I'm still knocking this thing down to the ground. You know that, don't you?" He laughed uneasily, as if to convince himself of something.

"I'm sorry," Emma said, laughing, too. "I didn't mean to be inappropriate." Emma didn't really know why she thought he was about to kiss her. She knew that he had a crush on her when they were younger. And that fight they'd had seven years ago, God, that fight. Had she really thought that a kiss from her would cause him to halt plans on the development? Or was it more complicated than that—had she actually wanted to kiss him? Being in the house again was doing strange things to her mind. Maybe it really *was* haunted.

"Do you want to see the attic?" Leo spun on his heel and walked to the other side of the kitchen.

"No, thank you."

"Still scared?" he asked, looking very much like his fifteen-year-old self, searching for mischief. When he smiled, she could see the boy he'd been back then.

"I think I am," Emma admitted, and laughed despite herself.

"Well, I'm glad," Leo said. And then, under his breath: "Wouldn't want you knocking me off the widow's walk."

Emma furrowed her brow.

"Bad joke," he said. "Sorry."

"Hey, can I ask you something?" Emma said.

"Sure."

"When we were interviewed, back when Fleur died," Emma said. "Why did you tell the police that Fleur was pushed?"

"Because she was."

"You saw that?" Emma asked. "Did you actually see it happen? Because I didn't. I recall seeing them fight, and then we rushed out of the tree to try to get help. Next thing I saw was Fleur falling to the ground."

"He was a Nazi, Emma. I think it's obvious what happened."

"But you didn't actually *see* it?"

Leo looked down at his shoes. "Did I ever tell you that I reported Felix for being a Nazi living in the United States?"

Emma didn't reply. She couldn't form the words.

"Multiple times, actually," he said, meeting her eye. "But they always wrote back citing insufficient evidence, or some lawyer speak like that."

"The plates," Emma said under her breath.

"I sent them one," he said. "But they said that people collect strange things. It didn't mean anything."

"Were they still here when you bought the property?"

"Yup. I'm going to donate them to the Holocaust Museum," Leo said. "My assistant's working on the logistics. They're right where we left them."

He ran his hands along the molding, searching for the button. And then, the wall released itself, opening the secret door to their former hiding spot.

Emma walked through the door, ready to see the hidden plates with the swastika. It was as if she wanted to make sure that they were still there. Like if the evidence of evil was contained, there could be evil no more.

But the plates were gone.

Emma pointed at the empty shelves. "I guess your assistant already boxed them up and shipped them off," she said.

Leo's face had gone slack. He walked through the pantry, running his hands along the shelves. "No."

"Um, yes," Emma said. "She's clearly much more efficient than you give her credit for."

"No, that's not possible," he said, his face a question mark. "There's a very specific way they handle these donations. We have a video call set up to show them the plates. My assistant wouldn't have sent them without the go-ahead from the Holocaust Museum."

"I guess the house really *is* haunted," Emma said, laughing uneasily.

"This isn't funny," Leo said. "This means someone was inside the house. Someone who stole everything that was in this pantry."

12

Then

Age sixteen

When Emma told her mother why she didn't want to have dinner at the main house, she was careful not to use the word *haunted*.

"You used to beg me to eat dinner over there each night," her mother said. "On nights when I insisted we eat here, you'd sulk. And you'd sneak out for breakfast before I was even awake most mornings."

"Things are different now," Emma said, her eyes cast down at the floor.

"I see that you now spend your free time with Leo, and not Henry," Mila said.

"I just hate the house," Emma said.

"Is this because of Fleur?" Her face wrinkled at the mention of Fleur's name. Even in death, Emma's mother still could not muster up a positive feeling about her.

"It's because the house is haunted," she blurted out.

Her mother let out a laugh. "Haunted?"

"Yes, haunted. Leo and I have proof."

"Is this because you don't like the new chef?" Her mother was right—Emma hated the new chef. No matter what she made for them, it never tasted as good as what Fleur used to cook.

"The house is haunted," Emma said under her breath. "I know it."

"I can assure you, it's not haunted," Mila said, laughter still in her voice. "Anyway, you'll need to get over this before Saturday, because you're expected to be at the benefit."

Emma had forgotten all about the benefit—one of Agnes's pet projects. Each year, the van der Wraaks threw a big, lavish black-tie party to raise money for the Long Island Ballet. Agnes had done ballet as a child, and was passionate about it. Her parents had her enrolled at a prestigious ballet academy, and she had planned to pursue dance professionally. Then, World War II and the horrible Hunger Winter that came toward the end of it changed everything. Unfortunately, because of the severe malnutrition Agnes suffered during the war, a career in ballet was no longer feasible for her. But still, dance remained an important part of her life. One wall of her home gym held a barre, and Agnes had a teacher come twice a week to run her through the old drills she did as a girl. She also donated her time by teaching kids ballet on Sunday mornings. She donated her money by throwing this annual benefit.

When the house had been built in 1899, they'd created a grand ballroom on the first floor. Most of the Gilded Age mansions on the Gold Coast of Long Island had grand ballrooms, necessary to host the many decadent society parties of the day. These days, the van der Wraaks didn't entertain nearly as much as the family for whom Rolling Hill was originally built. They used the space as a living room and library mostly, but for parties like the ballet benefit, it was as if time moved in reverse. They cleared the room and restored it back to its original purpose.

Each year, the benefit was an impossibly glamorous evening. Men in their sharp tuxedos, women in complicated, beautiful gowns. The smell of expensive perfume permeating the air. The house was completely transformed, with delicate white fabric covering the walls, a dance floor set up in the center of the ballroom, and fresh flowers on every available surface (and even some floating down from the ceiling).

An extravagant cocktail hour featured a caviar bar, three different types of meat at the carving station, and a table with a gigantic five-tiered seafood tower. Dinner was a duet of filet mignon and lobster, with truffle mashed potatoes and grilled vegetables on the side. And then, right when guests thought the night was coming to an end, a surprise: after dessert, the ballet corps treated the guests to a performance.

"You can bring Leo as your date," Mila said to her daughter, her face brightening at the idea.

Emma did not want to bring Leo as her date. Because despite everything—the way he treated her at school, her mother's warnings prohibiting it, the fact that his grandfather may or may not have been evil—Emma still wanted to go with Henry.

But how could she help it? He'd been the center of her life for most of it. She knew he felt it, too—they were a foregone conclusion. They'd be together, and get married one day. The bride and groom in her beloved Chagall. Maybe they'd even live at Rolling Hill. She'd be the maid's daughter no more. Emma knew that one day, she was destined to live inside the main house. One day Henry would wake up and know that Emma was the one. She, the princess, pure of heart and soul.

The night of the party, Emma walked over to the main house with her mother. Leo was standing, waiting for them, by the back door.

"You look beautiful, Emma," he said.

Emma couldn't bear to look at Leo, dashing in his tuxedo, so she looked toward her mother instead.

"I didn't know you two were coming together," her mother said, clasping her hands together like a little girl. "I'm so pleased."

"We're not," Emma said at the same time as Leo said: "I would be lucky to have such a wonderful person as my date."

Mila headed off into the party, and Leo held his arm out for Emma to take. Not wanting to offend him, she threaded her arm with his and let him lead her to the bar.

"Think they'll let us get some champagne?" he whispered to Emma.

"Do I look twenty-one?" she asked hopefully.

"Definitely not," he replied.

Emma looked down at her dress, a strapless white organza dress with intricate black floral embroidery. She'd felt so grown-up that night, putting it on. Her mother rarely let her buy new clothing, but that year, for the benefit, she'd taken her to the department stores in Garden City. They'd shopped all morning, going from store to store, and then had lunch at Lord & Taylor—Waldorf salads and peach iced tea, which felt like the height of glamour. She couldn't remember the last time she'd had that much alone time with her mother, and putting on the dress that evening had made her gleeful, remembering the day.

"What's wrong?" Leo asked.

Emma closed her eyes for a moment. "Nothing."

"I thought women wanted to look younger, not older," he said, brushing off an imaginary piece of lint from his arm. "Did I say the wrong thing?"

"No." But he had. Couldn't Leo see that she wanted to look older, not younger? Look like the sort of woman who'd be invited to a glamorous benefit like this? Not only there because she was the maid's daughter?

"Let's try to get some champagne anyway," Leo said, and gave Emma's shoulder a squeeze.

They quickened their pace as they strode up to the bar. The bartender didn't need to say a word. He simply shook his head, their signal to leave.

"I don't look twenty-one, either," Leo said, "if that makes you feel any better."

Henry walked past them and swiftly took one of the flutes of champagne that were lined up on the bar. Turning to face Emma and Leo, he asked: "What? You two aren't drinking?"

"We got shut down by the bartender," Emma said.

Henry furrowed his brow. "Well, then, don't get it from the bartender." Henry handed his drink to Emma. He then extended his arm and reached over to a passing waiter's tray, swiping two more glasses of champagne.

"Whoa," Emma said. "Thank you."

"Yeah, thanks, man," Leo said. He tried to make his voice sound appreciative, but Emma could tell—he was disappointed that he hadn't been able to get the champagne himself.

"Don't sulk," Emma said to Leo. She swatted his arm playfully, and was surprised to notice how strong he felt. How the fine fabric of his tuxedo jacket allowed her to feel the muscle below.

"Taste it. It's delicious," Henry said.

Emma took a sip, and the bubbles tickled her nose. She didn't think it tasted delicious. She thought it tasted sour and not at all sweet enough. Wasn't champagne supposed to be sweet?

And then, as if reading her mind, Leo said: "I prefer the prosecco I used to drink in Italy. Sweeter."

"Well, excuse me," Henry said, laughter in his voice. "I'll tell my grandfather to order some prosecco for next year's gala."

"I'll hold you to that," Leo said. And then, with mischief in his eyes: "Let's down this champagne and get out on the dance floor."

"That sounds like a great idea," Henry said, quickly drinking the rest of his champagne. "Emma, would you like to dance?"

Emma didn't remember saying yes to Henry. She didn't remember putting her champagne glass down, or whether or not she'd finished it. All she could remember was this, being swept up in Henry's arms, dancing. And seeing Leo looking impossibly sad on the sidelines as he watched.

"I know you go to the pool house with Leo every night," Henry said, breaking the spell Emma had fallen under. She'd been busy imagining the rest of her life with Henry.

Her eyes fluttered open. "What do you mean?"

"Don't deny it," he said, a small smile playing on his lips. "I've seen you."

"It's not like that," Emma said.

Henry pulled her closer. "What's it like, then?"

"We're just friends."

"Friends don't sit together in the dark. What are you doing there, all alone with Leo every night?"

"Nothing," Emma said. She felt heat rising in her cheeks.

"I thought the cabana was our place," Henry said. "It's where we had our first kiss."

"Why do you care? It's not like you ever kissed me again," Emma said, suddenly speaking very fast. "How come you never kissed me again?"

Henry angled his head down toward Emma. "I didn't know you wanted me to."

"That's a lie," Emma said, surprising herself with her directness. She'd never spoken her mind like this with Henry before. Was the champagne to blame? "I think you knew. Of course you knew."

Henry pressed himself closer to Emma. She could feel every part of his body, moving against hers on the dance floor. His chest, so strong, his arms, holding her tight. His hips, matched up perfectly against hers. She looked over Henry's shoulder to see if Leo was watching them still, but she couldn't find him through the crowd.

"Okay, so maybe I knew," Henry said. Quietly, into her ear, he said: "My grandfather doesn't want me to date you. He told me that you are off-limits."

Emma felt Henry's words like a knife to the heart. But then she remembered: "My mother said the same thing."

Neither one spoke; Emma wondered if Henry was reading the same subtext in the air: his grandfather and her mother didn't want them to date because they were carrying on an affair with each other.

The band started another song, a slower song, and Henry leaned toward Emma. "If I tried to kiss you now, would you let me?"

"Yes," Emma whispered. And then, in case he didn't hear her, she said it again, this time louder: "Yes."

Henry closed the remaining space between them and kissed her. And it was every bit as magical as the first time. Even more so, she thought, in the middle of the dance floor at his grandparents' house. Where anyone could see them. Where everyone could see them.

This is it, she thought. *This is the moment when everything will change.*

13

Now

Emma felt most at ease when she was at someone else's catered affair. She loved the bustle of the work, the excitement of being part of someone's big day. When she was working a party, it was five hours where she was so busy that she didn't have time to think. Didn't have time to go over everything that had gone wrong the day before.

Emma did one last walk-through of the room. She could hear the minister finishing up the wedding ceremony, and soon guests would be filing in, hungry. All of the servers stood at attention as she passed by, ready to begin. There were two bars, both fully stocked, and additional servers stood in the walkway to the cocktail hour, holding silver trays with frosted martini glasses.

The minister announced that it was time to kiss, and Emma sneaked a peek at the happy couple. She loved watching this—the first kiss that two people shared as a married couple. It seemed so momentous, like the start of something. But today, watching the first kiss reminded her of Leo, and how she'd embarrassed herself by closing her eyes, thinking he was about to kiss her.

She turned around and headed back to the kitchen. She told herself that she needed to rush back because it was a faux pas for the caterer to be standing in the center of the cocktail hour. But really, if she told herself the truth, she'd know that she was rushing back to the kitchen because the kitchen was the one place her mind could clear. Cooking was always so meditative for Emma—it always helped her find calm.

"How are we doing?" she called out as she entered the kitchen. Today's affair was at one of her favorite venues, Oheka Castle in Huntington on Long Island. The former country home of financier and philanthropist Otto Hermann Kahn, it was built over a five-year span, 1914 to 1919, on 443 acres, with a French château interior of over 10,900 square feet. It was said Kahn built it because Jews were not allowed to join the clubs and golf courses in New Jersey, so he came to Long Island and built himself an estate that had everything he needed.

Now Oheka operated as a hotel and event venue and sat on a modest 23.2 acres. The mansion was fully restored to its Gilded Age glory, and was surrounded by beautifully mani-cured grounds. And the best part? Instead of having to bring her own equipment and create a kitchen out of thin air, like she'd done for the Shelby wedding at a farm out in Montauk the weekend prior, Oheka had a professional kitchen for her to use. And she'd done so many affairs there that the kitchen felt like her own.

"Ready, Chef," Emma's event manager, Francisco, said.

Francisco Day was one of Emma's two event managers on staff. He came to her from a reentry program, designed for incarcerated men to transition back to civilian life. Francisco had interviewed for a position at Pierre Toussaint's world-renowned restaurant, *La Ferme*, where Emma herself had trained, but he hadn't had the training required for a traditional French kitchen. Pierre had called Emma and suggested that with some training, Francisco could be a real asset.

Pierre was right.

Emma taught Francisco everything she knew, and he quickly became one of the most valued members of her team. Within a year, Francisco was one of her event managers. He moved out of his halfway house and into his own place. He met a lovely woman named Blanca, and they'd been together for over two years. She was plain, in contrast to Francisco, who had enormous brown eyes that you could get lost in, lined with thick black lashes. He had a full head of black hair, which he slicked back each day, making him look like a movie star from the 1950s. He adored Blanca, which Emma knew for sure because Blanca called him *Franny* and Francisco allowed it.

"That's what I like to hear," Emma said with a smile. "Have you tasted everything?"

"Yes, Chef," Francisco said, holding out a plate for her. He loved using the formal address of respect—*yes, Chef*—even though they weren't technically in a restaurant kitchen, and he wasn't only her event manager. He was one of her best friends.

Emma looked at the plate, filled with a sampling of the hors d'oeuvres they'd be serving at the party—grilled baby lamb chops topped with mint pesto, caviar and crème fraîche on top of potato crisps, ahi tuna on crispy rice, seafood paella served in miniature cast-iron skillets, and a martini glass filled with truffle mashed potatoes, topped with braised short ribs.

"Service!" yelled a server at the door. The kitchen immediately went into action as servers took their first round of hors d'oeuvres out.

One of the newer servers picked up her tray incorrectly, and the entire thing crashed to the ground. "Oh my God!" she said, bending down to pick up the mess. "I'm so sorry."

"Luckily that platter had the vegetable kebabs," Francisco quietly said to Emma, his arms folded as he watched service begin. Francisco wore his chef's coat with the sleeves rolled up past the elbows. Emma always told him to order the short-sleeved version, but Francisco had a very specific sense of style. His love of beautiful things was what had gotten him arrested in the first place—he'd done time for running a ring of car thieves who specialized in high-end and classic sports cars.

"It's only some veggies and some broken plates," Emma told the server. "Nothing to worry about."

"I feel so awful," the server said.

"We've all been there," Francisco told the server. "Everyone, keep going. We'll clean this up."

"Everything's broken," the server said, still in disbelief that she'd dropped her first platter filled with tiny plates.

"It's just a bunch of plates," Francisco said. "Plates break."

"Francisco's right," Emma said. "It's just a plate. Easily replaced."

As two of the kitchen crew guys got brooms and dustbins to help out, Emma couldn't help thinking about the plates that went missing at Rolling Hill.

Only someone who had lived in the house and knew the house's secrets would have broken in to steal the plates. But most of those people had died or moved on. The only ones still around were Leo, and…well, she'd rather not think of him.

Of course, telling herself not to think of him had the exact opposite effect. Now, her thoughts were filled only with him. When they were kids, a vote of two to one always won out. Whether it was which bike trail to take or whether they'd swim in the pond or the pool, Emma could always convince

Henry to outvote Leo. Perhaps if Leo wouldn't listen to her about the fate of Rolling Hill, all she needed was one more person on her side. Emma pulled out her phone and scrolled. She found the contact she was searching for and hit Call.

PART TWO:
FRAMING

14

Then

Age seventeen

They hooked up secretly all year, far away from the eyes of his grandfather and her mother. Late at night, Emma and Henry would meet, under cover of darkness, at the indoor tennis court to fool around.

It was their new place; a place where they were a closed universe of two. No one used the indoor tennis court, for one, and Linwood didn't stop in on his walk-throughs of the property at night. They'd find each other on the chaise lounge couches on the far end of the court, where it was dark, untouched by the outdoor lights that illuminated the patio area around the building. Sometimes Henry would bring lantern lights, and sometimes he'd bring blankets for them to cuddle under. One time, they stayed out so late that they fell asleep afterward, and Emma woke up with a start at 5:00 a.m., just in time to sneak back into their respective homes and their respective beds.

Emma wished her mother could see how much she needed

Henry. Couldn't she tell that Henry understood her in a way that no one else could? Two fatherless kids, both with holes in their hearts that needed filling. Both untethered from the world in a way that they couldn't explain, both feeling afloat when thinking about their immediate futures after high school. Would Henry be the man that his father once was? Would Emma be the woman that her father would have been proud of?

Leo was still her best friend, but he didn't understand her in the same way that Henry could. Leo looked forward to high school graduation, couldn't wait to see the look on his father's face when they handed him the diploma. Emma knew that on graduation night, she would only feel her father's absence more intensely, the same way that she knew seeing Henry's grandparents in the audience would only remind Henry of the people who wouldn't be there.

Every night, they'd meet in secret. She would give herself so completely to Henry, and she would feel more like herself than she ever had.

It was the happiest she'd ever been in her life.

15

Now

Home court advantage. That was what Emma was hoping for. That was why she'd invited him to her old haunt, Pierre Toussaint's Michelin-star-rated restaurant. In some ways, the people who worked at *La Ferme*, The Farmhouse, were like family to Emma. She still met up with them for dinners on the odd Monday night and the occasional drinks, late night Sunday, after finishing up a party.

"*La meilleure table, bien sûr,*" Pierre said. "*Pour toi.*" *The best table, of course. For you.*

"*Merci,*" Emma said, and sank into the plush dining chair. Pierre took such pride in his restaurant, and the love he put into every detail of the place showed. The table was formal, yet welcoming. An ivory tablecloth, neatly pressed and crisp. Crystal wine goblets, perfectly clean, not a water stain in sight. A small sterling silver vessel, packed tightly with pale pink roses, between the two plates. The roses were so perfectly formed, so lush, they nearly looked fake. But the faint aroma announced that they were real. If Emma ever opened a restaurant herself, she would model it on what Pierre had created.

Pierre took her hand and gently kissed it. *"Bonne chance, oui?"* Pierre was wishing her luck; he could tell that Emma was nervous about this dinner.

"Oh, it's just dinner," she said.

"Bien sûr que c'est," he replied. *Of course it is.*

When he walked in, Emma felt the world slow down. He walked right to her table, like a film star making his grand entrance, and she could see the man he had become and the boy he had been, all at once. His boyish good looks had transformed into handsome ruggedness. His hair, still a thick dirty blond, was styled the same. His face wasn't as soft, though his lips were still full. Emma noticed a slight shadow of stubble across his jaw.

"Emma!" Henry said, leaning down for a hug as she started to stand up. It made for an awkward embrace.

"Thank you for coming," Emma said to Henry. She hadn't been sure if he'd accept her invitation.

"This is where you worked, isn't it?" Henry asked, taking in the room. "I've never been here before."

"It's one of the best French restaurants in the city," Emma said quietly. "I'm surprised it wasn't on your radar."

"Because you think I'm so fancy." Henry's clear blue eyes crinkled at the edges.

Emma knew that he meant it as a joke, but she couldn't help but feel embarrassed.

It felt strange, this. To be sitting across the table from Henry, the boy she'd loved her whole life. Only now he was a man. And it was fifteen years later.

"Bonsoir," the server said in a thick French accent. Emma couldn't tell if he was really French or not. Pierre often hired

actors as servers, and had them speak in a French accent. *Good for tips*, he would say. "I am told by Pierre that you are a famous alumna of this esteemed institution."

"I hope he's not going to embarrass me tonight," Emma said.

"Embarrass you? No," he said. "Get you drunk on free champagne? Yes." With a wave of the hand, a bottle of Veuve Clicquot appeared at the table.

"My favorite," Emma said with a smile.

"Pierre knows," the server said. And then, to Henry: "May I interest you in a glass of bubbly?"

"Absolutely," Henry said. When the servers left the table, Henry raised his glass: "To old friends."

"Old friends," Emma said. She tried to maintain a smile, but found it difficult. Was that all they'd been, in Henry's mind? Friends? He'd been so much more than that to her. Surely he knew that.

"Did you know that Leo had bought Rolling Hill?"

"I hadn't really given the place a thought once my grandparents sold it, to be honest. They were happy to move into the city and downsize. It was good for them. And with my grandmother gone now, it's better for my grandfather to have a smaller place."

"You don't feel any connection to the house?" Emma asked. "You know Leo wants to tear it down?"

"Someone was going to, right?" Henry said. "The developer my grandparents sold it to went bankrupt, and the property sat empty for years. I think Leo might have bought it in foreclosure, if I'm not mistaken."

"So you did know."

"I might've heard something about it."

"And you don't care what he does with it?"

"Not really," Henry said. "It was my home for a long time. But it hasn't been for years."

Emma sat with his words. It had been Henry's family home, and he felt no connection to it anymore. Emma didn't live there—her parents *worked* there—yet she felt that tearing the house down would be akin to cutting off a limb. Why was that? Was it because as long as the house was still standing, she could keep her father alive in her memory?

Emma wasn't quite sure what to say to Henry. She stuck with the truth: "I don't want him to tear it down."

"Well, if you've got millions of dollars stashed away some-where, I'm sure Leo would be happy to sell it to you."

Emma laughed. "Right."

"I'm impressed with what Leo's done," Henry said. "He's incredibly successful. We should both be proud of him. We knew him when."

Emma smiled. An image of Leo, as a teenager—long hair and that ever-present smile—flashed through her mind. Henry was right; they knew him when. Although they'd both lost touch with Henry, Emma had stayed friends with Leo after high school, through their early twenties. The question, Emma thought, was whether or not they still knew Leo now.

"I'm in touch with the Glen Cove Historical Society," Emma said. "Maybe you'd be willing to meet with us, help us out a bit in our efforts to halt the destruction of Rolling Hill?"

Henry's expression changed from soft to hard. "I have no interest in interfering with Leo's work in any way. As far as I'm concerned, he's the owner of Rolling Hill now. He can do what he wants with it."

"I'm going to help the Glen Cove Historical Society," Emma said, her voice almost a whisper.

"Why would you do that to Leo?" Henry regarded her. "This isn't just you breaking his heart when we were teenagers. This is interfering with his professional life. His work. You can't do that."

Henry's words hit her like a dagger. She took a sip of water.

Henry put his head back, cracked his neck. "Look, I don't mean to sound angry. But I'm not sure that you realize what's at stake here for Leo. This is a big project, a multimillion-dollar deal that will keep him busy for years. If you hold him up in litigation, you'll cost him big bucks. Is this about the house, or is it about Leo?"

"It's the house," Emma quickly replied. "Of course it's about the house."

"You sure about that?"

"That house has historical significance," Emma said. "And emotional significance."

"Why? With all due respect, Emma, you didn't even live in the main house."

"My father was happy there," Emma said. "We were happy there."

"Your father wasn't happy in that house," Henry said, an edge to his voice now there that hadn't been before.

"Why would you say that?" Emma asked. Those whispers, the year after her father died. She'd never forgotten them. Questions about how much time Mila was spending with Felix. Talk about how quickly she'd gone from the maid to the head of the household.

"You know what?" Henry said, tossing his napkin onto the table. "This was a mistake. My coming here was a mistake. I'm sorry."

"Wait, you're leaving?" Emma said, scrambling for words.

Henry stood. "I think it's for the best."

"No, you can't leave."

Henry walked around to Emma's side of the table and kissed

her cheek lightly. "If you speak to Leo, please send him my best."

"You can't leave," Emma said, louder this time.

But despite Emma's protestations, Henry walked out of the restaurant.

16

Now

Emma knew what they were doing was wrong. Henry had been very clear—he wanted nothing to do with halting the development of Rolling Hill. Still, when Stella suggested they have lunch on the Upper East Side and "accidentally" bump into Henry, she couldn't resist. Stella had cleverly followed him on Instagram and noticed that he had lunch at Sant Ambroeus a few times a week.

Emma was glad that Stella had called her after their late-night fries at the diner. Stella was funny, for one, and also, Emma didn't need to explain to Stella why she was upset about Rolling Hill. Stella understood. Stella knew.

Henry's art gallery, the one his grandfather used to own, was on Madison Avenue, only a few blocks away. Van der Wraak and Son, it had been called. It was only now that Emma realized how devastating the name must have been for Felix— named for him and his child who had tragically died young.

Emma had only been to the gallery a couple of times with

her mother, when running errands for Felix, but she knew the way without even thinking about it. It was one of those memories from childhood that was seemingly unimportant at the time, but that had been seared into her brain without her trying.

"Knight, table for two at one o'clock," Stella told the hostess, a beautiful blonde with hair like spun silk. She was wearing a slim-fitting pencil skirt and ridiculously high heels. Emma usually wore rubber clogs at work, so the dressiest she'd get on her days off were a pair of ballerinas or fancy sneakers. She rubbed the toe of her white sneaker onto the back of her other leg.

"Are you sure this is going to work?" Emma asked as they were led to their table.

"He comes here all the time. On Instagram, he calls it his office cafeteria," Stella said. "And if he doesn't show, it's still a win. We get to have a nice lunch either way."

Right then, Emma caught sight of Henry, sitting at a table for two, nestled in the back of the restaurant. He looked so impossibly handsome in his pin-striped suit. Crisp white shirt, silk flower tucked neatly into the buttonhole of his suit jacket's lapel, the way his grandfather used to do. Felix had an entire wardrobe of these silk flowers. Today, Henry wore one in bright pink.

Upon seeing him again, Emma was struck by two things: how strong a resemblance he had to his grandfather, Felix, and how strong an attraction she still felt to him. It was animal, visceral. She felt heat flame her cheeks and then run down the length of her spine.

"Well, isn't this a lovely surprise," Henry said, getting up from his table to say hello as they reached the back of the restaurant. He took Emma's hand and gave her a gentle kiss on the cheek.

"This is my friend Stella Knight," Emma said. "She's Fleur's niece."

Emma waited for Henry to react to the mention of Fleur—but Henry didn't flinch. "Nice to meet you."

Emma and Stella were seated at a table on the other side of the room.

"Now what?" Emma whispered to Stella as she glanced at the menu.

"He's looking our way," Stella said, her head down in her own menu. "Now we wait."

Emma could feel her palms get sweaty. She didn't belong in a restaurant like this, alongside all the Upper East Side ladies who lunched. Neither did Stella. Everyone here seemed impossibly fancy, and Emma couldn't help but feel like she and Stella stood out like sore thumbs. Emma had tried to fit in, wearing her Dior earrings, a group gift from her friends for her thirtieth birthday. She fingered the delicate bumblebee and number eight charms that hung down from the pearl. "Maybe we should go. I've lost my appetite anyway."

"We're here," Stella said. "We might as well enjoy our lunch. By the way, I love your earrings." She winked.

"Shall I start you off with drinks?" a server asked.

"Iced tea," both women said at the same time.

"Jinx," Stella said, "buy me a Coke!"

"I'm sorry," the server said, "was that two iced teas or two Cokes?"

Both women broke out in laughter.

"Iced tea for both of us, please," Emma said.

"Great minds," Stella said as the server left the table. "When she comes back to take our lunch orders, let's say them at the exact same time again."

Emma couldn't help but laugh once more. Regardless of whether this plan would work or not, she was having fun. Even though she hadn't had many girlfriends growing up, now she did, and Emma treasured her female friends. She didn't want to be too presumptuous on her "second date" with Stella, but could tell that she was going to turn into a good friend.

Right after they ordered their lunch (lentil salad for Emma, a pasta dish for Stella), Henry stopped by the table again. "It was so good to see you, Emma," he said. "My two o'clock just canceled. Any chance you two would like to skip dessert here and meet me at my office for some coffee?"

An hour later, Henry's assistant came in with a tray of tea, coffee, and *speculaas* cookies. Emma remembered those treats as Henry's favorite when they were kids. Delicate shortcrust biscuits, as thin as they were crunchy, they were filled with the flavor of nutmeg, ginger, and cloves. Fleur used to make them all the time for Henry, but Emma hadn't eaten one in years. She took a careful bite—they were so messy to eat— and it felt like she was back in Fleur's kitchen.

"Would you like some coffee or tea?" Henry asked, seated on a dark red velvet sofa. Emma and Stella had settled into the armchairs.

"Coffee, please," Emma said, just as Stella did, too. They looked at each other and laughed.

"Jinx," Stella said softly.

"I owe you a Coke," Emma said.

"Two Cokes, really." Stella took a bite of her *speculaas* cookie, and it crumbled into her lap. Henry passed a napkin to her.

"What a nice surprise to see you in my neck of the woods," Henry said to Emma. "Do you live up here?"

"I'm downtown," Emma said. "I was only uptown having lunch with Stella."

"Do you live nearby?" Henry asked Stella. He smiled at her expectantly, but Stella ignored the question.

Stella took a folder out of her tote bag and handed it to

Henry. "We're trying to save Rolling Hill. And we'd like for you to help us."

Emma cringed at the way Stella got down to business so quickly. Emma hated small talk, but surely Stella could tell that a little light conversation would be necessary before launching into a big ask?

Henry flipped open the folder. "I don't think I need to see a bunch of information about the house I grew up in."

"Right," Stella said, laughing self-consciously. "But we wanted you to see the merits of granting Rolling Hill historical status."

Henry took a deep breath. "As I've already explained to Emma, I don't think this is a good idea. And it's not fair to our old friend Leo. I would never do anything that would hurt him."

Emma couldn't help but think of the things Henry had done that had hurt Leo. But that wasn't why they were there.

"Please consider it," Emma said.

"I'm sorry," Henry said, taking care to meet Emma's eye. "But the answer is no."

"Oh," Emma said, and reached down to gather her bag so that she could leave quickly. How stupid she'd been. She hadn't been able to change his mind back when they were teenagers, back when he was hiding their relationship. What had made her think she could change his mind now?

"It was nice to meet you," Stella said, standing, and putting out her hand for Henry to shake. "If you change your mind, please be in touch."

"Nice to meet you, too," Henry said. And then: "Would you mind if I talked to Emma privately for a moment?"

"Of course," Stella said. "I'll wait for you outside."

Henry closed the door to his office and sat back down on the sofa. He patted the space next to his, Emma's cue to sit down next to him. "How much do you know about this person?"

"You mean Fleur's niece?" Emma asked. Again, Henry

didn't react. They were so close, she could smell his familiar scent—the faint notes of lavender and sage drifted over to her. A slight bit of nutmeg. From the cookies, she now realized.

Henry narrowed his eyes. "How do you know that she's really Fleur's niece?"

"Because she told me," Emma said, laughing, as if Henry's question was the most ridiculous thing she'd ever heard.

"Why haven't we ever met her before?" Henry asked. "Did Fleur ever mention a niece to you?"

"Why would she lie about something like that? How would she even know who Fleur was if she weren't related to her?"

"Because of all this research she's done," Henry said, holding up the folder.

"That's absurd," Emma said. "When did you become so paranoid?"

"I don't think you should trust her," Henry said. His forehead wrinkled as he rubbed it gently. "Something is off."

"Off?" Emma said. "What's this? Are these your art dealer superpowers of perception?"

"Art dealers do need to know how to read people," Henry said.

"And what are you reading off Stella, exactly?"

Henry smiled. "I'm just trying to protect you."

Emma laughed out loud. Protect her? "I don't recall you ever protecting me in the past."

"I did." Henry sighed.

"Really?" Emma asked. Quietly: "You broke my heart."

"Things were so much more complicated then."

"It didn't seem complicated to me," Emma said. "I loved you. And you said that you loved me, too. Only you didn't show it in public. Do you have any idea what that did to me?"

"I'm sorry about that," Henry said. "Maybe I could make it up to you now?"

"I'm *asking* you to make it up to me now," Emma said. "Help us get Leo to change his mind. After everything, I think you owe it to me."

Henry took a moment before he responded. He glanced up, and their eyes met. "Why do you care so much if they tear down the house?"

"It's where I lived with my father," Emma said.

"Oh, Emma—" Henry began, taking her hand in his.

Emma pulled her hand back into her lap. "I think the real question is, why *don't* you care about Leo tearing down the house?"

"It was only a house," Henry said simply. "Only a thing."

"Your entire life is things," Emma said, pointing at the artwork on Henry's walls. She assumed that Henry, like his grandfather before him, kept the art he was actively trying to sell on his office walls. Emma spotted two Manets and a small Degas sculpture on the coffee table. She imagined herself taking a painting off the wall, throwing it to the ground, and stomping on it. Then they'd see who cared about *things*.

"Right," Henry said. "I mean, no. My life is more than just things. But either way, I don't care what happens to Rolling Hill. And you shouldn't, either. Your father's memory is not at that estate. Just like the memory of my parents isn't there, either. It's in your heart. And that's what you should honor."

"You don't have to help me," Emma said, "but I'm going to save that house."

17

Now

"There are so many options," Leo said. He sat across from her, at the round table in her conference room, as they planned the menu for his grand opening party.

He rubbed the side of his face, and Emma watched as his fingers moved. Catching herself staring, Emma looked down at her notepad and drew tiny circles on the page.

Emma knew that he'd never make it to the grand opening party—she was hopeful that, with the help of the Glen Cove Historical Society, they'd get an injunction to halt construction—but she still couldn't resist the opportunity to show off for Leo. He was clearly very successful, just like she knew he would be, and she wanted to show him that she'd done well for herself, too. She was not merely *the help*.

"How do people choose?" Leo said as he watched the promotional video that ran on the large flat screen on the wall.

Emma couldn't help but smile. She prided herself on the number of options she made available to her catering clients.

She felt a surge of satisfaction, seeing Leo overwhelmed by the variety. They'd done that on purpose, of course. Emma wanted clients to feel taken care of, as if anything they could dream of, they could have.

"I recommend you choose five hot hors d'oeuvres and five cold. It creates a nice balance," Emma said, pulling out the first page of the folder she'd given to Leo. As she reached for the folder, their fingers touched. Emma immediately pulled her fingers back from where she'd touched Leo. They felt hot, electrified.

Leo didn't move as he watched her react.

"If," Emma said, "you even get to the grand opening, that is."

"If?"

"I told you about the Glen Cove Historical Society. I'll be helping them get an injunction so that you can't tear down Rolling Hill. There's a meeting next week."

"Seems like a conflict of interest, no?" Leo raised his left eyebrow.

"Your deposit is fully refundable," Emma said. "Or you can simply move it over toward the next party you throw. I'm glad we're back in touch."

Leo looked up at Emma and regarded her for a moment. "Are you?"

Her voice barely a whisper: "Of course I am. You were my best friend." Emma found she could not meet Leo's eye.

"Best friend," Leo muttered. He furrowed his brow as he flipped through the folder of menu items. "It's only a cocktail party. What is all this?"

"In addition to the passed hors d'oeuvres, we do three passed *experiences*, which are like hors d'oeuvres but super-sized."

"Tacos and tequila?"

"Yes, that's a fun one," Emma said. She hit the remote control, and the screen filled with a picture of a tray of "tacos and tequila"—a delicate fish taco perched on top of a tequila shot. "Guests love to eat the taco in two bites and then down the shot of tequila. That might be for a rowdier crowd, though." Emma hit the remote control, and another photograph popped up.

"Is that what you think my clientele would like?" Leo asked, examining the photograph of a miniature champagne flute, topped with a blini covered in caviar and crème fraîche.

"Well, that's what I like," Emma said, under her breath. Working in the food industry had given her a taste for all sorts of foods she never thought she'd eat—escargot, sweetbreads, goat meat.

"What's that?" he said, pointing at the screen.

"This one's a house specialty," Emma said. "Seafood paella served in miniature skillets, with the sangria on the side."

"How come the paella's not on top of the sangria?" Leo asked. "Isn't the gag that the food gets put on top of the drink?"

"Yes," Emma said, remembering how Leo always had a way of putting things—*the gag*. "But the skillets are too hot. They're not always on top, anyway." She flipped to the next slide. A tiny beer bottle, with delicately fried onion rings around the bottle, like a ring toss.

"Ha!" Leo said. "So you eat the onion rings, and then drink the beer?"

"That's the idea," she said. "We like it to be fun and playful. Without any compromises on the quality of the food."

"This is a lot," Leo said, fanning himself with the menu pages.

"There's no rush. Take that home with you."

"When do we need to finalize the menu?"

"We've got plenty of time," Emma said. "When did you say your event was?"

"We'll be breaking ground within the next couple of weeks," he said. "Then we're hoping to have model homes up in another few months. Let's call it six to nine months from now?"

"What's breaking ground?"

"Oh, it's a symbolic ceremony where we dig into the earth for the first time," Leo said. "We invite everyone who's involved in the project—the New York office of my company, the investors, our lawyers—and it's mostly a nice way to officially begin. To memorialize the moment."

"What are you serving?"

Leo laughed. "Are you trying to get more business off me?"

Emma shrugged. She didn't quite know what she was suggesting.

"I usually take everyone out for lunch afterward," Leo said. "Somewhere in town. So we can all get to know the neighborhood we're becoming a part of."

"You could do a nice picnic," Emma said, thinking out loud. "The excitement is in being on the property, right? Seeing what's to come?"

"I suppose."

"So, why not do a picnic lunch afterward?" Emma suggested. "We could do beautiful picnic baskets, and each table would have a different one. We'd fill them with wine, cheese, and gourmet sandwiches. We can get these French sodas that I love. They come in all different flavors, and then people could walk around to each table, sampling each basket."

"Why does the soda need to be French?" Leo said, suppressing a laugh.

"Made with real sugar," Emma said. "No high-fructose corn syrup."

Leo laughed out loud.

"They're delicious when you use them as mixers with the wine. You can do the grapefruit soda with a nice medium-bodied red…"

"Now we mix the soda with wine?"

"You're making fun of me," Emma said, realizing a beat too late. "You've got to try it." She walked over to the miniature fridge and pulled out a French soda. She poured a glass for Leo and waited until he took a sip.

"Tastes like soda."

"You know that it's better than regular soda."

"Actually…" Leo said. He took a second sip. "You know what this reminds me of? The soda I used to drink when I was a kid in Italy."

"And now try it with this," Emma said, opening a bottle of pinot noir. She poured the wine into Leo's glass.

Leo took a sip of the new drink. *"Bellisima."*

Emma grabbed Leo's glass and took a sip herself. It was good. "I think you mean *deliziosa.*"

"Oh, you speak Italian now?"

"Un po," Emma replied. "The summer I left the restaurant, a few friends and I backpacked through Italy for a few weeks."

"I see," Leo said, taking the glass back from Emma. He took another sip, his lips touching the glass where hers had just been. Emma felt her face flush; it was a surprisingly intimate gesture. "The drink is delicious. But we both know I wasn't talking about the drink."

18

Now

Emma slumped onto the chaise in her office. The Morgan wedding had gone two hours longer than expected, and while that meant more money for her, double pay for her staff, she was exhausted. She couldn't even sleep in—she'd had back-to-back appointments all morning, capped off with menu selection for the Bower Sweet Sixteen—and now all Emma wanted to do was to close her eyes.

"Knock knock," a familiar voice said, accompanied by actual knocking on the door.

Emma's eyes fluttered open.

"Is now a bad time?"

"No, not at all," Emma said, sitting upright and trying to appear more awake. She swept one hand through her hair, smoothing it, and held her arm out, inviting Henry to sit on one of the chairs across from the chaise.

"Were you sleeping?" Henry asked as he sat down. He raised his eyebrows: "At work?"

"The Morgan wedding ran until 2:00 a.m. last night," Emma said, suppressing a yawn.

"They have weddings on Tuesday nights these days?"

"They have weddings every night of the week these days," Emma explained. "Easier to get the venue you want, cheaper... It's exhausting. But good for business."

"I see," Henry said. "Well, I just stopped by to ask if you wanted to have dinner with me tonight."

Emma was sure she was still asleep. "Dinner?"

"Yes," Henry said. "You know, the meal after lunch? Are you free tonight?"

"Tonight?" She mentally pulled up her calendar—Francisco's crew was doing a small birthday party in Westchester this evening, and she had Samantha's crew doing a bridal shower in the afternoon. Emma herself didn't necessarily have to be at either one, though usually she would have stopped by both events to oversee, make sure things were going smoothly.

For a split second, she thought about how her mother and Henry's grandfather had forbidden them to date.

But they weren't kids anymore.

Emma took a deep breath before answering. "Sure."

"I'll pick you up at seven," Henry said. He smiled warmly. "It's a date."

No one drove in Manhattan. Emma expected to be picked up in a cab, or even to simply receive a text, telling her where to meet Henry. But at seven o'clock on the dot, he appeared at her office. In a car.

Henry drove a dark green convertible, top down. He stood outside the car, leaning on it as he waited for Emma. When she came out of her office building, his face lit up. Henry gave her a gentle kiss on the cheek before he opened the car door for her, and then shut it once she was safely inside.

As a child, Emma's father had explained why Rolling Hill was called the Audrey Hepburn Estate. She'd watched the movie *Sabrina* countless times. And now, here she was, living it out in real life. Her very own Larrabee boy, here to sweep her away to a life of adventure. Henry had the best of both Larrabee brothers: he was handsome like David, but smart like Linus. Humphrey Bogart and William Holden, all wrapped up into one.

It was a strange sensation, cruising down the streets of Manhattan in a convertible. Emma usually traveled by subway, or in a catering van. This feeling of having the wind in her hair as they drove was a foreign one for her. And it was bizarre to be stopped at a traffic light and have so many people walk by, with the rooftop down. Emma felt exposed. But Henry seemed totally relaxed, in his element.

Emma spent her life on the precipice, convinced that this would be the day when everything fell down. A remnant of her father dying suddenly when she was a kid, it was a feeling that she could never fully shake.

They crossed the bridge and made their way into Queens. Emma searched her mind for Queens restaurants—where was he taking her? She remembered an amazing gastropub that she'd been to in Bayside. Or perhaps they'd do a tour of the delectable dim sum restaurants in Flushing. That was something she loved to do for Sunday brunch. She didn't think that Henry would know of a hidden gem she hadn't discovered yet, but then he pulled into the parking lot of Citi Field. It was completely empty, and Emma had that feeling of being exposed again—riding around in an expensive convertible in an empty parking lot.

But then they turned the corner, and the place was packed. Cabs and buses were dropping people off, and tons of cars were parked around a big semicircle of trucks.

"We're here," Henry said, smiling.

"We are?" Emma still wasn't sure what was happening. They got out of the car and walked toward the action. And that was when she realized what she was heading toward— food trucks. The kind you'd see on city street corners, doling out shawarma and falafel. About ten or fifteen of them, lined up in a huge semicircle. Picnic benches were set up all around the outside of the trucks, and tall bar tables were set up on the inside. "These are food trucks."

"Yeah," Henry said, glee in his voice. "Isn't it great? Once a month, a bunch of them line up here, and you can walk from truck to truck, trying everything. Have you ever been here before?"

"I definitely have not." Emma had taken Henry to one of the finest French restaurants in Manhattan, and he'd taken her to a parking lot so they could eat while standing up.

"Okay, let's do a lap, see who's here tonight, and then we can start sampling."

"I'm not good enough for a real date?" Emma thought, but didn't say. Or rather, meant to think, but not say. But the words had fallen out of her mouth, unbidden.

"This *is* a real date," Henry said, his expression that of a wounded animal. "I thought you would like this. I thought it would be fun, trying out lots of different foods."

"Where do you take the girls you really like?"

"I thought we could have fun here, since you're a foodie."

"After all these years," Emma said, "I can't believe you're still hiding me away. I am such an idiot."

"Emma," Henry said.

Emma scanned the parking lot. She could easily hop into one of the cabs that were letting people off.

"This is the sort of place you bring a girl when you don't

want to bump into people you know," Emma said. "I need to go."

Without waiting for a response, Emma turned around and threw her hand in the air. One of the cabs that had just done a drop-off swerved to the side to pick her up.

She cried all the way home to Manhattan.

19

Now

Henry's name lit up on Emma's phone, but she wasn't sure if she should answer it. The date had been a mistake. And a massive disappointment. It was her childhood all over again—her, falling hard for Henry; him, keeping her at arm's length. She would never be Sabrina, with the two Larrabee brothers fighting for her affections.

She let the call go to voice mail and hopped out of the cab.

Leo walked out of the construction trailer to greet her. "Hey!"

"Hey," Emma said.

"Thanks for coming out here," he said. "Things have been nuts, preparing for the groundbreaking."

"I'll be quick," Emma said. "I'll walk you through the picnic basket options, and I'll leave you with the folder so that you can decide on your own time." She gave Leo a close-lipped smile and followed him back into the Sales Center.

Emma and Leo sat down together on the leather couch. The

cushions were soft, softer than Emma had imagined they'd be, and she felt herself melting into them, completely taken in by the comfort of her surroundings. She placed her bag by her feet and took out the folder with the menu choices for Leo's groundbreaking ceremony. She set it down next to the tray on the ottoman. The rattan tray held thick coffee table books—all on Audrey Hepburn, except for the one on the bottom, *Vogue on Hubert de Givenchy*.

"Cute," Emma said, pointing at the stack of books.

"Did you know," he asked, "that when Audrey Hepburn had her first meeting with Hubert de Givenchy, he had no idea who she was?"

"I did not know that," Emma said.

"When he was told that *Miss Hepburn* wanted to meet with him, he mistakenly assumed that his meeting was with the Hollywood star *Katharine* Hepburn, and not *Audrey* Hepburn."

"Really?"

"Yes," Leo said. "At that time, Katharine Hepburn was already a big star, and Audrey was just starting out. *Roman Holiday* hadn't come out yet. Billy Wilder sent Audrey to Paris to get her wardrobe for the movie *Sabrina*. When Givenchy opened the door, he was surprised to see her standing there, and not the other Miss Hepburn. But even though he was initially disappointed to have the wrong Hepburn, their friendship became one of the most important collaborations of actress and designer of all time."

"Interesting," Emma said. "I wonder what *Miss Hepburn's* family would think of you using her name to sell cheap condos and town houses."

"They won't be cheap," Leo said, bumping his leg into hers. "And anyway, that wasn't the point of the story."

"Oh, that story had a point?" Emma joked.

"I suppose not," Leo said, laughing self-consciously. "Let's move on. What's on the menu?"

Emma smiled. "I have a few ideas for you." She passed him the folder she'd made up.

Flipping through it: "Are you always this thorough?"

"I like my clients to have lots of options," Emma said.

"You do like lots of options," Leo said, fanning the pages out onto the ottoman. He pointed at the third page. "Let's go with this. Cheese platters that pair with wines, the sandwiches on different artisan breads, the pastry basket."

"Are you sure?" Emma said. "Our clients usually like to sit with the menus for a bit. Think about it. I can help explain all the choices."

"No," Leo said. "This is it. I assume that every choice you offered me here was a good one, right?"

"Of course," Emma said.

Leo handed her the page with the menu he wanted. "Okay, so then I made a decision."

"Okay, then!" Emma parroted back. "I'm impressed with how decisive you are. I wish all of my clients could be like that."

Leo looked at her carefully. "When I see something I like, it's easy for me to decide."

"Great," Emma said. Nervous energy was building up in her body from the intensity of Leo's gaze. "That's it, then!"

"Before you go," Leo said, "do you want to do another walk-through of the house?"

Emma didn't respond. She didn't really need to.

The deal was this: Leo would take Emma through the house one more time, but she had to go up to the attic with him.

They shook hands and made their way inside the house.

"Can I interest you in some more crystal doorknobs?" Leo

said as they walked into the main foyer. "You do realize that now, whenever I see one of them, I think of you?"

"That's sweet," Emma said, careful to keep her voice steady, noncommittal. What she didn't say was this: she'd brought the crystal doorknob home with her that night, and asked her super to install it onto her bedroom door the following day. Whenever she saw it, she thought of him, too.

As Emma walked up the steps, she ran her hand along the banister, thinking of how every inch of the house told a story. Who carved the wood? Who built the curved staircase? As she touched the banister, she felt a warmth in her chest, thinking about all the times her father had run his hands along that same place as he polished the wood, making it gleam. Looking down, she could practically see it: her hand over her father's hand.

"So many memories," Emma said.

Leo took her to the narrow staircase that led to the attic. Hard to believe she'd only attempted to climb these steps one other time in her life—that time with Leo when they were kids. Emma felt like she'd memorized every square inch of the house. It was bizarre to think that there were parts of the house they'd never really explored.

"I hope you don't mind cobwebs," Leo said, leading the way. He held his arms out in front of him, breaking the silky webs as he ascended.

Emma held her breath. She definitely *did* mind cobwebs.

"No crystal doorknobs up here, I'm afraid," he said as they made it up to the attic.

Dust was suspended in the air. Emma felt as if she couldn't breathe.

"Maybe this was a mistake," Emma said, suddenly desperate to be anywhere but there. She sneezed.

A sharp gust of wind blew in, and she screamed. Leo rushed to her side. "I've got you." He put his arms around her.

"Sorry," Emma said, backing away from him. "In my head, I know that this place isn't haunted, but try telling that to my heart."

"It's haunted by the past," Leo said. "Are we going to talk about what happened? Between us?"

Emma opened her mouth to respond, but found that she didn't know what to say. He was talking about that horrible fight they'd had seven years ago. The reason they hadn't spoken. But what else was there to say? He was her best friend, her rock.

Until he wasn't.

20

Now

The Glen Cove Historical Society meeting was exactly how Emma had pictured it in her mind. She was the youngest person there by about fifty years.

"Why, hello. Welcome," a woman said to her as Emma walked in. She wore a navy cashmere twinset and a double strand of pearls. "I'm Gladys."

"It's nice to meet you. I'm Emma."

"This is Edith and this is Myrtle," Gladys said, pointing across the room to two women who were similarly attired: cashmere twin sets, double strands of pearls. Emma wasn't quite sure which one was wearing the yellow and which one was wearing the green. Was Edith in the yellow and Myrtle in the green? Or the reverse? "And that's Vivian. She's in charge. It's so nice to have another young person joining us."

"Um, I'm actually meeting someone here. Do you know my friend Stella?" Emma assumed that when Gladys referenced having "another young person" she was talking about Stella, and not herself.

"Yes, of course!" she said. "Stella! I was hoping to impress you with the one other young person who comes to these meetings; that's too bad that you already know her. I'm afraid you've beat her to the punch this evening. She's not here yet, but she will be. Hasn't missed a meeting in months, that one. But please, help yourself to some coffee and some nibbles. We'll get started in a few minutes."

Emma checked her watch. She'd purposely come only a few minutes before the meeting began. That way, less chitchat.

She texted Stella: I'm here! She was surprised when she didn't see the three dots that meant Stella was writing back to her. They'd planned to meet here tonight. Their third date.

The building had been hard to find. Nestled at the end of a leafy street, you could easily drive by without realizing it was there. It was a tiny home, with a spacious parking lot out front. Once inside, Emma wondered if the meeting place for the Glen Cove Historical Society was itself a historical landmark. She took a cup of coffee and circled the meeting room. If it had landmark status, there would probably be a plaque or some other indication.

A table held pamphlets for other projects the Glen Cove Historical Society was working on—an old carriage house by the water, a building in town that presently housed three restaurants, and Rolling Hill. Emma picked up the pamphlet and leafed through.

The photographs in the pamphlet were ancient. Some of the pictures predated the van der Wraaks, but the bulk seemed to be from their time living there. There were floor plans for the main house, and photographs of nearly every room. Emma wondered where they'd even gotten them from, given Henry's lack of interest in helping.

The sound of a gavel hitting the table rang out. "Let's call this meeting to order!" Vivian cried out. All the other women, about fourteen of them total, hurriedly found their seats.

Emma raised her hand. "Excuse me, but do you think it would be possible to wait for Stella? I know that she's planning to meet me here."

"Who's Stella?" one of the ladies asked. It was either Edith or Myrtle. She was wearing the yellow twin set.

"Wasn't she that graduate student?" the other one answered, the one in the green twin set.

"I don't believe she was a grad student. We connected because she has a personal connection to Rolling Hill," Emma said.

"No, that's not right," Gladys said. "I distinctly remember she told me that she was a graduate student. I recall it because she said she was at Columbia, and that's where my Charlie is."

"How *is* Charlie?" either Edith or Myrtle asked.

"Great," Gladys said. "Charlie's great! But anyway, that Stella said she was doing her thesis on Gilded Age architecture, so she came to some meetings and was trying to get the blueprints to the mansion on the Rolling Hill Estate."

"And then we all told her the story of why people call it the Audrey Hepburn Estate," the woman in the row behind Gladys said.

"You must have her mistaken with someone else. I met her at Rolling Hill a few weeks ago," Emma said. "She told me that she was the niece of the cook, Fleur, who worked there when I lived there."

"You're a van der Wraak?" Gladys asked. "I thought they only had one son."

"My mother was the maid there," Emma said. "And then later, she ran the house for Felix van der Wraak."

"So you would know if she was the niece or not," Gladys said, her brow furrowed.

"Well, I'd never met her before."

"I thought you said you met her a few weeks ago?"

"Right," Emma said. "I meant I never met her when I lived at Rolling Hill as a child. I met her a few weeks ago, and that's when she told me who she was."

"Well, it doesn't matter who she is," Vivian said, motioning her hands in the air as if swatting away an insect. "The meeting starts promptly at eight, and we've already lost a few minutes with this chitter-chatter. Let's begin. You can catch your friend up when she arrives."

With that, Emma found a seat toward the back. She carefully placed her tote bag on the chair next to hers so that Stella would have somewhere to sit when she arrived.

But she never did.

Exactly forty-five minutes after Vivian first hit her gavel down, the meeting was adjourned. Gladys rushed to Emma's side and plied her with questions: How old was she? What did she do for a living? Might she be interested in a fix-up with her grandson, Charlie? (She was not.)

Emma stayed at the meeting, chatting with the women while they nibbled on the cookies Edith had made (it was Edith in the green sweater set, Myrtle in the yellow). Emma was surprised to learn that Edith's special ingredient in the cookies was cream cheese. She tried to tell herself that she stayed after the meeting was over because she was enjoying the company of the women she'd just met. Not because she was still waiting for Stella to show up.

By 10:00 p.m., Emma was tired and ready to head back into the city. Edith gave her a ride back to the train station.

She caught the 10:16 train back into Manhattan, and the quiet trip left her alone with her thoughts. Had Stella lied about who she was? Was she really only a grad student, trying to find something to make her thesis more special?

Either way, Emma thought, it didn't matter. Stella was yet another person who'd let her down. She didn't need Stella. Just like she didn't need Henry. She'd get what she wanted on her own, the same way she always had.

Anyway, the women at the Glen Cove Historical Society were pretty good at getting things done on their own. The meeting's big announcement was that they'd officially filed injunction papers to halt the development of Rolling Hill.

21

Now

You could always tell a native New Yorker from a tourist by the way that they walked. New Yorkers tended to walk quickly, and in the direction of where they were going. Tourists tended to walk with their heads in the air, admiring the sights and sounds of the city, staring up at the skyscrapers.

Emma walked quickly. Especially on nights when she didn't have a party to work, Emma left her office swiftly, as if she had wings.

"I'm sorry."

Emma almost missed him as she made her way out of the office that evening. She looked up to find Henry, standing outside her building again, leaning against his car. It was so jarring to see him there. Spending the afternoon two days prior with Leo was giving her whiplash of sorts. Henry. Leo. Leo. Henry.

"It's fine," Emma said, shaking her head in a way that indicated that quite the opposite was true. "It was stupid to think that things would be different. You have nothing to be sorry for."

Henry opened the car door. "Can we try this again?" His smile was so assured. He had the smile of a man who wasn't ever told no.

"No, thank you," Emma said. "It's my only night off this week, and I have a date with a hot bath."

She brushed by him and made her way toward the subway.

"Emma, wait!"

Emma knew if she turned back, she might cave. And she wasn't going to repeat the mistakes of the past. She wasn't going to spend years of her life again pining after someone who didn't love her back. She put her head down and quickened her pace.

She felt his presence before she saw him. "Emma, please."

Emma looked up from the sidewalk and turned to face Henry. They both stopped at the corner, waiting for the light to change. Henry put his arm around Emma's shoulder.

She quickly brushed it away. "I don't think so."

"Why not?" Henry asked. "We still have a connection. I know you can feel that, too."

Emma looked him in the eye and lied: "I feel nothing."

"I think you misunderstood my intention the other night," Henry said. "I honestly thought you'd love the food truck rally."

"I didn't."

"I mean, you didn't try it."

Emma shook her head.

"Well, then, let's try again," Henry said. "Let's have dinner. We can go anywhere you'd like."

"I really don't want to," Emma said. "This was a mistake. It was a mistake then, and it's a mistake now."

"It's not a mistake," Henry said, reaching out for Emma's

hands. "And it wasn't a mistake then. My grandfather and your mother wouldn't allow us to see each other. There were reasons it couldn't happen then."

Emma had heard that excuse before. "Right." Emma pulled her hands away from his and put them into her jacket pockets.

Then the skies opened up. Rain fell, one of those sudden storms that are quick and heavy, with no sign of letting up. The people around them immediately scattered, all searching for shelter. The forecast hadn't predicted rain. Emma took her tote bag and raised it over her head.

"We should go."

"Give me another chance," Henry said. He was getting drenched by the rain, but he didn't move. "I messed up then, and I messed up the other night. But I won't mess up again."

She was getting soaked, her tote bag no match for the torrent above, but she didn't dare move. She wanted to hear every word of what Henry was telling her. Then, remembering suddenly: "Your car! The top is down!"

"I don't care about the car," Henry said. The rain fell down harder, the sound of the drops reverberating off the city sidewalks. He spoke louder: "I care about you. I want you to give me another chance."

"Give you another chance from the last week?" Emma asked, her voice a bit louder, too. "Or from when we were kids?"

"Both. Either," Henry said. "All of it. Can we start over?"

"Didn't we try that the other night?" Emma asked. "It didn't work."

"Start over with the do-over, then."

Emma didn't know how to respond. She'd wanted to be with Henry since she was five years old. Had planned out their wedding hundreds of times. But this? Now? So much had happened between them. Could they really start over again? Emma decided to stick with the truth: "I'm afraid that you'll hurt me again."

"I know," Henry said. The rain beat down as he spoke. "I won't."

"I need to think about this," Emma said.

"I understand," Henry said. And then, with a sheepish laugh: "I should probably try to salvage my car."

"Goodbye, Henry," Emma said, and leaned toward him to kiss his cheek goodbye.

"Goodbye, Emma," he said, as her lips grazed his cheek.

And then, she kissed him. Not another kiss on the cheek. A real kiss. Emma pressed her lips to his and kissed Henry, right there, in the middle of the sidewalk, in the pouring rain. She didn't know why she'd done it. She hadn't planned on doing it. But kissing him on the cheek, being so close, she'd had only one thought: *more.* So, she kissed him. And he kissed her back.

He tasted like the fresh rain that was beating down on them. Kissing Henry felt familiar, like she'd never stopped kissing him. Kissing Henry again felt like coming home.

22

Then

Age seventeen

When spring came, the school hallways were filled with whispers about the prom, and Emma held out hope that Henry would ask her. In her head, she knew that they couldn't go together. They were forbidden to date. Her mother and his grandfather could never find out they'd been together; she knew this intellectually. But her heart? Her heart was another thing entirely. In her heart, she imagined that Henry would stand up to his grandfather, insist that they were in love, and make him understand. Her mother, too.

Each day, she'd sit with Leo at lunch, staring at Henry. Waiting for him to come to her. Waiting for him to do the one thing she knew he could not.

"So I was thinking that maybe we should go?" Leo said.

"What's that?"

"Earth to Emma," Leo said, tapping on the cafeteria table. "Have you listened to a word I've said?"

"Of course I'm listening," Emma said, even though she knew full well that she had not been.

"Really?" Leo said. "Repeat it back to me."

"Something something something," Emma said, still staring in Henry's direction, "we should go."

Leo studied Emma. She felt his eyes burn the side of her head, so she turned to face him.

"I was trying to ask you something important," he said.

"So ask!"

"It was nothing."

"I'm sorry," Emma said. She took care to look directly in Leo's eyes. "What did you want to ask me?"

Leo reached for her hand from across the table. "Will you go to the prom with me?"

"What?" Emma pulled her hand back from Leo's as if it was on fire.

"I'm asking you to be my date for the prom," he said, his voice now a bit smaller.

"Oh," Emma said. "I'm sorry, I just—"

"You know what?" he said. "Forget it. It was stupid anyway. I thought we could go as a gag. Make fun of the whole thing."

"I'm sorry," Emma said. "I was distracted. Forgive me."

Emma saw his face soften. He would forgive her. Of course he would. He always did. "Forgiven."

"Good," Emma said. And then, her voice a whisper: "Anyhow, I'm pretty sure that I'll be going to the prom with Henry."

"Henry?"

"Lower your voice." Emma looked around the cafeteria to make sure no one had heard Leo.

"He doesn't even talk to us at school," Leo said, making no effort to keep his voice low. "What makes you think he would ask you to the prom?"

"Shhh." Quietly, she explained: "We sort of have been seeing each other at night."

"Is that why you never want to meet at the pool house anymore?"

Emma giggled and nodded her head.

"You're hooking up with Henry?"

"Yes," Emma said, surprised at how gleeful it made her to tell someone else the secret she'd been hiding for so long. "But you can't tell anyone, because his grandfather and my mother don't want us to date. It's forbidden."

"You're hooking up with the guy who won't acknowledge us at school?" Leo said. "Please tell me that you haven't slept with him."

Emma lowered her eyes. How could Leo know? Was it written across her forehead? Was it seeping out of her pores?

"My God, Emma," he said, raising his voice. "Really? How could you have so little respect for yourself?"

"Lower your voice," Emma said. "People are starting to stare."

"But don't you want them to hear?" Leo said, now searching around the cafeteria. He spoke louder. "Isn't that why you're doing it? Don't you want them to know that you're sleeping with Henry van der Wraak?"

"Shhh!" Emma chastised him.

Leo put his head down into his lunch. "You're too good for him. He doesn't deserve you."

"He's not a bad person," Emma said.

"A good person wouldn't keep your relationship a secret," Leo said, his eyes soft. "Someone who really loved you would scream about it from the rooftops."

"He would," Emma said. "Of course he would. It's his grandfather—"

"Who is a Nazi," Leo said, cutting her off.

"He's not a Nazi," Emma quietly said back.

"Who killed Fleur."

"He didn't kill Fleur," Emma whispered. "Keep your voice down."

"Regardless of whether or not he killed Fleur," Leo said, "Felix van der Wraak is definitely an evil Nazi."

As Leo spoke, Emma felt a presence behind her. She looked up just in time to see Henry walking by their table.

23

Now

The sun was setting, making the grounds especially beautiful. Kissed with golden hues of deep orange and pink, the sky was magic. It hadn't rained in days, so the garden's lawn wasn't soaked through the way it had been in prior years. And the air was clear, without an ounce of humidity pulling it down.

Emma adored catering the annual fundraiser at the Long Island Museum of Fine Arts. She enjoyed doing good work for a worthy cause, and the people who ran the museum were a pleasure to work with. Each year, it was a fun party. Her favorite sort of experience: enjoyable, while also giving back.

Emma usually worked the party with Samantha's crew. She loved the energy of the seven-person all-female team. They got along with each other, and the guests as well. And even better? They did meticulous work.

Samantha came to Emma from a downtown celebrity chef restaurant. After two years in that kitchen, she'd developed an eating disorder and a diagnosis of generalized anxiety disorder, and had been trying to find a job where she had more control over her schedule, more control over her life. Emma's company offered her both of those things. Before going to culinary school, Samantha had paid her way through UCLA as a model. But she was so much more than a pretty face. Emma admired how smart and innovative Samantha could be; Samantha loved that with Emma, she could work in the food industry in a way that allowed her to live a healthier life.

Emma walked over to do a last-minute check of the bar, and she saw Henry heading toward them.

"Did the party start?" Kendall, the bartender, asked. Kendall always bartended at Samantha's parties. Unlike Francisco's team, where he moved everyone around for each party so that they'd learn every aspect of the trade, Samantha's team was ordered. Everyone had their role, everyone had their specialty.

Kendall was a former tattoo artist, even though she didn't look the part at first glance. She looked like Grace Kelly, with her soft blond hair and crystal blue eyes. But that's where the likeness ended. Both of her arms were covered in sleeve tattoos, and Samantha told Emma that Kendall also had four piercings that couldn't be seen when Kendall was fully clothed.

"No," Emma said, smiling at Henry as he got closer. "He's a friend I invited."

"Handsome," Kendall said. "Should I make him a drink?"

"Yes," Emma said, but then immediately realized that she didn't know what Henry liked to drink. She quickly covered herself: "Do tonight's specialty cocktail. He can be our guinea pig."

"Coming right up," Kendall said. "One for you, too."

"You know I don't drink on the job."

"Right," Kendall said. "I'll make yours a mocktail, but put it in the champagne flute."

"Perfect."

By the time Henry had made it across the lawn and to the bar, Kendall had two perfect cocktails waiting. The evening's drink was called Surrealist Spritz and it had vodka, elderflower liqueur, French grapefruit soda, and a dash of champagne. The flutes were pretreated with dots and stripes of purple food coloring to give the drink its surreal twist.

"Hey, you," Henry said, and bent down to give Emma a gentle kiss on the cheek.

Emma introduced him to Kendall, and they took their drinks with them as Emma did the rounds and checked on the last-minute details.

"I'm glad you could be here," Emma said, eyeing each table to assure that everything was ready for the party.

"I'm glad you invited me," Henry said. "I made a small donation to the museum to cover my plate."

"You didn't have to do that. You're here as my guest."

"Well, this way I can stay out of your hair a bit because they seated me at a table. Anyway, it's a tax write-off for me since I'm in the business." He leaned down to kiss her. She could taste the vodka on his lips, the sweetness of the cocktail.

"That's too bad," Emma said. "Things sometimes get a little out of control in the food service tents."

"I like out of control," Henry said, unable to conceal a smile as he leaned closer to whisper in her ear. "Do they get out of control before the event begins?"

"I think that can be arranged," Emma said, tilting her head up for another kiss.

Right then, the president of the museum board approached, breaking the spell. Emma took a step back and crossed her arms behind her back, ever the good caterer. As she threw her arms back, she felt her mocktail turn over and drip down the leg of her pants.

"Emma," the president said, "I see that you've found our

last-minute donor. Mr. van der Wraak, we can't wait to hear what you think of our modest little collection."

"I'm looking forward to touring the museum," Henry said, patting his hair back into place. "It was my friend Emma, here, who suggested I come tonight."

"Why, thank you, Emma."

"It wasn't completely charitable—he's the guinea pig taste testing tonight's specialty cocktail." Emma hoped her face wasn't too flushed from her kiss with Henry.

"I can't wait to try it myself!" the president said. And then, turning to Henry: "We simply cannot thank you enough for your generous donation. A few members of the board would like to thank you personally."

As she ferried him away, Henry looked back at Emma with an expression that said: *I'll be back*. Emma gave a gentle wave and tried to control the stupid grin that had taken over her face.

The six-piece orchestra began to play, and Emma took this as a cue that the party had officially begun. Guests made their way to the back of the museum as servers handed out cocktails and small bites.

Emma headed back toward the food service tents. Now that the cocktail hour was underway, she'd check on the entrées for the dinner service. She'd do her final tastings of the food, and make sure everything was ready to go.

"Look, it's Emma!"

Emma spun around at the mention of her name. Leo's father, Enzo, was making his way toward her. She was surprised to see him there, but he fit in seamlessly with the Long-Island-fancy crowd: still handsome, looking dashing in his summer-weight ivory suit. But he looked older, so much older, especially with his ever-present limp, for which he now used a cane. Emma supposed that was what her father would have looked like, too, if he'd been granted the privilege of growing older.

Emma rushed over to greet him. "Enzo, how lovely to see you."

Enzo kissed Emma on both cheeks. "Hello, stranger. Leonardo said you would be here. I'm so glad that the two of you are back in touch."

"I'm catering the event," she said.

"How wonderful," he said. "Then you'll have to tell me what to eat. What's good."

"Everything's good," Emma replied with a broad smile.

"*Papa, ti ho preso da bere,*" Leo said, *Dad, I got you a drink*, approaching with two of the specialty cocktails. He handed one to his father.

"*Guarda chi ho trovato, Leonardo,*" Enzo said. *Look who I found*.

"Hey," Leo said, his voice soft as he gave Emma a kiss hello. He put his hand on her arm as he did so. Suddenly, Emma felt warm in her chef's whites, the heat from Leo's hand traveling up her arm and then down her spine.

"What are you doing here?" Emma said. Then, hearing herself, she hedged: "I mean, I didn't expect to see you today. And your father—what a treat after all these years!"

"It's a treat to see you, too, *bella*," Enzo said, taking one of Emma's hands in his and giving it a squeeze.

"I'm becoming part of the community," Leo said simply. "I'll be building out here for two years, at least, so it's never too early to start getting involved."

"Right," Emma said, thinking of what to say next. She looked out at the party—it had filled in quite nicely—and caught a glimpse of Henry, talking to the museum director.

"Someone's certainly in a good mood," Leo said, bringing Emma's attention back to the conversation.

"I'm not allowed to be happy to see an old friend?"

"I love the enthusiasm," Leo said. "But, I don't know, something's different."

"I'm just happy." Emma shrugged and tried to focus her attention on Enzo and Leo.

"Oh," Leo said, a light bulb practically appearing next to his face. "This is about the injunction, isn't it?"

"No," Emma said, furrowing her brow. Then, remembering herself: "But yes! I am very excited about that. Now maybe you'll reconsider this ill-conceived plan of yours."

"You realize that the Glen Cove Historical Society doesn't care about my development, right? They just don't want the house to be knocked down. And the injunction only covers the main house. So, even if they win, I can still tear down the staff quarters, the pool house…even your old apartment."

"It's still a win."

"I can use the main house as a clubhouse for the people who live at Hepburn. You'd be okay with that?"

"Well, no," Emma said. "Can't you just sell it as a single-family home? That's what it's meant to be, anyway."

"All of this is moot," Leo said. "They're not going to win. The house is not going to be granted historical status, and I can go along with my plans, the same as before."

"Oh."

"But still, you're not sad," Leo said. "So, what is it that's making you so happy?"

Emma shrugged.

"She's in love," Enzo said, his finger tracing a circle in the air. "You can see it on her face."

Leo's face brightened. "Are you?"

"I'm not in love," Emma said, her voice unnaturally high.

"Falling in love," Enzo said, beaming. "The face does not lie."

"I'm not."

Leo smiled shyly at her. "Of course you're not. I'm not, either."

Emma didn't respond.

"Anyway, we shouldn't be monopolizing your time when you're working." And then, to his father: "*Papa*, let's go mingle."

Enzo gave Emma a double kiss before making his way into the crowd. Leo leaned in to give Emma a gentle kiss on the cheek goodbye, and she couldn't help but notice that his lips lingered for a moment longer than was friendly. "I'll see you in a bit."

Emma put her fingers to her cheek, to the spot where Leo had kissed her. She felt frozen in place, like she'd forgotten what she was doing at the party in the first place.

A server walked over and asked her whether the crab cakes were gluten-free (they were not), breaking her from her reverie. After a quick rundown about which appetizers were gluten-free (the tuna tartare, the sea bass skewers, and the bacon-wrapped dates), the server went back out into the crowd.

Emma surveyed the party. She was pleased with tonight's service. The rest of the servers were walking around with trays at a nice clip, and the cocktail hour seemed to be moving along at a good pace.

Emma felt a presence behind her. She could smell Henry's fresh scent, unchanged since they were kids: lavender and sage, a hint of nutmeg. Before she could turn around, he leaned down and said: "I think you said something about things being out of control in the tents?"

Emma took Henry's hand and led him to the tents where her team had set up. At this point, Samantha's whole team would be in the front tent, ferrying out the hors d'oeuvres, prepping for dinner service. Emma brought Henry to the back tent, which served as a makeshift pantry for the events.

It would be empty right before the party, and Emma planned to take full advantage of that fact.

"Oh, this is very cool," Henry said as his eyes took it in. "I'm so impressed by your level of organization."

"That's why I brought you here," Emma said. "So that you could marvel at the way I organize a pantry."

Henry smiled. Emma grabbed him by his suit lapels, drawing him close, and they kissed. She pressed her body against his, and she could feel him immediately respond. How different things were now that they were adults. Sneaking around still, sure, but there was something about the fact that they were adults now and didn't actually need to sneak around—they both had their own apartments, privacy—that made it so much more delicious.

Emma slipped Henry's suit jacket off and he puzzled over her chef's whites.

"How on earth does this thing come off?"

Emma laughed as she helped Henry with the buttons. "Like so."

"That's unexpected," Henry said as he realized that Emma didn't wear anything underneath her grand chef jacket. "That is seriously sexy, Emma."

"When you're in the kitchen, you're supposed to refer to me as Chef."

"Oh, really?"

"Really," Emma said.

"Yes, *Chef*," Henry said, and kissed her neck. She let her hands travel down Henry's body, and he took a nibble of her shoulder.

"Emma?" A voice called out, and Emma almost fell over as Henry stood at attention.

"One minute," Emma said, fixing her hair, smoothing her smudged lipstick back into place. She quickly fastened her jacket buttons and motioned for Henry to hide. She walked out into the aisle.

"Leo!"

"Your event manager said you'd be back at the tents."

"Here I am!" Emma could still feel herself breathing hard. She willed her breath to slow down.

"I thought I'd surprise you."

"Mission accomplished," she said.

"I thought we'd continue that conversation about whether or not you're in love," Leo said as he moved closer to Emma.

"Hey, Leo," Henry said, stepping out from behind the rack of dishes.

"Henry?"

"Good to see you, man. It's been a while," Henry said, putting his hand out for a shake. Leo stared at it for a moment, and then looked back at Emma.

"You're with him now?" Leo said, his face a question mark. "Again?"

"It's complicated," Emma said. "It just sort of happened."

"Which is it?" Leo said. "Complicated? Or just happened?"

"Both," Henry said, laughter in his voice. "It's complicated, given our history. But it just happened. And I'm really happy that it did." Henry looked at Emma, and Emma couldn't help but let a dopey smile take over her face.

"Are you kidding me right now?" Leo said.

"Leo," Emma said.

"Hey, I get it," Henry said. "We've had a complicated past, the three of us. Who would have thought it would be the three of us, here on Long Island, back together again?"

"Emma, you can't do this," Leo said.

"We're adults now," Emma said. "The past is the past."

"You can't be with him," Leo said.

"Enough, Leo," Henry said, his congenial manner replaced by something a bit tougher. "You're out of line here."

"I don't care," Leo said. He turned toward Emma and spoke to her as if she were the only one standing there: "Don't do this to yourself again."

"Hey," Henry said, taking a step closer to Leo. "I'm going to have to ask you to leave."

"This isn't your *house*," Leo replied, shrugging his shoulders. "You don't own everything here like you did when we were kids. You can't ask me to leave."

"Then I won't ask," Henry said, his voice calm and measured. "I'm telling you. Leave."

And that was when Leo punched him.

24

Then

Age seventeen

"So, what do you think?" Henry asked Emma one night, as they lay on the couch, after. "Do you believe Leo? Do you think my grandfather's a Nazi?"

"Of course not," she said, answering quickly. Truth was, Emma didn't know what to believe. Surely her mother wouldn't work for a Nazi?

"Well, he's not," Henry said, running one finger across her shoulder blade. "He's not a Nazi. He's not even German. He's Dutch. My grandmother, too."

"He's so mean to you."

"That doesn't mean he's a Nazi," Henry said. "And anyway, he's not mean. He's tough. He's European. I don't think that European men of that age, men who lived through the war, are the happy, smiley type. He's seen things we can't even fathom."

"I'm worried about you, is all," Emma said. "Sometimes I think it's too much, the way he yells…"

"You only see one side to him," Henry said. "I promise, he has a softer side as well"

Emma had never seen a softer side to Felix. Maybe her mother had?

Then, as if he were reading her mind: "And I hope you don't believe the other rumors, either. About my grandfather and your mom."

"Of course I don't," Emma answered quickly. Too quickly. The fact that she hadn't even thought about it before responding gave her away completely. The answer was canned, already planned out. Emma tried not to think about how much time her mother spent with Henry's grandfather. To admit that Felix and Mila were having an affair would be too much to bear.

"Good," Henry said. "They work together. That's it."

"I know."

"But speaking of trust," Henry said, "are you sure you can trust Leo?"

"What do you mean?" Emma asked. Her eyes instinctively went toward the staff quarters, to Leo's apartment.

"Accusing my grandfather of being a Nazi," Henry said, waiting until Emma's gaze drifted back to him. "Talk about out of left field, right?"

"I think he was jealous," Emma said.

"Of what?" Henry asked.

Emma furrowed her brow. "Of this. Of us."

"You told him?"

"He figured it out," Emma said.

"Oh," Henry said, understanding. "So, he was hurt. I get that. But I mean, why would he bring my grandfather into it? And why does he think my grandfather is a Nazi?"

"Oh," Emma said, unsure of what to say. Should she tell Henry about what she and Leo found in the secret pantry all those years ago? Would that betray Leo's trust? Would Henry be mad that they'd never said anything before? Emma didn't know.

"It doesn't really matter. All that matters is this." Henry kissed Emma gently on the lips.

"I think he was upset because he asked me to go with him to the prom and I said no," she said.

Henry pulled back. "Why'd you say no?"

Emma felt her cheeks flush. Wasn't it obvious? Was he going to make her say it?

"Oh," Henry said. And then again: "Oh."

"You don't have to ask me," Emma said, and immediately chastised herself for saying it. She wanted Henry to ask her. She was dying for him to ask. Why would she let him off the hook so easily?

"I've been through it a million times in my mind, but I don't see how we could go together," he said.

"Of course," Emma said, feeling her insides deflate. She'd given him an out, and he'd taken it. What else did she think would happen?

The silence seemed to stretch on endlessly. Emma tried to think of something to say, anything that would diffuse the tension that had worked its way between them, but she couldn't find the words.

"You know what?" Henry said, filling the quiet with his nervous energy. "We should go. I'll talk to my grandfather tomorrow."

"What?" Emma wasn't quite sure if she'd heard Henry correctly, or if she was simply imagining that he was finally saying what she'd wanted him to say for so long.

"Yeah, I will," he said. "I should have done it a long time ago."

"Really?"

"Of course," Henry said, sliding closer to Emma.

Emma smiled, as their faces drew so close together, they were practically kissing.

"Emma," Henry said.

"Yes?"

"Will you go to the prom with me?"

25

Now

A sucker punch, Henry would later tell Emma, though Emma wasn't sure that was the case. She'd seen the punch coming a mile away. Hadn't Henry?

Henry fell to the ground, and Leo stood over him, waiting for the fight to begin. But it didn't. Emma knelt down next to Henry, to comfort him, to make sure he was all right.

"I'm fine," Henry told Emma, but the hand covering his eye, nursing it, told another story.

"You're not fine," Emma said. "I'm going to get you some ice."

Emma stood up to get a bag of ice, trying to think of what to say to Leo. But she didn't have to worry about that, because by the time she turned around, Leo was gone.

Emma brought the ice over to Henry. She wrapped it in a bar towel and pressed it to his face.

"Ouch."

"Trust me," Emma said. "It'll help."

Emma had seen her share of fistfights in the kitchen. This was the first time she'd witnessed a fight between guests at one of her catered events, but there was a first time for everything, she supposed.

Luckily, no one at the museum seemed to have noticed the fight going on in the back tent, and the rest of the evening went on seamlessly. Henry spent the duration of the party icing his face (and licking his wounds) in the tent, and when the event was over, they drove back to the city together.

The next morning, Henry's eye had a bruise. Dark and swollen, it marred his otherwise beautiful face. Emma couldn't help but gasp when she saw how pronounced the damage from one punch could be.

"You can't go to work like that," Emma said as Henry used his French press to make coffee.

"I think it gives me street cred," Henry said as he pushed down, and the coffee began brewing. He checked out his reflection on the back of a spoon. "The Upper East Side doyennes will know who they're dealing with."

"The Upper East Side doyennes will be terrified if they see their favorite art dealer sporting a shiner. I have some concealer that will work wonders."

Henry poured the coffee into a mug and handed it to Emma. As she sipped, she picked up the newspaper and flipped to the City section. A headline announced: "Neo-Nazi leader arrested, suspected of stealing artifacts from concentration camp."

Emma read on:

Police arrested Stella Knight, a 42-year-old woman, on suspicion of stealing priceless artifacts from a Long Island mansion.

The artifacts in question were from the Amersfoort concentration camp in the Netherlands and have been

returned to the owner of the property, who will be donating the pieces to the United States Holocaust Memorial Museum. Knight is head of the purported Neo-Nazi
organization the Supreme Reich, whose members claimed
ownership over last year's racist graffiti, which was sprayed
on the door of a Queens synagogue on Yom Kippur.

Emma put the paper down.

"What's wrong?"

Emma silently handed the paper to Henry. His eyes quickly
scanned the article, and he looked up to Emma. "I see. Are
you all right?"

"How did you know?"

"What do you mean?"

"How did you know?" Emma repeated. "You told me not
to trust Stella. And now, this."

"Just a vibe," Henry said. "Working in my field, you learn
to become finely tuned to people—who's for real and who's
wasting your time. Who is lying, who's telling the truth."

"She's the leader of a Neo-Nazi organization," Emma said.
"This is a bit more than *just a vibe*. It says here that the Supreme Reich is an organization whose mission is to revive the
ideals of the Third Reich in today's modern world. Aryan su-
premacy, anti-Semitism..."

"Then I'd say you dodged a bullet." Henry picked up his
coffee and took a sip.

Emma was missing something. She could tell. She might
not have been intuitive enough to know that Stella had been
lying to her, but she could tell that Henry was hiding something from her now. He wouldn't meet her eye, and he seemed
unfazed by the discovery that the person he told Emma to
watch out for had turned out to be a Neo-Nazi. Pure evil.

Were Henry's powers of deduction so finely tuned because

his own grandfather was a Nazi? Was that why he was so readily able to recognize Stella for who she was?

Emma examined Henry's face for a clue, from the clear crystal blue of his eyes to the ever-present stubble on his chin. What was he keeping from her?

Though Henry had Stella's number, he seemed unaware that Emma was wondering about who he really was. He refilled their coffee cups and with a broad smile, asked: "Would you like me to make pancakes?"

26

Now

"Hello, dear, I'm calling with some unfortunate news."

"Who is this?" Emma said, pulling her phone away from her ear to see if she recognized the phone number.

"Why, it's Gladys, of course," she said. "From the Glen Cove Historical Society." Emma was about to ask how Gladys had gotten her number, but then she remembered: when she went to the meeting, she'd signed in with all of her information, including her cell number. Anyway, Gladys wasn't one to let the conversation lag by waiting for Emma to say more. "I'm sorry to tell you this over the phone, but it couldn't wait. Unfortunately, the injunction did not pass muster. Leo and his company will resume building over at Rolling Hill. I'm so sorry."

"Oh," Emma said, wondering to herself why Leo hadn't delivered this news himself.

Gladys continued on: "Leo's legal team was very aggressive. Here at the Glen Cove Historical Society, we've worked on many such projects, and I've never seen something like this move through the courts so quickly."

"Oh," Emma repeated, seemingly the only word her mind could formulate.

"If I wasn't so angry," Gladys said, her voice a conspiratorial whisper, "I'd be impressed. But you didn't hear me say that!"

"Right, of course," Emma said. "Of course."

"I know how disappointed you must be," Gladys said. "I wish I had better news for you today."

"I understand," Emma said.

They ended their call, and Emma stared dumbly at her phone. Of course this would happen. She should have expected it all along. It was silly to have held out hope.

Right then, a text popped up on her home screen from Leo: **How's next week for the groundbreaking?**

27

Now

Emma did something that morning that she'd never done before: she overslept.

It was the day of Leo's groundbreaking ceremony, and the alarm on her cell phone hadn't gone off. She rushed around Henry's apartment to get ready, make herself presentable as quickly as possible, but once they were cruising down the Long Island Expressway at lightning speed, an unwelcome thought came to mind: Had she done it on purpose? Was it subconscious, this desire to oversleep and miss Leo's groundbreaking ceremony?

When they pulled into Rolling Hill, Francisco's van was already there. The catering tents were set up, and Francisco's team was moving about. Emma jumped out of the car, promising to meet up with Henry once she'd checked in with her team. She tried to act as if everything was normal, going according to plan. As if she'd meant to arrive a full two hours after her crew.

"How are we doing?" she asked Francisco.

He regarded her for a moment. "All good, Chef. We're ready for service."

The picnic baskets were lined up neatly, ready to be set down on the picnic tables, which a crew of four men was unloading from a truck.

"Thanks for taking the lead," Emma said.

"Everything's under control, Chef." Francisco smiled at Emma, but the smile didn't reach his eyes. There was something else that Francisco was communicating in his half smile, but it was only once he walked back toward the tent that Emma could place it: concern.

Out in front of the house, Leo's assistant made a big show of the shovel she'd spray-painted gold. She dramatically handed it over to Leo, and he carried it around with him as a prop as people pulled up to the property. They both wore dark gray hard hats with the *Hepburn* logo printed in white on the front.

Leo spotted Emma by the catering tents and rushed over to greet her. "I wasn't sure you were going to show," he said.

"Of course I'm here," Emma said. "I'm a professional."

"Was today bring your boyfriend to work day?"

"Henry and I wanted to support you," Emma said. "Can you two kiss and make up now?"

"I don't think so."

"He still has a bruise."

Leo looked back toward where Henry sat, schmoozing with some of the board members of the art museum. "He absolutely does not."

"Bruised ego?" Emma offered.

Leo shook his head and gave his gold shovel a twirl.

Emma couldn't help herself: "That's a very big shovel."

"It's a very big piece of property," Leo said, dangling the shovel from his hip, like the phallic symbol that it was.

Emma looked around the property—it looked sadder, darker, than the last time she'd come. Almost as if the estate itself knew that it was about to be destroyed.

"I hope you'll join us for lunch afterward," Leo said.

"It's not really appropriate for the caterer to eat with the guests," Emma said. "But thank you."

"You can be *my* guest," he said. "Change into regular clothes after the ceremony, and no one will even know that you're a caterer acting inappropriately. I hope you can sit at my table and eat with me. It would make my father happy."

"Well, if you're going to invoke Enzo," Emma said, "then what choice do I have?"

"And now I know I'll get the best basket, because you'll be at my table." Leo smiled like a little boy.

"They're all the best," Emma said. "You'll just get the basket with my favorites."

"Not that horrible grapefruit soda," Leo said.

Emma rolled her eyes. "Obviously the grapefruit soda."

"Okay, fine. For you," Leo said, "I'll drink grapefruit."

He walked off to greet more guests, and Emma went back into the tent to check on service.

"The picnic tables are set up," Francisco said. "Do you want the baskets on the tables now? Or should we wait until after the ceremony?"

"Let's keep them cool in here," Emma said. "We have enough servers to quickly get them out onto the tables once the ceremony wraps up."

"You sure?" Francisco asked, and Emma did a double take. Francisco had never doubted Emma's judgment before.

"What's that?" Emma asked.

"Nothing," Francisco said. "Yes, Chef."

"Okay, then."

"Samantha said there was a fight at the museum benefit," Francisco said.

Emma squinted her eyes as she looked at Francisco. "What's going on right now?"

"It isn't like you to lose focus," Francisco said quietly.

"I haven't."

"Yes, Chef."

"I'm going out to watch the ceremony."

Emma left the tent, her face hot from her conversation with Francisco. She stood toward the back of the crowd. She hadn't lost focus. Of course she hadn't.

Emma saw that Henry had taken a seat far away from where Leo would be conducting the ceremony, the very back row, and all the way off to the side. Emma walked over to join him. Henry caught her eye and patted the seat next to him, her cue to sit down.

But Emma didn't want to sit down. Not yet, anyway. It felt like her legs were being controlled by an invisible force, taking her directly to Leo.

He stood in the front of the crowd, speaking quietly with some members of his company.

"May I please borrow Leo for a moment?" she asked.

"Is there a problem with the food?" Leo asked, turning toward Emma as they moved away from his associates, so that they could have privacy.

Emma could see Enzo sitting proudly in the front row, smartly dressed in a lightweight navy suit with a red tie. He wore an enamel pin with the flag of Italy on his lapel, and when he saw Emma, he gave her a wide smile and a wave.

"No, everything's fine with the food."

"Is this about the grapefruit soda again?" Leo laughed at his own quip, and leaned in toward Emma. Their private joke.

"Please don't do this."

"Someone's very upset about the grapefruit soda," Leo said, laughter in his voice. "I'm only messing around, you know."

"You know what I mean," Emma said.

"I do," Leo replied, his tone shifting from jocular to business. Still, there was a softness in his voice. "But you know that it's a done deal."

"Let me walk through the house one more time." Emma could feel beads of sweat forming on her forehead. Her breath felt rushed.

"Emma," Leo said, furrowing his brow. "It's over."

"It doesn't have to be," Emma said. "Please. You're making a mistake. This place was our home."

"It was not our home. It never was. It didn't belong to us."

"It was *my* home," Emma said.

"Home is not a piece of real estate," Leo said. "This house? It's just a pile of bricks and some dirt. Keeping this place standing isn't going to bring your father back."

"But his memory," Emma said. "It's still home."

"Home isn't a place. A house is a physical space, but a home? Home is the people you want to be with, the ones you come back to at the end of a long day. It's the life you create for yourself, not an actual place. How can you not know that after all these years?"

Emma tried to come up with another argument, a last-minute Hail Mary that would make Leo change his mind. "Please."

He whispered: "I'm sorry, Emma, but it's over. Demolition begins next week."

PART THREE:
ROUGH MECHANICS

28

Then

Age seventeen

"But I don't understand," Emma said. She'd already bought the dress, the shoes. The dress had come from a fancy boutique in town that didn't accept returns.

"I'm sorry," Henry said, unable to meet her eye. "It was a mistake. I tried, but I couldn't do it."

Emma could think of many things that were a mistake. Hooking up with Henry secretly. Believing that he'd come through for her, after all this time of hiding her away, all this time letting his grandfather and her mother dictate their lives. Planning to go to the prom with him in the first place, when she knew he'd never go through with it. She hadn't wanted to admit it to Leo, and certainly not to herself, but deep down, she knew. She'd always known.

"Brittany asked me to go with her," Henry said. "So I said yes."

"Brittany, of all people?"

"Emma, it's easier this way."

★ ★ ★

The night of prom, Emma didn't know what to do with herself. Her mother couldn't understand why she'd changed her mind about going. She urged her to go by herself, or with Leo. After all, the prom was a rite of passage, something that every girl should partake in. But her mother didn't understand. Emma didn't want to go to the prom. She'd barely wanted to finish out her last days of high school. She couldn't wait to get away from Henry.

Event planners flitted about the house. Henry was throwing the pre-prom party, and the hallways would soon be filled with classmates, all ready to experience the best night of their teenage lives.

The entryway would serve as party central, with tables of mock cocktails and small sandwiches. Couples all planned to take photographs on the grand staircase. Emma's mother, Mila, was in charge of the party prep, overseeing the party planners.

"I'm sorry," she'd told Emma as she walked out the door that morning. "It's my job."

Emma understood. She wasn't mad at her mother. Not really. She reserved the majority of her rage for Henry. Their entire lives, it seemed, had built up to this. She could forgive his cowardice, his insistence of hiding her away, if he'd simply taken her to the prom. Emma locked herself in her room—she didn't need to torture herself by watching Henry and Brittany pose for photos.

But minutes before the guests arrived, she changed her mind. She threw on her party dress and made her way toward the house. Her mother was right. It was her prom as much as it was Henry's. She opened the back door to the house and walked through to the front entryway.

It was magical. Her mother had done a stunning job. The

room was filled with silver and gold balloons, and the air seemed to have been tinged with glitter. Everything glowed.

"You look beautiful, my sweet girl," her mother said when she spotted her.

Emma's eyes immediately filled with tears. Why, she wasn't quite sure. It was as if that simple act of kindness, calling her beautiful, using her pet name, had sent Emma over the edge. She'd been an exposed nerve all day, and her mother's gentle declaration of love had seemingly made her explode.

"Thank you," she said. "But I made a mistake. I can't do this."

Emma fled. Mila tried to follow her, but right at that moment, the first limo pulled up the driveway.

Emma quickly ducked into the shrubbery and watched as Brittany and her friends exited the limo. Emma's mother greeted them, offering each girl a fruit punch in a martini glass, and she felt an overwhelming sense of shame seeing her mother show kindness to these girls who had tortured her.

Emma darted across the front driveway to the Japanese maple tree. She quickly hoisted herself up and into the branches so she could observe the pre-party unseen. But when she got onto the first branch, she found something unexpected in the tree.

Leo.

"What are you doing here?" she hissed.

"Same thing as you, I guess," Leo said. "Only I didn't get the memo about the dress code." He pointed at his jeans and sneakers.

"Let me up," Emma said, and then pulled herself up to the branch where Leo sat, both of them hidden away by the leaves. Instinctively, she ran her fingers over the spot where Henry had carved their initials.

"You know," Leo said, his eyes unable to meet Emma's, "we could have gone to the prom together. We still can."

"You don't understand," Emma said. A few more limos drove up, and kids piled out, all looking shiny and fresh in their expensive dresses and tuxedos.

Emma watched as her classmates started posing for pictures on the staircase. From her vantage point, she had a direct view of the steps through the windows. Henry had his arms around Brittany, and she laughed wildly.

"What don't I understand?"

"I've been in love with Henry for my entire life," Emma said. "Since before I could even put a name on what the feeling was. You can't just get over something like that. It's impossible."

"I know."

"And how could you possibly understand that?" Emma said, turning to face Leo.

"Don't you know?"

"Know what?" Emma kept her eyes glued on the party inside as she spoke.

"Nothing," Leo said. "Nothing at all."

29

Now

"I can't believe that he's actually going to do it."

"Of course he's going to do it," Henry said as they sailed along the Long Island Expressway in Henry's convertible, top down after the groundbreaking ceremony. "He needs to demo and clear the main house so that he can build the development."

Emma turned and stared at Henry. That was not the response she wanted to hear. Perhaps if she glared at him, he'd see how angry his answer had made her. But with the top down on his car, his hair blew in the breeze, making him appear even more carefree and handsome than usual. Emma felt her anger melt away the longer that she looked at him. Henry van der Wraak was a hard man to stay angry with. A fact Emma had always struggled with.

After the ceremony, Emma and Henry had indulged in the baskets that Emma's company had made up. Emma had never done that before—completely blown off service at one of her events—and she was surprised at how easy it was. While Henry made himself comfortable at a table with the art museum board members, Emma sat at Leo and Enzo's table and acted like a guest: requesting refills on her wine from the servers passing by, talking about the food as if she hadn't helped prepare it herself, and wondering aloud when dessert would come out.

After dessert was served (freshly baked chocolate chip cookies, served warm in miniature skillets with vanilla gelato on top), Emma swiped one of the party favors for herself—an apple cinnamon popover in parchment paper with a jar of brown sugar butter on the side, all tied up in a burlap bag with a drawstring. A small tag read: "We hope you'll *pop over* to pick out your dream home soon!"

She'd planned to stay back, help out with cleanup. But she couldn't bring herself to talk to Francisco again and found herself in Henry's car instead.

"I know that he said he was going to do it," Emma said, "but I didn't think he actually would. I thought I could stop him."

"I think you need to let the past go. Let the house go," Henry said.

Emma considered Henry's words. Could she let the house go? She supposed she'd have to. Leo had won; she had lost. He would be demolishing the house the following week. Still, she thought, there had to be something else she could do.

When Emma didn't respond, Henry broke the silence: "It's his work. And work is important."

Emma felt like she was a child again, listening to her mother explain how important Felix's work was.

"Are you listening to me?" Henry asked, taking a hand off the steering wheel to put it on Emma's knee. "If someone told you not to cater some affair, would you listen?"

"Catering an affair isn't an act of destruction." Emma found that she had to raise her voice just to be heard over the wind racing by. "I create things. I don't destroy them."

"Okay, so not a perfect comparison," Henry said, setting both hands back on the steering wheel. "But you know what I mean."

"But *why* do you think he's doing it?" Emma asked. She was now almost yelling, the wind creating a soundtrack of white noise. "You knew that Stella couldn't be trusted. You seem to have art dealer superpowers of perception. Why do you think he's *really* tearing the house down?"

Henry slowed the car down as traffic built up on the highway. More quietly: "I think he's wanted to do it for a long time."

"What?"

"I think he was really unhappy at that house."

"I was, too, but you don't see me tearing it down brick by brick."

Henry looked over at Emma. "You were unhappy?"

"You know what I mean."

"I'm afraid I don't," Henry said, turning his head back to focus on the road.

"I was happy," Emma said. "But I was also unhappy that one summer."

"Because of me?"

"Because of you," Emma said. And then quickly: "Also, because my father died when I was little, and I never really had the sort of relationship with my mother that other girls seemed to have so easily with theirs." Emma wondered if she was letting Henry off too readily, by saying the truth about him, about them, but then couching it between the other hard truths about her childhood.

"I'm sorry," Henry said without hesitation. "There were

so many things I couldn't say to you then, but let me tell you how sorry I am now."

"You don't have to—"

"Let me say this," Henry said, his hands gripping the steering wheel a little bit tighter. "I'm sorry about the way I treated you when we were kids. I was wrong. I was horrible. And I'm lucky that you gave me another chance. I'm happy that we're together, and I'm going to do everything in my power to let you know that every day. I'm going to make up for the stupid things I did back then. If you'll have me, that is."

Emma sat with his words for a moment. Of course she would have him—had there ever been any doubt? She'd been his for her whole life, even when they were apart. He knew that. He had to have known that.

But here he was, bringing up the past. Henry had just told her that she needed to let the past go, but Emma wasn't sure she could. After all, wasn't that why she was here, in a car with Henry, speeding along the Long Island Expressway?

Was she a fool to give him another chance? Maybe she was. Leo certainly seemed to think so, seemed surprised that Emma had let him back into her life after all that had happened. How could she be with Henry after the way he treated her when they were young? Was she a fool, setting herself up for a heartbreaking disappointment once again?

They say: *fool me once, shame on you, but fool me twice, shame on me.* Was Henry about to fool her again?

Henry disrupted her reverie. He reached over and interlaced his fingers with hers, gave her hand a squeeze. "Emma Jansen," he said. "I love you."

30

Now

It was all-hands-on-deck in the prep kitchen. They had a four-hundred-person black-tie wedding the following night, and they'd spend the entire day doing prep, getting themselves ready for the massive amount of work to come.

Samantha handled the sauces and marinades while Emma worked with some of their more junior team members to cut and prep vegetables and garnishes. Most chefs hated this tedious part of prep work—after all, working with the proteins was more showy, and considered more difficult to do—but Emma relished it. She found the act of slicing and dicing, being meticulous, to be meditative. Her mind would clear as she created perfect tiny pieces of vegetables, each one the exact same size. And even if her thoughts did take her to unpleasant places, it wasn't exactly like she could do anything about it with her hands full of raw onions. No matter what thoughts came to mind, she had to keep chopping.

She was showing one of the new chefs how to cut multiple pieces of basil at the same time when Francisco turned up the television.

"Out on bail," the reporter said, "is Stella Knight, who'd been arrested last week on suspicion of stealing priceless artifacts from a Long Island mansion. Head of the purported Neo-Nazi organization the Supreme Reich, a judge ruled that she could be released due to insufficient evidence."

Emma watched as Stella walked out of the detention center, and toward a waiting car. She couldn't believe that this was the same person she'd met at Rolling Hill. The same person she'd sat at a table across from at lunch. The thought of having shared a meal with someone with those beliefs made Emma feel physically ill.

"Ms. Knight," the reporter said, chasing after Stella as the cameraman kept focused on the back of her head, "why did you do it?"

Stella didn't respond to the reporter, or any of the other reporters. Before the car pulled away from the curb, Stella looked out the window and smiled.

Emma dropped the knife she was holding. It bounced from the rubber mats on the floor onto her rubber clog, and she bent down to pick it up. When she righted herself, she realized that the whole kitchen was staring at her.

"Wasn't that the woman you told me about from the Glen Cove Historical Society?" Francisco asked.

"Yeah," Emma said, staring at the television, hoping that they'd say more. But they'd moved on to the next story. How was she supposed to let the past go when bits of it kept creeping up into her future?

"Back to work, everyone," Samantha said. "We pay you to make food, not to watch TV."

The entire kitchen put their heads back into their work, and Emma excused herself.

Francisco followed her out of the kitchen and into the hall-way. "You okay, Chef?"

"I'm fine," Emma said, sitting down against a wall in the hallway, rubbing her eyes. "It's just the onion."

"Yeah," Francisco said, sliding down next to her. "Chopping onions is a bitch."

"The worst."

"You wanna talk about it?"

"Nothing to talk about," Emma said. She kept her gaze straight toward the wall across. She couldn't figure out how to process Stella's release. The realization that she was a horrible judge of character. If she had misjudged Stella so completely, what else was she wrong about?

"Well, I have some news that may cheer you up," Francisco said, his voice softer. "Blanca's pregnant."

"Francisco, that's wonderful!" Emma said, and hugged her friend. The news was the exact thing to take her out of her head and completely change her mood. "I'm so happy for you two."

"Thanks," Francisco said, nodding. "We're pretty excited."

"I assume you'll let me cater the shower?" Emma said.

"Yes, Chef," Francisco answered, smiling. "Of course. We'd be honored."

"Good."

"Listen," Francisco said, rubbing his fingers along his jaw-line, "just because you befriended one bad egg, it doesn't have to mean anything."

"What does it say about my judgment?" Emma said. "Pretty bad."

Francisco did not tell Emma that he was worried about her. (He was too smart to make that mistake again.) He reminded her about how good her judgment could be by simply turn-ing his arm over to show Emma his tattoo of a sharp knife.

He'd gotten it once Emma declared his knife skills *better than hers* and then promoted him to event manager.

Emma looked down at the tattoo. She knew what Francisco was telling her. He didn't need to say a word. That was what real friendship was, Emma thought. The ability to communicate without saying a thing.

31

Now

Kissing Henry was different from before. He no longer kissed like a boy, back when they were younger, constantly sneaking around, rushing.

Now, Henry kissed like a man.

He felt comfortable giving Emma a kiss wherever they were, be it a trendy downtown restaurant, the intermission of a Broadway show, or on the sidewalk while they waited for the light to change so they could cross the street. He didn't rush; he took his time. He took his time with other things, too.

It was a Sunday afternoon, and they were at the wedding of one of Henry's friends from college. Emma knew, from the many weddings she'd catered, that being asked to accompany someone to a friend's wedding was a big deal. Whenever she brought snacks and sandwiches to the bridesmaids during picture time, she'd hear them talk. Taking someone you were dating to a wedding escalated the relationship from *casually dating* to *serious*.

Emma usually didn't make plans on Sundays. In the morning, she was generally too tired to function after catering a Saturday night party. She needed to conserve all her energy for whatever Sunday affair she'd be working. But today, she'd sent Samantha to handle the Russo baby christening herself. It was an after-church brunch in their backyard with an omelet station and a carving station. She and her team could take care of a job like that in their sleep—it was hard for Emma to admit, but she wasn't needed.

So Emma found herself free from work for the day. She put on a tea-length black dress with delicate ties on the shoulders. It had a demure boatneck in the front, but it plunged into a deep V in the back. When she'd seen the dress in a vintage shop window, she couldn't resist trying it on—it looked exactly like the little black Givenchy dress that Audrey Hepburn wore in *Sabrina*. She paired the dress with black kitten heels, bought two years ago when she went to Paris for the wedding of a friend from CIA, along with delicate pearl earrings that had belonged to her mother. Emma rarely wore the things that had once belonged to her mother. But the more time Emma spent with Henry, the more she longed for her. Emma was desperate to tell her, all this time later, that she'd been wrong. Henry was the right one for her. Just like Emma had always known.

Emma felt pretty. The deep V plunged so far down that Emma could feel Henry's strong hand on the skin of her back as they walked through Central Park together, on their way to the Boathouse, where the wedding would take place. As they walked across the park, toward the wedding, Emma's toes felt pinched by the heels, but she would not let that dull her excitement for the day. As soon as they got to the Boathouse, she and Henry were enveloped by a crowd of his college friends, and Emma tried to contain her smile as he referred to her as his *girlfriend*.

Henry draped his arm around Emma's shoulders through the ceremony, and when the couple kissed, Henry leaned over to kiss Emma. Exhausted as she was from the Moore wedding the night prior, Henry's kiss made Emma feel like she could conquer the world.

Still, she couldn't help but critique every level of the hospitality at the wedding. As Henry passed her a flute of champagne, she noticed that some of the servers didn't have freshly pressed shirts. When she reached for a passed appetizer, the server didn't seem to know what was inside (baked brie inside puffed pastry, with raspberry preserves and walnuts). And when the cocktail hour was ending, they didn't seem to know how to move the crowd into the main room. Emma always took pride in the way Samantha could gracefully, yet forcefully, herd a party from one room to the next.

Emma hated seeing the dinner plates set out directly onto the table. She never felt that a table was truly set until there were chargers underneath each plate. It was something that was always hotly contested at the office—Emma was strongly for, and Francisco couldn't see the purpose. Samantha loved them, because they helped save the linens, guarding against small spills, and Francisco would counter that they were barely useful, and merely a holdover from the older, more stuffy types of service. Emma would argue that a charger plate could help keep entrées hot, since the charger plate caught the heat from underneath the plate, but Francisco couldn't be convinced. He thought they were pretentious and a waste. Emma thought of him every time she saw one. (Or when she didn't.) She made a mental note to dress the tables at Francisco and Blanca's baby shower with chargers, just to see her friend's reaction.

"Isn't this beautiful?" the woman seated to the right of Emma asked her.

"Bold choice not using chargers," Emma said, pointing at her dinner plate.

The woman furrowed her brow and turned her attention back to her date.

Emma cursed her inability to make proper small talk. Weddings were filled with small talk. She thought about texting Samantha to get some ideas. She should have asked her for tips when she saw her the night before.

Henry seemed to be having no such difficulty.

"You're so right," he was telling a couple seated on the other side of the table. "They really did get lucky with the weather today."

As the woman across the table responded, Emma could barely hear what she was saying. The music had started up, and the table centerpieces were so tall that she couldn't see who was speaking. Wedding faux pas number 532, as far as Emma was concerned. The table centerpieces should be low, so as to encourage conversation.

Still, Henry seemed to be following along with the conversation seamlessly. "I was once going to a wedding on Fire Island, and it started to pour while we were still on the ferry on the way over. By the time we got there, most of us were drenched. And then, we still had to walk over to the restaurant from the ferry. The theme was *barefoot barbecue*, which was good, because my shoes were completely ruined by the time I got there!"

Everyone laughed at Henry's Fire Island anecdote, and Emma tried to laugh along, too. "A bad guest experience is so funny," she muttered under her breath.

Henry turned to Emma. "Should we see how the guest experience out on the dance floor is?"

Emma felt her face burn red as she realized that Henry had heard her. "I'm sure those shoes were very expensive," Emma said as she took his hand.

He led her out to the dance floor, right in the center of things. "They were. And so are these shoes, so careful where you put those kitten heels."

"I may spend most weddings in the kitchen," Emma said, smiling, "but I still remember how to dance."

Henry pulled her close, and they swayed to the music. As she danced with Henry, she realized something about her day: she'd forgotten to simply have fun. For the remainder of the afternoon, she told herself that she would be a wedding guest, and a wedding guest only. She would not critique the affair, and she would make small talk with the people at her table. (Henry wasn't the only one who could talk about the weather!) She would eat, dance, and drink, just like everyone else.

"Do you think they have a pantry here?" Henry whispered in Emma's ear. "Like the one you set up at the art museum benefit?"

Emma bit her lip. Not only did the Boathouse have a pantry, but she knew exactly where it was, having catered her fair share of parties at the venue. "Yes," she whispered.

"Then what are we waiting for?"

32

Then

Age seventeen

"I'm right here," Emma said as she heard the door to the indoor tennis court open.

She knew Henry would come for her. Even though she'd seen it with her own eyes, she didn't think that he'd actually go to the prom with Brittany. Of course, he'd find a way to be with her. So, as the pre-prom party took place inside the main house, she'd gone to the indoor tennis court. The place where they would meet, late at night. The place where she'd given herself so freely to him, the place that she'd come to think of as theirs.

Emma waited. And waited. She sat on the tall chair that would normally be reserved for an umpire during a game. She knew he'd come. And when he did, they'd hug and rush off to the prom, the way it should have been all along.

Only it wasn't Henry. It was Leo.

"Don't look so disappointed," Leo said, walking over to the chair and gazing up at her. "When you ran off, I thought you went back to your apartment. Why would you come here? Of all places…"

Emma didn't respond.

In an instant, Leo understood. "This is where you used to meet him, isn't it?"

Emma climbed down from the umpire chair.

"Why do you let him treat you like this?"

Emma sighed. "I've been in love with him all my life."

"He doesn't deserve you."

"You don't get it."

"I think that I get it perfectly," Leo said. "Maybe it's you who doesn't. You're in love with a guy who just took another girl to the prom. Now, whaddya say we do some damage to this prosecco I swiped from the house?"

"I'm not in a very celebratory mood."

Leo opened the prosecco bottle anyway. He had forgotten to bring glasses, so he took a swig directly from the bottle. He held it out for Emma.

"No, thank you."

"It's gooood," Leo said, stretching out the *o* in *good* so that it sounded like a song.

"Okay, fine," Emma said, and took a small sip. Leo was right; it *was* good. It was better than good. It was sweet and delicious, the bubbles tickling her nose, and Emma wanted more of it.

They finished the bottle in less than ten minutes. Emma danced around the tennis court, giddy from the alcohol, which had gone directly to her head. She tripped over her shoes, and somehow fell onto the tennis net, bringing it down completely.

"Oops," Emma said, crumpled on the ground.

"You okay?" Leo asked as he put out his hand and picked Emma back up.

"I'm fine," Emma said. "I'm better than fine."

Leo walked over to the side and reattached the net to the pole. He laughed. "You seem fine."

He bounced his hand onto the net, now newly rehung.

Emma immediately crashed her body into the net and tried to knock it back down again.

"What are you doing?" he asked.

"I thought it would be funny if I made the net fall again after you put it back up."

"Oh, it wasn't attached properly before," Leo said. "That's why it fell so easily. It won't fall down again."

Emma felt a tiny burp escape her lips. "I wish it would fall down. I wish I could tear this whole place down."

"If you want, I can unattach the net?"

Emma walked over to the couch, the place where she'd slept with Henry countless times. She pulled the French mattress off the top and stomped on it. Then she jumped up on the frame and stomped on that, too. For a moment, she heard her father's voice in her head: "Clean house, clear mind." She felt a pull, thinking about how much pride he placed in keeping Rolling Hill in pristine condition, as if it were his own home. But she pushed the thought away as quickly as it had come.

"Again, I feel the need to ask," Leo said, "what are you doing?"

"I hate this couch," Emma said. "I hate this stupid couch, and I hate this whole indoor tennis court." She jumped again, and when she landed, her foot went through the wood, leaving a huge hole in the couch's frame.

"Are you okay?" Leo rushed to the couch, but Emma had already extricated herself from the hole and had moved on to her next target.

"I'm great," Emma said. She went over to the back wall and grabbed one of the tennis rackets. In one swift motion, she lifted it high over her head and brought it down, hard, onto the back of a nearby chair. The strings looked uneven and out of place, but not quite broken. Emma swung again, and this time, it did the trick. She went through all eight rackets that hung on the wall, each in varying shapes and sizes. Emma didn't know why one family of three needed quite so many rackets.

"I think maybe we should go," Leo said.

"You can go," Emma said, "but I have a few more things I need to do." She threw the racket she was holding down to the ground, and walked over to the table and chairs next to the court. In one swift motion, Emma picked up the chair and threw it directly toward the center of the court. She then picked up another one and did the same thing.

"Well, I'm not going to leave you here," Leo said as he picked up a third chair and crashed it down.

Once the eight chairs and two tables were in the middle of the court, they moved on to the benches. Once those were overturned, they switched on the automatic ball serving machine. Tennis balls flew through the air as they surveyed the damage.

"Needs one more final touch," Emma said, and went to retrieve a ball basket from the side. She turned it over, and bright new tennis balls covered the ground. Leo found another one and did the same thing. They went into the back, and they found three more. They kept spilling brand-new tennis balls until the floor became bright yellow.

After, when the indoor tennis court was in shambles, Leo sat down on the ground next to Emma.

"I can't believe we just did that," Emma said, her breath still hard.

"Want me to help you clean it up?" Leo asked, his face open and honest.

"I'm not going to clean it up," Emma said. "Let Henry clean it up."

"I think we both know that Henry's not going to clean it up," Leo said. "He has people for that sort of thing."

They both laughed out loud.

Leo turned toward Emma. "Do you feel any better?"

"I didn't feel bad," Emma said quickly. "I feel fine."

"I guess I meant to say: How did it feel?" Leo asked.

Emma looked at Leo. "It felt good."

33

Now

This was not a productive use of her time. She was supposed to be getting ready for Henry to pick her up, but instead, she was stuck in the past, once again. Googling Stella Knight and the Supreme Reich.

She didn't know why she was doing it. After all, Stella was out of her life, and with the house being razed to the ground, she had no reason to be in touch with her anymore. Still, she found she couldn't stop.

She'd stumbled upon an op-ed about the rise of anti-Semitism in America, and the Supreme Reich was name-checked as one of the largest organizations on Long Island, with strong ties to the KKK. (Emma immediately googled this, and was shocked to find various KKK outposts all over Long Island.) The op-ed went on to describe the various types of white supremacist groups, how they differed and how they were the same. The one thing the groups held in common with all of the Neo-Nazi groups popping up all over New

York State: the belief in a "pure master race." Reading about Nazis living on Long Island, Emma couldn't help but think of Felix, and the research she and Leo had done back in high school.

Her phone rang. "I just got off the FDR. I should be at your building in ten minutes," Henry said.

"See you in ten."

Emma gasped when she looked at the time. She'd wasted the last hour in a haze on the internet. She quickly slammed her laptop shut and rushed into the bathroom. She dabbed some perfume onto her neck and brushed some blush onto her cheeks. Then she quickly put on the earrings she'd left out to wear, as well as a cuff bracelet. Samantha always said that a woman's jewelry was her armor, and Emma couldn't help but agree in that moment. Once adorned, she felt like a different version of herself—refined, pretty. She was ready for her night out.

Emma tossed her phone into her clutch, and pulled out a nude lipstick. She dabbed some on, and then did a final check of her outfit. It was a black shift dress, on loan from Samantha, and she'd paired it with her kitten heels and a bright red bag.

Emma had never been to an auction before. She'd never had any occasion to step foot inside of Sotheby's, the famous auction house on the Upper East Side, but tonight, she was unexpectedly giddy at the thought of going.

Henry picked her up in his convertible, and they drove uptown with the roof down. He held her hand as they drove, and Emma felt the rest of the world melt away. At the first stoplight, Henry pointed at where the top should have been, and asked: "Is this okay with your hair?"

Emma laughed before responding: "It's fine. I like the fresh air."

She couldn't help but think of the sort of woman Henry van

der Wraak was used to dating. Certainly the sort of woman who would rather arrive at the venue with her hairstyle intact. A woman who worried about what her hair looked like, whereas Emma usually wore hers inside a bandanna at work. A woman who got weekly manicures, whereas Emma cut her nails short, all the better to do prep work in the kitchen. For a moment, Emma wondered if that's what Henry would prefer—for her to be a woman who cared about things like her hair. But Emma wanted to enjoy the ride. She would shake out her waves, made even more wild from the wind, when they got to Sotheby's.

Emma couldn't recall what type of art they'd be seeing tonight. From the moment Henry said *Sotheby's*, all she could think about was that auction she'd read about in 2018, when a Banksy shredded itself shortly after being sold. Emma felt that all manner of unexpected things could occur at an auction. She couldn't wait to find out what the night held in store.

There would be a cocktail party first, and Emma knew the caterer. She was an old friend from CIA, and since they both worked in the Tri-State Area, their paths crossed quite often. They each constantly referred to the other when they were overbooked. But knowing the caterer meant more than simply seeing an old friend. It meant an evening spent getting served before everyone else, getting slipped special treats from the kitchen, not to mention the bar. Tonight would be fun.

Henry pulled up directly in front of Sotheby's, and Emma was surprised to see they had valet parking. Valet parking was not really a thing in Manhattan. At her city parties, the biggest perk was when a host paid for guests to park for free in a nearby garage. This was next level.

They made their way inside, and Emma's friend, Sophie, immediately swept in for a hug.

"Henry, this is Sophie," Emma said. "The *second* best caterer in Manhattan."

Sophie laughed as she shook hands with Henry. "So, you
two know each other from culinary school?" he asked.

"I could tell you some stories about this one," Sophie said.

"Please don't," Emma said, her smile wide.

"I'll wait until you've had a bit more to drink," Sophie said.
She bumped her hip into Emma's. "Okay, work beckons…"

"I'll come find you before we go," Emma said, and Sophie
made her way toward the kitchen.

"We forgot to ask her about the pantry situation," Henry
said, leaning down to whisper into Emma's ear. He took a
nibble. "Ah, that's okay. I'm sure we'll find it on our own."

He gently kissed Emma, and they walked into the reception.
Henry introduced her to various colleagues, and Emma found
that the art crowd didn't do small talk. She liked them immediately. No one talked about the weather, or what brought
her here, or what she did for a living. They asked her about
her favorite artists, whether she preferred paintings or sculpture, and what she thought of the pieces that were up for sale
that night. She'd been having such a nice time talking that
she hadn't realized it when Henry drifted off to one side of
the room, leaving her on the other.

"Emma?" a voice asked from behind her. Familiar, like
she'd known it all her life. She knew the voice, but somehow,
she could not place it.

She spun around, and seeing his face had the same effect.
She knew him, but she did not. He looked exactly the same,
and entirely different. He looked frail, with a wheelchair and
an aide to push it forward. "Felix," Emma said, unsure of
whether she should shake his hand, or lean in for a double
kiss, or simply run away.

She didn't have to decide. Felix's aide brought his wheelchair toward her, and he took her hand and pulled her in for a double kiss. "How long has it been?" Felix asked.

"I don't know," Emma said, her eyes searching the room for Henry. Seeing Felix again made her unsure on her feet—did he know that she and Henry were dating? Did Henry know that his grandfather would be there that night?

"Grandfather?" Henry said, his face a question mark as he walked over to Emma and Felix. The expression on Henry's face answered her question: he did not know his grandfather would be there. Henry put his arm protectively around Emma's waist. That answered her other question: there was now no doubt as to the fact that they were dating. He turned to his grandfather's aide. "Anne, it's nice to see you. This is Emma, my girlfriend."

"Nice to meet you," Anne said, offering Emma a smile and a nod.

"You two are an item?" Felix asked Henry. His face held the stern expression that Emma remembered from her youth. Was Felix going to chastise them for dating, the way he had when they were young? Was he going to forbid Henry from seeing her?

"We are," Henry said, his voice confident and strong. He gave Emma's waist a squeeze.

Felix cleared his throat. "Ah, well. Emma and I were catching up."

"I didn't know you'd be here, Grandfather," Henry said.

"I'm still the van der Wraak in van der Wraak and Son, aren't I?"

"Of course," Henry said. "It's just—"

A server walked over to them and interrupted Henry's thought. "Sophie said that you two get the special treatment tonight." She handed them plates filled with appetizers, along with the specialty cocktails for the evening.

"Thank you," Emma said. "Please thank Sophie for me. Would it be too much trouble—"

"Two more plates," the server said, reading her mind, "coming right up."

Emma smiled. "Thank you."

"Our Emma is a VIP, it seems," Felix said.

"Emma is one of the city's most in-demand caterers, and her friend is catering this event tonight."

"You're a chef?" Felix asked, his face suddenly sad.

"Yes," Emma said. "I studied at CIA."

"You work for the CIA?" Felix asked.

"Culinary Institute of America," Emma said.

"So you cook," Felix said, taking a long, uncomfortable pause before his next words came out: "Like Fleur."

"Yes."

Emma's phone rang, and she shuffled her drink to the top of her plate so that she could pull it out of her purse. Emma checked the caller ID—Leo.

They hadn't spoken since the groundbreaking ceremony, and Emma didn't think that they would again. They were both so angry—she, that he tore the house down, even though she begged him not to; he, that she was with Henry. She assumed this would be like the last time, that Leo wouldn't speak to her for another seven years.

"Would you all please excuse me?" Emma said to the group, and walked over toward a window for some privacy. Before she could say hello, Leo spoke. "You need to come here as soon as possible."

"Are you okay?" Emma asked. "What's going on?"

"Don't bring Henry," he said. "Come alone."

34

Now

Leo was waiting at the edge of the property when Emma arrived in a cab from the train station the next morning.

It looked like a crime scene. The police had secured the entire job site, and Emma had to show her identification before Leo could bring her onto the property. They drove up to the house in his red Jeep, which had four-wheel drive for the dirt roads, but no actual doors or windows. Emma buckled in and held on to a handle next to the windshield.

"I didn't think you would ever want to see me again," Emma said. Dirt kicked up as they drove up the hill, and she squinted her eyes to see Leo.

"This is bigger than just you and me."

"What is?"

"I think it's better if you see it."

"See what?" Emma asked, but her question was soon answered. Where the main house once stood, there was nothing. The house had been razed to the ground, and now all that remained was a foundation. It looked like a concrete maze, built deep into the ground.

More cops swarmed the property, along with a number of men in dark suits. It looked like something out of a movie.

Leo parked right in front of the house. Or, to be more accurate, where the house used to stand. They got out of the car and made their way to the ladder that led down to the foundation.

"Is this safe?" Emma asked as she followed Leo, who was moving quickly.

"I've got you," Leo said, and held out his hand. Emma stepped onto the ladder, and Leo used one hand to steady her at the waist.

"What is this?" Emma asked as they got down to the floor of the foundation. "All this concrete is scary." She had to look up to see the sky, to avoid feeling claustrophobic.

"Remember all those secret hallways and rooms?" Leo asked. "There's more."

"Down here?" Emma asked. "I recall the house had a basement, but it was mostly storage rooms for the art and old clothing."

"Did you know there was a subbasement?"

"A what?"

"A subbasement," Leo said. "A basement below the basement."

"Of course not," Emma said. "I was too scared to go past the stairs of the attic. I don't think I was ever in the basement, much less a subbasement."

"We were in the basement that one time," Leo said. "But we felt a breeze, which supported our theory that the house was haunted, so we hightailed it out of there."

Emma immediately remembered. "That's right. We went down there to look for evidence, and we were convinced that the ghost of Fleur was the breeze that lived down there. That's when we got the Ouija board."

He nodded and led her around the hallways. A crowd of men in suits stood around an opening in the concrete.

"Subbasement," Leo said, pointing.

They walked directly to the cut in the wall. A set of steps awaited.

"So, this was hidden?" Emma asked. "All these years?"

"Yes," Leo explained. "It was a false wall, just like the one we found for the secret pantry behind the kitchen."

"I'm not going down there," Emma said.

"We're going together," Leo said, and grabbed a handheld lantern from one of the men in suits. "Here, take this."

Emma took the lantern. "Who are all of these people?"

"Let's go," Leo said, and disappeared down the dark stairwell.

35

Then

Age seventeen

Emma stayed in her room as the cops swarmed the estate. It wasn't that she was scared. Mostly, she was embarrassed.

That morning, her mother had told her that some teenagers had broken into the indoor tennis court during the pre-prom party and vandalized it. Thrown furniture around, broken tennis rackets, and filled the floor of the court with brand-new tennis balls. Mila seemed particularly angry about this part—the waste of it all. She and Felix had already telephoned the police, and she expected that this *nonsense*, as she called it, would take up most of her day. Emma got back into her bed. She couldn't face what was going on out there, and anyway, she had a raging headache from all of the prosecco that she and Leo had downed the night before.

How could she have destroyed the tennis court? What had she been thinking? It was bad enough that Henry had utterly, completely broken her heart. Did she need to retaliate like that? Was that really the way to get him back? Of course not. But then, Emma realized: she hadn't done it because she wanted him back. She did it because she knew she never *could* get him back. She did it to end things, once and for all. Taking Brittany to the prom was the end of everything. They could never come back from that. And in some far-off part of her mind, Emma knew that she didn't want to.

But now her mother had gone and gotten the police involved. What if Henry told them that she was the one with a motive? What if Henry told her mother everything?

A gentle rap on her window shook Emma from her reverie. She poked her head out of her comforter and saw a tiny pebble hit the glass. She stood up and walked to the window. It was Leo, lazily throwing tiny rocks, leaning against the railing of the staircase, seeming as if he had not a care in the world. As if he had nothing to hide. As if they hadn't trashed the indoor tennis court the night before. As if cops weren't crawling all over the property.

Emma caught his eye and then motioned with a flick of the wrist for him to come up. She opened the front door and waited, her blanket still wrapped around her shoulders.

"Aren't you looking lovely today, Miss Jansen," Leo said. "You didn't have to get all dressed up on my account."

"Come in," Emma said, pulling him through the threshold and then slamming the door behind him. "We can't act suspicious today."

"Well, walking around with your comforter as a disguise is not at all suspicious. Get dressed." He took a seat at the kitchen table.

"We can't go out." Emma peeked out the window and then sat down in a chair next to him.

"Did the cops put you on house arrest?" Leo asked. "And, yes, please, I would love something to drink."

"There's diet iced tea in the fridge," Emma said, making

no move to get it. "And we can't leave. What if the cops want to talk to us?"

"See, now *that* sounds suspicious." Leo got up from the table and poured two glasses of diet iced tea. "Let's go do something. Is there anything playing at the theater at the mall?"

"I think I'm going to stay here," Emma said.

"Well, if the cops are going to come talk to you," Leo said, "don't you think you should have a last hurrah first? I mean, if you're going to jail and all..."

"You think we're going to jail?" Emma's eyes widened, and her mouth fell open.

"No one is going to jail," Leo said, laughing. "Go get dressed. Lunch is on me."

One double feature, two tubs of popcorn, and one serving of bourbon chicken from the mall later, Leo dropped Emma back off at home. By then, the cops had left. Things had quieted. And anyway, being with Leo for the day had made Emma forget all about Henry and the prom. It made her forget all about what they'd done the night before (and its consequences).

Emma floated back upstairs to her apartment as if on a cloud. Leo was right—there was very little that a double feature couldn't fix.

"You're home," her mother said as soon as she let herself in. Emma froze in place. Her mother never waited up for her.

"I went to the mall with Leo," Emma said, searching her mother's face for a clue. Why was she waiting for her? "I guess the cops left?"

"The cops left," Mila said. "I realized it was silly. After all, we can have Linwood clean things up and take care of the furniture repairs. The tennis rackets..."

"That's good news," Emma said. She was eager to rush off

to her room, but something about the way her mother was glaring at her told her that she wasn't yet excused.

"You'll help, of course," Mila said, holding her daughter's gaze. "You can start tomorrow."

Emma didn't answer.

"Henry will be helping out as well"

Emma waited for her mother to say more. She felt as if this were worse than if she'd been subjected to a police interrogation. Anything she said to her mother would surely be used against her.

"I thought it was so odd that Henry offered to help Linwood clean up," Mila said, her voice calm and measured. "But then I realized. You two have been carrying on behind my back, despite my warnings."

Emma wanted to deny it, but she couldn't find the words. She began to quietly cry.

"When the police searched for evidence, they found a stash of condoms hidden inside the side table next to the couch." Emma didn't respond. Mila cleared her throat. "At least you were being safe. But I warned you about him."

"I was in love with him," Emma whispered.

Mila walked over to Emma and put her arms around her. "Oh, my sweet girl, I know. I know."

Emma buried her head into her mother's shoulder. "I'm so stupid," she said between tears.

"You're not stupid," Mila said. "You are smart and special. One day you will find someone who deserves you."

Her mother's kindness only made Emma cry even harder.

36

Now

Emma didn't follow Leo, at first. She was terrified. What could possibly be in a hidden subbasement that could only be discovered once the house was torn down to the ground? Emma was sure she didn't want to know.

"We were right all along," Leo said, and his voice echoed up to where Emma stood. "Are you coming?"

Emma turned around to leave. She shouldn't be here. But then, just as quickly, she spun back on her heel. She couldn't leave Leo. And she had a feeling that she'd regret not seeing what Leo wanted to show her.

She held her lantern out in front of her face with one hand, and ran the other hand against the concrete wall so that she wouldn't fall. Once down in the subbasement, she no longer needed the light. Men in suits had the entire space illuminated.

"Now maybe people will believe what I said about Felix van der Wraak," Leo said.

Emma looked around, and couldn't process what she was

seeing at first glance. It took her eyes a moment to adjust. It took her brain a beat longer. What she was looking at was this: a subbasement filled with Nazi relics. In one corner, there were Nazi uniforms, pressed and hung up neatly, as if they were waiting for the time when they could be worn again.

Against the back wall, there were six shelves filled with books and files. A man in a suit was cataloging each one.

Another corner had more of what Emma and Leo had found as kids—plates, serving platters, and other pieces of china, all with gold Nazi insignias, right in the center. A man in a suit was packing them up, filing them away.

"Are you with the Holocaust Museum?" she asked him.

"I'm with the Department of Justice."

Emma stepped back, and nodded her head. She tried to keep her composure, but his words had rocked her to the core, made this all the more real.

"Are you all right?" Leo asked.

"I can't believe what I'm seeing."

"I know," Leo said. "It's a lot to take in."

Emma tried to formulate a thought. *A lot to take in* was the understatement of the century. They'd lived their whole lives in this house, when all the while, this was lurking beneath. Pure evil. And they didn't know. They lived their day-to-day lives here and didn't know. They ate their meals, danced in the ballroom, and played hide-and-seek, all while this was beneath their feet.

Emma turned toward Leo, about to say something. But when she tried, she found she was unable to speak.

37

Now

Leo and Emma were silent on the drive back into the city. Emma knew what they had to do. They would talk to Henry, and tell him the truth: his grandfather was a Nazi, after all. Emma thought it was the kind thing to do. Within hours, the Department of Justice would sort through all of the evidence, and even though Felix was now an old man, living with constant care from an aide in his Upper East Side apartment, he would be arrested and tried for war crimes.

"Maybe this doesn't mean what we think it means," Emma said, her mind racing. "There could be a perfectly logical explanation for all this."

"Maybe," Leo said.

But they both knew they were lying. They'd discovered an entire subbasement filled with things that Felix was hiding. And there was only one reason for a person to have Nazi artifacts hidden in a subbasement: Felix was a former Nazi, hiding out in the United States.

Leo had been right all along.

Now, with proof of who Felix really was, Emma figured out the rest. Despite what she'd been made to believe as a kid, she now knew that Felix had, in fact, killed Fleur. At the time, Felix had told the police that he and Fleur had quarreled about missing antiquities from the house. But that wasn't why they'd fought. Fleur must have discovered Felix's secret, and he killed her for it.

The plates. The treasure trove of artifacts. The library of Nazi records. All proof of his evil. The only thing that tied Felix to his former life. The evidence that could get him deported and land him in jail, branded a war criminal.

"Do you think Agnes was a Nazi, too?" Emma asked.

"Even if she wasn't," Leo said, "she was married to a Nazi. She loved a Nazi. It's almost worse."

"Maybe she didn't know," Emma said.

Leo turned to look at her for a brief moment. "She knew."

Neither one said the thing that hung in the periphery, the thing Emma really needed to know: *What did my mother know?* Emma closed her eyes. Had Mila known the man she worked for was a Nazi? They'd spent countless hours together in his office. Emma couldn't believe that her mother would knowingly work for a Nazi. The thought was too much to bear.

When they got to the Upper East Side, they parked in front of Henry's gallery, van der Wraak and Son. Emma had texted him, so he was expecting her. He wasn't expecting Leo to come along, too, but that was the least of her problems. Even after the hour-long drive into the city, she still hadn't landed on what she would say to Henry. How did you tell someone that everything they thought was true about their life was actually a lie? How did you tell someone something that would make their world come crashing down?

Emma didn't know.

"To what do I owe this pleasure?" Henry asked gracefully as Emma and Leo walked into his office. She knew that he was expecting only her, and she saw his eyes narrow when Leo came in behind her. Emma could feel her palms go clammy, felt her face heat up.

Henry motioned to the dark red velvet sofa, and Leo and Emma sat down, side by side. Emma noticed the slightest twitch in Henry's jaw when he realized that Emma had chosen to sit with Leo, leaving Henry on the armchair next to the couch.

"I think it's best if we tell you," Leo said. "And not mince words."

Henry looked at Emma. "Is there something going on between the two of you?"

"Oh, God," Emma said. "No, that's not why we're here."

Leo winced. "We just came from the house," he said.

"Oh," Henry said, sitting back in the chair. "Is that all? You had me worried."

"My crew demoed the house, down to the foundation. But then we found something that wasn't supposed to be there. A subbasement."

"What?" Henry said.

"There was a subbasement, hidden in the foundation. They immediately stopped demo, because that wasn't in the blueprints. But they found something down there. The subbasement, this hidden room, was filled with Nazi artifacts."

Henry didn't speak.

"Remember in high school, when you overheard us talking about how your grandfather was a Nazi?"

"Yes," Henry said, his voice droll. "I remember that."

"That was because Emma and I had found a plate with a Nazi insignia in a hidden pantry, off the kitchen."

"I see."

Emma reached over and took Henry's hands in her own. She gave them a squeeze, and said: "I'm so sorry."

"We're sorry to be telling you this," Leo said. "But we felt that we should warn you. The subbasement was filled with Nazi paraphernalia. Plates, serving platters. Munitions, jewelry stolen from the people killed in the camps, gas masks. Old uniforms and records. Tons and tons of records. The DOJ is there now, cataloging everything. We believe they'll be taking your grandfather into custody tonight, if they haven't already done so."

"It was kind of you to try to warn me," Henry said. "But it's not what you think."

"Oh, Henry," Emma said. "I'm so sorry. We'll be here for you. I'll help you get through the trial."

"There's not going to be a trial," Henry said simply.

Emma studied Henry's face. Surely he must be hiding how he was feeling. She grasped his hands tighter, a show of support.

"With all due respect," Leo said, "I overheard the agents talking about your grandfather, strategizing when they'd take him in."

"You didn't tell me that," Emma said, turning to Leo.

"Well, you didn't think I was going to let him get away with it," Leo asked, "did you?"

Henry cleared his throat. "I have no doubt that the Department of Justice has already contacted my grandfather, but it's not to arrest him."

"It's okay," Emma said. "I'm not going anywhere. I'll be there for you, no matter what."

"You won't have to," Henry said.

"And how can you know that when there's an entire subbasement of proof that says otherwise?" Leo asked, his tone no longer friendly.

"Because my grandfather wasn't a Nazi," Henry said. "He was a Nazi hunter."

38

Then

Age seventeen

Henry was already at the indoor tennis court, helping Linwood with the cleanup, by the time Emma arrived. She checked her watch; she was perfectly on time.

"I thought you could help gather the balls," Linwood said, handing Emma one of the tennis ball hoppers. He stared down at the ground as he gave it to her. Emma wondered if he, too, had figured out what had gone on at the indoor tennis court late at night for the past year. Just like her mother had.

"Sure," Emma said, and took the hopper. It was a steel wire basket, and you simply had to press down on a tennis ball in order to pick it up. The balls were soft, pliable, and they bent slightly to pass right through the wires on the bottom. Once through, the ball then popped up into the basket. It was relatively easy, in terms of what needed to be done. And sort of fun, though Emma wouldn't admit that part to herself.

Henry was helping Linwood carry the furniture outside to determine which pieces could be salvaged, and which would need to be sent out for a little more attention. The chairs and tables seemed to need only a little paint and new glass tops. The wood frame of the chaise couch would require a bit more TLC.

Emma kept her head down as she worked. Shame flamed through her body. Shame over trashing the tennis court, shame over the extra work she was creating for Linwood. Shame over how Henry had treated her. How she'd allowed herself to be treated. It took all of her energy to keep herself from crying.

Henry walked back into the indoor tennis court and gathered the rackets, all eight of which needed to be restrung. The nylon strands stuck out, all at different sizes and angles, making Henry look like an alien with hairy claws. "Can I talk to you?"

"I don't think that's a good idea," Emma said, and continued collecting the balls. She willed herself to stay steady. She pictured herself tripping over one of the tennis balls and falling flat on her back, embarrassing herself even more.

Linwood announced that he was driving the truck into town, to take the couch frame to a repair shop, and that when Emma was done with the balls, she could leave. It was a small price to pay for the damage she'd caused.

"Thank you," Emma said, but Linwood was already out the door.

"Please, can we talk?" Henry asked again once Linwood was safely out of earshot.

"I don't think we have anything to talk about." Emma focused back down on her work.

"I think it's pretty clear that we do."

Emma didn't respond.

Whispering: "Emma, you trashed the indoor tennis court."

Emma tried to think of something clever to say, something about how he'd trashed her heart, so it was only fair, but their conversation was interrupted by Leo, who opened the door to the indoor tennis court loudly, making his presence immediately known.

"Thought you two could use some help," Leo said, smiling brightly as he traipsed across the court to where Emma and Henry stood.

Emma couldn't help but notice that he'd waited for Linwood to leave before setting foot inside.

"You don't need to be here," Henry said, his voice rough. "We've got it covered."

"I figured another set of hands couldn't hurt," Leo said, and grabbed a nearby ball hopper.

"I was actually hoping to be alone with Emma, if you don't mind," Henry said.

"And what if I do?" Leo asked. He put the ball hopper down and met Henry's gaze.

"Leo," Emma said, "it's okay. Let me finish this up and then I'll come by your place and we can go to the mall."

"Emma's right," Henry said to Leo. "This has nothing to do with you."

"I was the one who helped pick up the pieces last night," Leo said. "I was the one who was there for Emma, after what you did."

"So it was you?" Henry asked. "You're the one who did this? But why?"

"He didn't do it," Emma said. "It was me. I was mad about prom. Let's forget this and clean up. The quicker we get it cleaned up, the sooner we can leave and put it all behind us."

"It wasn't just Emma," Leo said, his voice firm, strong. "It was the both of us."

"Leo, you need to leave," Henry said. His voice stayed steady, but his cheeks flamed red. Taking a breath: "And, Emma, you and I need to talk."

"I have nothing to say to you," Emma reminded him. "And once I leave for college at the end of the summer, I plan to never see you again."

39

Now

"My grandfather wasn't only an art dealer," Henry continued. He spoke calmly and matter-of-factly. "He was a Nazi hunter, too."

"What?" Emma asked. The shock of what she had seen in the subbasement had not yet worn off; she could barely process another surprise like this.

"Yes," Henry said, "he hunted down Nazis who escaped to America after the war. At first, he did it primarily through tracking stolen artwork."

"What?" Emma asked again. She found herself unable to say anything intelligent, unable to come up with a response other than: *What?*

"That's the *real* reason my grandfather took to calling the house the Audrey Hepburn Estate. It was only after someone overheard him say it that he came up with the *Sabrina* cover story, since the house shared an address with the Larrabee estate.

"Did you know that when she was a child, Audrey Hepburn lived in Nazi-occupied Holland for five years? She saw such atrocities in the war that she never really spoke of that time of her life. But she was a part of the Dutch Resistance. Kids were tasked with carrying secret messages back and forth in their shoes, and Audrey was a part of that."

"I thought you just said she never spoke about that time in her life?" Leo asked.

"She didn't," Henry explained. "But her son has confirmed, in his book, that she told him about that part."

"It's too much," Emma said, putting her hands in front of her face. The whiplash of the past day was getting to her. "It's simply too much."

"I know," Henry said, reaching for Emma's hands. He took her hands in his own. His eyes were soft and gentle as they gazed into hers. "It's a lot to handle. But perhaps now it's time I told you everything."

"Please do," Leo said.

"My grandparents, like Audrey, were children who lived under Nazi occupation in the Netherlands during World War II. The things they saw, that they experienced...well, they were unimaginable. My grandparents had a hard time talking about it, too."

Henry called out to his assistant to bring in drinks. She came in with bottled waters. "Anyone need anything stronger?" he asked.

"Scotch," Leo said.

"Three glasses of scotch, please," Henry said to his assistant.

She left the room, and Henry continued: "They, too, were part of the underground Resistance, carrying messages along in their shoes. That's how my grandparents met, in fact. Childhood sweethearts. Years later, when they finally got to this country, my grandfather found work as an assistant in an art dealer's showroom. He was tall and strong, so he'd help carry the artwork in and get it ready for sale. He also helped catalog the art that came in. The grunt work, mostly. One day, he helped unload a painting that he recognized. The Chagall. Do you remember the Chagall? It hung in the—"

"Cabana," Emma interrupted. "I know. It was my favorite piece of art. The most beautiful thing I'd ever seen."

"It was beautiful, yes," Henry said. "But it had special meaning for my grandfather. That Chagall had hung in the dining room of his childhood friend's house. Jacob and his family were Jewish, and it was an important piece for them, since Marc Chagall was a Jewish artist."

"So…how did the painting end up in an art gallery in America?" Leo asked tentatively.

"I think you know," Henry said somberly. "Of course you know. During the German occupation of the Netherlands, Jacob's family was taken."

"They were sent to the camps?" Emma asked.

"Yes," Henry said. "But first, my grandfather saw his friend's father get shot, in broad daylight, in the town square. His entire family was rounded up after that."

"I didn't know there were concentration camps in the Netherlands," Leo said.

"They were mostly used as transport stations to ship Jews over to the concentration camps most people have heard of—Auschwitz, Buchenwald—but there were camps in the Netherlands. Herzogenbusch and its subcamps. Amersfoort, and a number of lesser-known camps."

"Did anyone from Jacob's family survive?" Emma asked.

"I'm afraid not," Henry said. "But my grandfather never forgot his friend, or his friend's family. That's why he immediately recognized the Chagall when it appeared that day at the gallery. There was no mistaking it—this painting had been stolen by the Nazis, and my grandfather knew it. My grandfather told the art dealer what he knew, and the dealer told him to keep his mouth shut."

Henry's assistant gently knocked on the door and brought in the scotch. Leo downed his in one gulp, and she quickly refilled his glass. Emma took small, measured sips of hers.

"My grandfather went directly to the government," Henry explained. "And from there, as they say, the rest is history. He began working with the Department of Justice, Office of Special Investigations, tracking down Nazis through stolen artwork.

"Once my grandfather was more established in the art world, he and my grandmother bought Rolling Hill. My grandparents sought out other people who'd survived the war to work for him. He thought it was the kind thing to do, a way to give back. But it turned out that the driver he hired was a Nazi, hiding out in the United States. When my grandfather discovered this, he, of course, secretly turned him over to the government. But not before that driver had put the word out that Rolling Hill was a safe harbor for others who needed to hide. From there, my grandparents were able to recruit suspected Nazis as house staff. They were able to monitor their actions, investigate them, and compile evidence to determine if they were, in fact, Nazis who served during World War II."

"Did we know any of them?" Emma asked, her voice tentative.

"I'm afraid so," Henry said, nodding. "Fleur was one."

Emma gasped. "So, your grandfather *did* kill Fleur?"

"He didn't kill her," Henry said, shaking his head furiously. "That was an accident. He planned to bring her in, and she tried to run. But she made the mistake of going upstairs—we think that she was planning to try to jump from a second-floor window?—and she encountered one of my grandfather's bodyguards. From there, her only option was to make her way up to the attic. My grandfather followed her, tried to lure her back down, tried to speak reason, but she chose to end her own life instead of facing deportation and trial for war crimes."

Emma covered her face as the tears fell.

Leo passed her a tissue from the coffee table. He rubbed her back in tiny circles as she wept.

"I know how you felt about Fleur." Henry reached out for Emma, but she wouldn't let him. One hand covered her face, and another tightly gripped the tissue Leo had given her.

"She was a coward," Leo said to Emma. "I know that we thought we knew her. But in the end, she was evil. And what's worse, she refused to answer for what she had done. She'd rather kill herself than face the consequences."

"But you know who wasn't a coward?" Henry asked gently. "Your mother."

Emma looked up from the tissue. She wiped her eyes and waited for Henry to say more.

"She started working for my grandparents as a maid, but when she discovered what they were doing, she joined them. She was such a brave woman, Emma. That's how she climbed so quickly, from maid, to house manager, to my grandfather's right-hand. They weren't having an affair. They were working together on secret projects."

"So, she was a Nazi hunter, too?" Emma asked.

"Yes," he said. "You should be really proud of the work your mother did over the years."

"My God," Emma said.

"So now you know the truth," Henry said. "But there's one more thing."

40

Then

Age seventeen

"Can I make it up to you?" Henry asked. "We still have the whole summer to spend together."

Emma stood, bewildered. Did Henry really think she'd speak to him again after everything that had happened? After he took another girl to the prom? After she'd destroyed the indoor tennis court in anger? After she told him that she planned to never speak to him again?

She looked at Henry as he stood before her, bright-eyed. Of course he assumed that they'd see each other all summer again. Pick up where they'd left off.

"Let's do something tonight," Henry said, the glint in his eye suggesting exactly what he had in mind when he said *something*.

"No," Emma said, surprising herself as the word fell out of her mouth. Had she ever said no to Henry before? Even once? She'd said no to Leo before, plenty of times. No to her mother, to her friends, her teachers. But never once to Henry.

He stared back at her as if she were speaking a foreign language. "Oh, okay," he said. "Tomorrow, then?"

"No," Emma said once again. She liked the power of the word. The way it felt in her mouth.

"Um, not tomorrow?"

"No, not tomorrow," Emma said. The word had fortified her, made her feel strong.

"I don't understand," Henry said. "Do you want to just meet up, late-night? I thought it could be fun to go out first."

Of course he didn't understand. Emma had made things so easy for him, all this time. She'd always been waiting there for him, in the wings, and she didn't care how poorly he treated her. She believed him every time he told her that things would change. Or maybe she simply forced herself to believe it.

But she wasn't going to do that anymore. She'd made a fool of herself, sleeping with him secretly, letting him hide her away. She'd allowed herself to be nothing, to pick up the scraps that Henry dropped on the floor.

"This is over," Emma said. "I don't want to meet up late-night. I don't want to go out with you. You took another girl to the prom, Henry."

"I thought you understood," Henry said. "You know that things are complicated."

"I know that you always *say* that things are complicated," Emma said. "But it's not complicated. If you wanted to take me to the prom, you would have taken me to the prom."

"So that's why you trashed the indoor tennis court?" Henry asked. "Because I didn't take you to the stupid prom?"

"I don't know why I trashed the tennis court, honestly," Emma said. She'd been trying to put her finger on exactly why she'd done it. She thought out loud: "But the indoor tennis court is the place we used to meet up. I guess I thought it was a symbol of us, or our relationship, or whatever you want to call what we were doing. I waited for you there, after the pre-prom party, certain that you'd show up. I was convinced you'd realize that you should ditch Brittany and take me at the last minute. When you didn't, I guess I lost it."

"You know that I couldn't take you," Henry said, his voice quiet. "You know that my grandfather and your mother have forbidden us from being together."

"Yes, I do know that," Emma said. "But why? Did you ever ask your grandfather why?"

"You know I can't ask him something like that. You know I can't speak to him like that. Why haven't you asked your mother?"

Emma didn't answer. They both knew why; neither of them could speak to Felix or Mila in the way that Emma was suggesting.

"That's what I thought," he said. "Can we just start over? Hi, I'm Henry."

Emma laughed, which made Henry smile widely. "It's not that easy."

"But it can be."

"I don't think it can."

"Give me another shot," he said, as if he already knew the answer would be yes. "Let's put all this behind us and have a great summer together before going off to separate coasts in the fall."

They never talked about college, about the fact that they'd be three thousand miles apart, Henry in Manhattan, and Emma in California. Emma considered what Henry was offering: to be together again, but only for the summer.

"I don't think so," Emma said, still unsure of the words as she said them. "Too much has happened."

"One more chance," Henry said. Then: "You know what? Give me ten minutes. Just ten minutes. I'm going straight to my grandfather's office, and I'll to tell him that we're to-gether. If I go and speak with him right now, will you give me another chance?"

Henry rushed off into the main house without waiting for an answer. Emma called out his name, tried to tell him that it was pointless, things were over, but he ran off so fast that he didn't even hear her call his name.

Emma considered what he was doing—this was what she had wanted for so long, wasn't it? All along she'd thought if they could just get the approval of Felix and Mila, or at the very least, convince them to stop forbidding them from see-ing each other, she and Henry could make things official. Be an official couple. They could go out, and not hide what they had. Maybe one more chance was exactly what they needed.

But none of that would matter. Emma waited ten minutes, thirty minutes, over an hour, and Henry never came back out of the house. She tried to remind herself that she already knew this about Henry. He was a coward. He would always let her down. He would never stand up for her. She told herself it didn't matter. She told herself she didn't care. And she spent the whole summer trying to convince herself of it.

Henry spent the rest of the summer avoiding her.

41

Now

"That's why we couldn't be together as kids, why my grand-father and your mother forbade it."

"Because your grandfather was a Nazi hunter?" Emma said. "All that time, kept apart. It was only so that I wouldn't discover that your grandfather was a Nazi hunter?"

"Yes."

"Shouldn't he have felt proud of that? Why would he have hidden all of that?"

"Well, it was for your safety, of course," Henry said. "And for theirs. If their identities were ever revealed, they'd be in grave danger."

"How would they be in danger?" Leo asked. "How would the Nazis come after them, if they were all in hiding?"

"There's more to it," Henry said, shaking his head. "It's complicated."

"Of course it is. You've been telling me that for my whole life," Emma replied.

"There are things you didn't know. Things you couldn't know."

"Why not?" Emma said. She took another sip of the scotch. The liquid burned on its way down her throat. "Your grandfather would prefer to have me think that he was a Nazi, rather than a Nazi hunter?"

"It's just—"

"There's something you're not telling me," Emma said. "Why did your grandfather forbid us from being together?"

Henry looked down at the ground. "It was what your mother wanted."

"My mother wanted me to think that Felix was a Nazi?" Emma asked. "The man she spent her life with, who she dedicated her life to?"

"Yes."

"But that makes no sense, Henry. You have to understand that none of this makes sense." Emma took another sip of her scotch, and then another. When she finished, Leo refilled her glass.

"I know, but it's the truth."

"Then there has to be *more* truth," Emma said. "What is it?"

Emma downed the glass of scotch in one gulp. Leo refilled her glass again. She was catching up to him—they were both on glass number three.

"Would you want to know the truth, even if it flipped your entire world on its axis?" Henry asked, his voice somber.

"My world has already been flipped on its axis today," Emma said, her voice uneven. She wasn't sure if it was the information she was learning, or the alcohol. "I found out this morning that everything I thought about the house I grew up in was wrong. And now, this afternoon, I'm learning that everything I knew about my mother was wrong. What else could there possibly be?"

"If I tell you the truth," Henry said carefully, "nothing will ever be the same again."

"Okay," Emma said, drawing out the syllables slowly.

"Emma, it's about your father."

Emma felt her heart fall into her belly. She put her hands down next to her on the sofa to steady herself. "What...what about my father?"

"It was their idea to keep this from you," Henry said, shaking his head. "I never agreed with it. You should know that." He pointed his finger at the table, for emphasis.

"Tell me." Emma barely recognized the sound of her own voice, deep and rough. Like she was growling, not speaking.

"I thought they should have told you when we were teenagers. You were always stronger than they gave you credit for..."

"Henry," Leo said, "you're rambling. Out with it."

Emma could barely hear Leo's words. She was stuck on what Henry had just said to her. "You've known something about my father since we were teenagers?"

Quietly: "Yes."

"And you never told me?"

Even quieter: "Yes."

"What is it?"

Henry looked like a fish out of water. He kept opening his mouth to say something, and then closing it again.

"What is it?" Emma asked, this time louder. Leo squeezed her hand.

"This is hard to say," Henry said, squaring his shoulders. "Emma, you know how I told you that my grandfather was not a Nazi, but a Nazi hunter?"

"Yeah." Emma waited for Henry to continue. It was so unlike him to be unable to find the words like this, so unlike him to lose his composure. He was repeating himself, something he never did. A thin layer of sweat had gathered on his brow, but he made no move to wipe it away.

"Emma," he said slowly and carefully, "your father was a Nazi."

PART FOUR:
FINAL FINISHES

42

Then

Age seventeen

"Wake up," Leo was saying to Emma in a dream. "Emma, are you okay? Wake up!"

Only it wasn't a dream. When Emma opened her eyes, she was lying on the grass next to the pool at Rolling Hill. In an instant, it all came back to her: Henry, throwing a graduation party when his grandparents and Emma's mother were in DC for the weekend. Emma, doing shots with the soccer team, and then wandering off.

"I'm okay," Emma muttered. Her mouth felt like it was filled with cotton.

"You're not okay," Leo said. "You passed out. What if you'd fallen into the pool?"

Emma felt the sensation of her body being lifted off the ground. A beat later, she realized Leo had picked her up. "Can you stand up?"

"Of course I can stand," Emma said in her most indignant tone. Once Leo let go of her, she immediately swayed. Leo caught her and put her arm over his shoulder, half walking, half carrying her all the way back toward the pool house.

No one seemed to notice them—the party was taking place in the opposite direction. Their fellow graduates were far too busy over on the grand lawn, right behind the main house. Some were dancing on the lawn. Others were at the keg by the main house, or at the bar set up in front of the staff quarters. The staff had been given the weekend off, and Henry had taken full advantage of that fact.

"Coffee," Leo said. "You need coffee." He punched in the code to the pool house door—Henry had declared it off-limits for the party, it seemed—and locked the door behind them. He set Emma down on the sofa and made his way into the kitchen. He quickly took out the coffee maker and got a pot brewing. The delicious smell of freshly brewed coffee filled the space.

Emma immediately felt sick. She jumped up and ran to the bathroom, where she stuck her head directly in the toilet. Moments later, she felt Leo behind her, gathering her hair for her as she heaved. He rubbed her back in tiny circles, telling her that she'd be okay.

"Don't look at me," Emma said. She was embarrassed for Leo to see her in this state. How could she have let herself get this drunk?

"I won't look," Leo said, still holding her hair. "Promise."

When Emma was finished, she picked her head up, and saw Leo sitting behind her, against the wall with his eyes closed.

"Do you need me to help you get to the sink?" Leo asked softly, eyes still closed, waving his arms around dramatically.

"No, I feel much better now." Emma turned on the cool water and splashed some onto her face. It felt good. She looked at herself in the mirror, and tried to fix her makeup. Her eyeliner had smudged so far down, it almost served as blush, and her lip liner had smeared all over her chin.

"Still not looking," Leo called out from the floor.

"Good," Emma said, opening the cabinet to search for some makeup remover. She took a cotton ball and cleaned up her face. She then dunked her head into the sink and rinsed out her hair. She took the wet hair and tied it into a knot. "Okay, you can look now."

"You feeling better?" Leo asked, meeting her eyes.

"I know I look worse since I took my makeup off," Emma said, "but I actually do feel better now."

"You look beautiful without makeup."

"I look terrible," she responded.

"Let's get you something to eat."

They walked back into the kitchen, and Emma sat down on one of the counter stools. Leo served her a cup of coffee and she took a sip. He rooted around in the freezer until he found a bag filled with frozen bagels.

"This should do the trick," Leo said. He popped two bagels into the toaster oven. "You need to soak up all of that alcohol."

"I think my stomach's completely empty."

"Still," Leo said. "You need grease." He went back into the freezer and pulled out more food: frozen pizza bagels, mini hot dogs, and frozen french fries. Probably leftovers from a party. He turned on the oven and put them all in to cook.

"How do you know so much about what to do when you drink too much?"

"Ah, the spoils of my misspent youth," Leo said.

Emma laughed. "What misspent youth?"

"Okay, busted. Everyone knows that you need grease to soak up alcohol. I guess I watch too many movies."

"Thank you for taking care of me," Emma said. "I feel bad

that you're missing the party. I can get the food out of the oven. You should go. Go, have fun."

"I *am* having fun," Leo said. The toaster dinged, and he took the bagels out, tossing them from one hand to the other as he realized how hot they were. "I'm with you."

Emma didn't know how to respond. It was so sweet and earnest. And after a year spent sneaking around with Henry, she wasn't really used to sweet or earnest. She didn't know what to make of it.

"But if you were having fun," Leo said, "we could totally go back out there. I'll be insisting that you drink water from here on out. You can put it in a martini glass if that makes you feel better."

"I'm having fun here. With you." Emma took a sip of coffee and a bite of the bagel. That first bite felt so good, filling up her empty belly. She quickly ate the rest.

"Good," Leo said, smiling widely at Emma. "Should we see if there's a movie on?"

"Yeah," Emma said. "That sounds good."

The party raged on in the backyard, right outside the pool house. But Emma and Leo spent the rest of the night inside, on the couch, watching a movie together, a world away.

43

Now

Emma felt like the world was underwater. One second, Henry was speaking to her, and the next, she was disconnected from mind and body. Unable to see clearly, unable to hear.

Your father was a Nazi.

Emma couldn't understand what Henry had just said. Her father, the man she loved with all of her heart and soul, was a Nazi.

She thought about the stories he would tell her as a child, casting her as the princess, pure of heart and soul, who would one day finally realize her destiny.

Purity.

Her mind stopped at the word. When she'd researched Stella and the Supreme Reich, that's what they stood for. Purity. Racial purity. The fairy tales that her father had been telling her at night were steeped in Nazi ideology.

Emma shook her head, tried to right herself. This couldn't be true. None of this was true. She knew who her father was—a kind and caring man. A man who worked hard. A man who wanted better things for his family. A man who would do anything for his daughter.

Emma couldn't reconcile these two thoughts: her father was a good dad. Her father was a Nazi. Both of those things could not be true at the same time.

"You're lying," Emma said to Henry.

"I'm not," Henry said. "I'm finally telling you the truth."

"This is low, Henry," Leo said. "Even for you."

"Even for me?" Henry asked. "What have I ever done to you?"

"You took the girl I loved," Leo said, his voice gravelly, "and you treated her like garbage. And now, this? I didn't think that you could hurt her any more than you have, but—"

"I love her, too," Henry said.

Emma took measured breaths. "It's not true. My father was not evil."

She stood up, ready to leave Henry's office.

"Come on, Leo. Let's go," she said, motioning for him to join her. She saw spots and stars in her field of vision as she tried to march out of the room.

The next thing she knew, Leo was holding her tightly. "You're okay," he said.

"Of course I am," Emma said, feeling the pressure of Leo's arms around her body. She felt light-headed, confused.

"You fainted," Leo whispered in her ear. "But I've got you."

It was only then that Emma realized she was staring up at the ceiling; Leo had caught her, and was holding her body up. He slowly helped her down to the couch as the room came back into focus.

"Thank you." Emma wiped her brow, where a thin layer of sweat had gathered. The back of her neck felt clammy. Henry passed her a bottle of water.

"I know," Henry said. "It's a lot to take in. Maybe this is enough for today?"

"Take sips of water," Leo said.

Emma slowly sipped her water, felt the strength returning to her body.

"I feel fine now," Emma said. She finished the bottle of water.

"I know that the truth is too much to bear," Henry said.

"You didn't even know him," Emma said. "He was just another person who worked for you. You didn't know the real him."

But as the words left her mouth, Emma had another thought. A less welcome thought. Maybe Emma was the one who never really knew her father.

"It was the secret that your mother wanted me to keep from you. It was the real reason we could never be together."

Emma remembered the year that her mother turned cold. When suddenly, she seemed to no longer love her father anymore. It made sense. What Henry was saying tracked with what she remembered from her childhood. That was when her mother must have discovered the truth.

Her father was a Nazi. Her father was evil, believed in a system of pure evil. He played a role in the genocide of six million Jews, along with the many other groups that the Nazis deemed racially and biologically inferior. Emma's mind reeled as she thought of the countless victims of the Holocaust. The lives her father had destroyed.

The father she had loved was a murderer.

"I can't believe I never knew," Emma said, her voice a whisper. "How could I never have known?"

"You were eight years old when he died," Henry said. "And your mother didn't want you to know. She did everything in her power to make sure you wouldn't find out."

"But then how did you know?"

"I found out when I marched into my grandfather's office that summer," Henry said softly. "It was after the prom. We fought, and I told you that I was going to confront my grandfather. I did, and...well, that's when he told me the truth."

"And then instead of telling me," Emma said, "you ignored me for the whole summer."

Henry kept his eyes turned downward. "Yes."

Emma turned to Leo: "Take me home."

44

Then

Age seventeen

"I told Henry that I never wanted to see him ever again."

Leo regarded Emma. They'd spent the morning together in the cabana, watching old movies. "Oh."

"Yeah."

"Should we pop in another movie?" Leo asked. "Or go to the mall for some lunch?"

"Lunch, I guess?" Emma said, though her voice going up at the end made it sound more like a question.

"You're not sure about lunch?" Leo asked. "Traditionally, it's the meal that comes at midday, and it's almost 12:30."

"I thought you might have something to say about what I just told you."

Leo stood up from the couch. His back was to Emma as he spoke. "I heard you. I don't know what you want me to say about it."

"Right," Emma said, shifting her weight on the couch. Suddenly, she felt like she couldn't get comfortable. "I thought…

I mean, didn't you ask me about going to the prom together...
Um, and the night of the grad party?"

Leo turned to face Emma. "I'm not a consolation prize."

Emma couldn't find the words to respond. Was that what
she was doing, treating Leo like a consolation prize, once she
didn't get the thing she'd really wanted?

"I wanted you to want me. To choose me over Henry. I
gave you so many chances. I don't want you to just settle."

"I..."

"You can't want me *only* because you can't have him anymore."

"Let's forget this," Emma said, her breath short in her chest.
She felt the sudden need to get up, get out, and move. To be
anywhere other than there. "I'm starving. Let's go to the mall."

Leo nodded and held the door as they made their way to the
garage. Neither spoke on the drive over to the mall, and after
a rushed lunch at the food court, Emma suggested a double
feature. Anything where they didn't have to talk. She hoped
that with enough time, the awkwardness would subside.

Between the two movies, they went to the concession stand
to refill their sodas and popcorn.

"You're not a consolation prize," Emma blurted out, right
as Leo squirted more butter onto their popcorn. "I just—"

"I know," Leo said. "You don't have to say it."

"I'm still a little messed up from everything that happened."

"Understandable," Leo said. "We're not going to trash another part of Rolling Hill again, are we?"

Emma laughed as they headed back into the movie theater
before the second film began. "No. I say we enjoy the summer before college begins and retire our vigilante ways."

"Sounds like a plan," Leo said. "Are you excited about
going out to California?"

"Excited," Emma said as they settled back into their seats. "Scared."

"Yeah," Leo said. "That's how I feel about Chicago."

"I think a fresh start will do me good."

"Here's to fresh starts," Leo said, holding up his soda for a toast.

"Fresh starts," Emma said as they touched their sodas together before taking a sip. She turned to Leo, about to say more, but right as she formulated the words, the next movie began.

45

Now

"You can drop me on the corner." She pointed to where Leo could pull over.

"I'm not dropping you off," Leo said, as if what Emma had said was the most ridiculous thing in the world. "You need to process what happened. *We* need to process it. Together."

"The last thing I want to do is to think about what happened," Emma said quietly.

"I don't think that either of us should be alone after what we learned." Leo pulled the car over to the side of the road and looked at Emma. He reached for her hand, but it was already unbuckling her seat belt.

"I won't be alone," Emma said, still turned away from Leo. "I've got friends."

"There was a time when we were the best of friends," Leo said softly.

"But we're not anymore," Emma said, her face turned toward the door. "You saw to that."

"I'm worried about you," Leo said. He put his hand on her shoulder gently. "When you get upset, you tend to destroy things."

"I'm pretty good at destroying things, no matter what my mood."

"We don't have to talk," Leo said, his voice uncertain. "We can go for dinner or something. A movie."

"I don't think so." She felt tears sting the back of her eyes. But Emma didn't want to cry anymore. She wanted to rage. As she sat with Leo in his Jeep, she felt like she might jump out of her own skin. "Thanks for the ride."

She hopped out of the car without leaving time for Leo to respond. He called out to her. "Emma! Emma, please come back."

But Emma didn't want to have a quiet evening with Leo where she could talk things over. Emma wanted to go someplace loud, so loud you couldn't hear yourself think. And she knew just the place—Kendall's girlfriend, Anka, owned a bar inside the L train subway station in Bushwick. A tiny space, you had to know where it was to get in. The door was unmarked, and hard to find, nestled in on the platform between the subway tracks and the north stairwell. Reservation only, it was completely packed every night.

Emma texted her work crew, and they all met at the bar an hour later. Anka had promised them free drinks for the evening, and Kendall had jumped back behind the bar to hurry up the process. Their third round of tequila shots was lined up, and Kendall helped herself to the first one. She nudged numbers two and three toward Emma and Francisco.

"Where's Blanca?" Emma asked Francisco. Big band jazz spilled out of the speakers, and Emma leaned in so that she could hear Francisco's response.

"This doesn't seem like the sort of place for a pregnant person."

"Right," Emma said, and downed a tequila shot from the bar. "Should I do her shot?"

"That one's Samantha's," Kendall said, but Samantha was already off in a dark corner making out with someone she'd just met.

"Maybe we've had enough to drink," Francisco said, picking up Samantha's shot and moving it down the bar.

"You can go," Emma said. "You're completely right. Go home to Blanca. Send her my love."

"I'm not leaving you alone," Francisco said, furrowing his brow. He looked over his shoulder at the crowd. A bunch of Brooklyn hipsters. Not exactly the threatening type.

"I'm not alone," Emma said, acutely aware that she was one shot away from slurring her speech. "Kendall's here."

Emma pointed at Kendall, and Kendall gave Francisco a bow.

"And Samantha's right there," Kendall said, pointing to Samantha and the random guy in the corner. "She's literally right there. Like you could reach out and grab her." She made an exaggerated grabbing motion with her arm, and Emma laughed out loud. Francisco made a face.

"Why don't you come back to the apartment with me?" Francisco asked. "Blanca can make you some of her famous chocolate brownies."

Emma had to admit brownies sounded really good. And Blanca's secret was the sour cream, which made them extra gooey, but Emma would never spoil things by telling her she'd figured that part out.

"Brownies. Yes, please," Emma said, leaning on the bar.

"Anka has some pot brownies back here," Kendall said, rooting around the bar.

"That sounds even better," Emma said, eyes opening wide.

"I'm not going to let you do this to yourself," Francisco said.

"I'm fine," Emma said. "Kendall, don't I look fine?"

"Fine!" Kendall said. A guy at the end of the bar tried to get her attention for a drink order, but she yelled out: "I don't really work here!" And turned her attention back to her friends.

"I'm serious," Francisco said. "Ever since Henry came back into your life, things have been different. *You've* been different. And now you're here, attempting to get blackout drunk for some reason, and I'm concerned."

"Aren't I allowed to cut loose every once and a while?" Emma said, taking the last shot of tequila. She immediately felt it go from her throat directly to her head. She held on to the bar for support. "I mean, I can go out and have fun."

"That's the thing," Francisco said. "You don't seem like you're having fun."

"This is fun," Emma said, and could feel her words all melting together.

"So fun," Kendall said.

Just then, Samantha joined them.

"What happened to your guy?" Kendall asked.

"He smells like cigarettes," she said. "You know I could never kiss a guy who smoked."

Emma wanted to make a crack about how she'd spent the last forty-five minutes making out with the guy, but found that the night was moving in slow motion. Francisco was right— she couldn't recall the last time she'd gotten drunk like this.

"I'm worried about you," Francisco said, placing his hand gently on Emma's forearm.

"You're not even a dad yet," Emma said, "but you're already acting like my dad."

"Emma…"

"And my dad, it turns out, totally sucked," Emma said. "So, maybe pick someone else to act like."

"What's that supposed to mean?" Francisco asked. Francisco didn't have a father himself—his had died of colon cancer when Francisco was eighteen months old—but he knew how close Emma had been to her father.

"Oh, this is really funny, actually," Emma said, her words all smashing into each other. She motioned with her hands for her friends to come in close, and they all leaned in. She planned to whisper, barely say the words out loud, but instead, she ended up screaming them: "Turns out, my dad was a Nazi!"

Francisco's face went pale.

"Ohmigod," Samantha said, putting her hand over her mouth as she gasped. "He was a Neo-Nazi like that girl you met?"

"No, dummy," Kendall said, climbing over the bar and giving Emma a hug. "She means like World War II shit. Are you okay?"

"I'm fine," Emma said. "I'm totally fine."

"You don't seem fine," Francisco said. "This is a lot to deal with. Let's go somewhere quiet so we can talk."

"Why does everyone keep saying that to me? First Leo. Now you. I don't want to talk," Emma said. "I want to drink." She put up her hand to flag down Anka.

"Why are you on that side of the bar?" Anka asked Kendall.

"Shhh," Kendall said. "State secrets."

"Emma just told us something devastating. Devastating!" Samantha said, her words also slurred. "So we need to drink more."

"You all seem pretty drunk to me," Anka said. "Francisco, why don't you help me get these three into the back office?"

Francisco nodded, and Emma shook her head in the opposite direction. "The party has just begun!" Emma said, or maybe she only thought it. Either way, she was not ready to go to Anka's back office and call it a night.

No more than three minutes later, she was passed out on Anka's couch.

46

Now

"Do I smell brownies?"

When Emma woke up, she didn't know where she was at first. The sheets were soft, and she was under a fluffy blanket. She did not own a fluffy blanket. She opened her eyes, and there were the pieces of a crib, ready to be put together, leaning against the wall. On a big plush chair with a matching leg rest, Samantha was fast asleep. Emma quickly realized that she was in the baby's room at Francisco and Blanca's place. Kendall must have gone home with Anka.

"Why do I taste cigarettes?" Samantha asked as she rubbed the sleep out of her eyes. "Are we at Francisco's?"

"Yes," Emma said, closing her eyes and massaging her temples. "My head."

"Oh, I know, mine, too," Samantha said.

"Glad to see you're up," Blanca said, peeking her head into the room. She cradled her belly, which looked a bit rounder than usual. "How are you feeling?"

"Totally fine," Emma lied. "How are you feeling?"

"Sick to my stomach most of the time," Blanca said. "I had to fight you two for the bathroom all night long."

"I know how to hold my alcohol," Samantha said. And then, as if on cue, she covered her mouth with her hand and made a run for the bathroom.

"I'm so sorry we're bothering you like this," Emma said. "We'll get out of your hair as soon as Samantha gets back."

"Don't worry," Blanca said. "I assume you'll be making it up to me with the amazing baby shower you'll be catering for me, right?"

"Right," Emma said, smiling at the thought. The only thing Emma loved more than catering parties was throwing parties for friends and loved ones. She had started planning the baby shower in her mind the moment Francisco told her that Blanca was pregnant.

"I got fried eggs," Francisco called out from the kitchen.

"Drink this first," Blanca said, passing a glass of water to Emma.

Once at the breakfast table, Emma filled Blanca in on everything—growing up at Rolling Hill, her relationships with Leo and Henry, how she felt about her father, and how she spent all that time with Leo, trying to figure out if Felix was a Nazi.

"And now, it turns out," Emma said, "it was my own father who was the Nazi."

"But that's not you," Blanca said simply. She looked at Emma intently.

Emma nodded her head and agreed. Of course that wasn't her. Just because her father was a Nazi, it didn't mean that she was inherently evil, too. Or did it? "How will I ever make up for what my father has done?"

"Let's deal with processing what you learned first," Francisco said. "We process the truth, and then, once you're okay, we work on next steps."

"Okay."

"Where did you leave things with Henry? Your phone has been blowing up with missed calls and text messages from him," Francisco said, handing Emma her phone. She hadn't even realized it wasn't in her pocket. And then, without waiting for an answer to the first question: "Are you going to call Leo? You have five missed calls. It looks like he was worried about you, too."

"Of course," Emma said. "I mean at some point I will figure out where I stand with Henry and call him back. And I'll call Leo back, too. Just not right now. Not until I figure all of this out for myself first."

"That makes sense," Samantha said, walking over to the table and eating a piece of toast in two bites, before she even sat down. "There's no rush here."

"And anyway," Emma thought out loud, "I clearly have the worst taste in people on the planet. First, it turns out Stella was a Neo-Nazi. And now I find out that my own father was one, too. And not a Neo-Nazi. An actual Nazi."

"You're a trusting person," Francisco said, refilling Emma's coffee cup. "Maybe too trusting."

"Not to mention how wrong I was about Henry, too," Emma said, her eyes down in her coffee. She always took hers black, but Blanca served it with cream, and Emma loved seeing the colors swirl as she poured it in.

"Henry seems like a good man," Samantha said. "Just because you had a few bad apples in your life doesn't mean that everyone was pure evil."

Francisco spoke softly, but his words hit Emma like a punch: "Everything's been different since you've been seeing Henry. I'm worried."

"Franny," Blanca chastised him. "That's enough."

"No, it's okay," Emma said. "Maybe you're right."

"I know it's breakfast," Blanca said as the egg timer went off and she hurried to the oven, "but I couldn't resist."

She pulled out a tray of Emma's favorite, her homemade brownies, and set them in the center of the table.

"We should plate these with some vanilla ice cream," Francisco said.

"You don't have to *plate* things when you're with us," Samantha said.

Emma picked up her fork and stuck it directly in the center of the tray. She put the sticky, gooey bite in her mouth and closed her eyes for a moment. "You should sell these."

"They're only really good fresh out of the oven," Blanca said. "To sell them, I'd have to use preservatives and stuff and change the essence. I kind of like making them for family only."

Emma took that word—*family*—and held it in her heart. She'd spent most of her life with only her mother to call family, and she'd always wanted more. The acknowledgment by Blanca that she'd created a family of her own warmed her insides.

"This will be better," Francisco said, popping a scoop of vanilla ice cream directly onto the tray of brownies.

"Just because I didn't plate it doesn't mean you should make a mess, Franny," Blanca said, her eyebrows knit together.

Samantha dug in and moaned as she took a bite.

"I guess not everyone thinks it's a mess," Francisco said to Blanca.

Blanca didn't respond. She put her spoon into the pint of ice cream and flicked it directly into Francisco's face.

"You're going to regret that," Francisco said to Blanca, enveloping her in a hug, and pressing their faces together.

"My makeup!" she cried out, laughing as the vanilla ice cream smeared all over her face.

"You don't need makeup to look beautiful," Francisco said.

"Yeah, right," Blanca said, kissing him and then checking her reflection on the side of the shiny toaster.

"We should get going," Emma said, but didn't make a move to leave.

"Yeah, you're right," Samantha said as she took another monster-sized bite with the perfect proportion of brownie and ice cream.

They all sat happily eating brownies and ice cream for breakfast, putting off the inevitable, when they'd have to actually leave and start their days. Emma enjoyed the food, the company, and the warm embrace she still felt from the mention of their little group as a family.

47

Now

"You missed our meeting last night."

Emma usually didn't answer her phone when she didn't recognize the phone number. But she'd been sleepwalking through the day, doing things she didn't ordinarily do, like eat brownies for breakfast at Francisco's (like sleeping over at Francisco's, to begin with), and so she'd answered the call. After all, what more could life possibly throw at her now that she'd discovered who her father really was?

"I'm sorry," Emma said. "Who is this?"

"Why, it's Gladys, dear," the voice said. "From the Glen Cove Historical Society. You really need to save my telephone number in your phone."

Emma laughed in response. "I suppose I do."

"You missed last night's meeting. I usually don't like indolents at my meetings, but I really like you."

"Me?"

"Yes," Gladys continued. "Don't sound so surprised! And

if I'm being honest, the Glen Cove Historical Society could use some young people who really care."

"Right," Emma said. She was unsure how to break the news to Gladys, and that was the fact that she didn't actually care. She had only really cared about the main house at Rolling Hill, and now that was gone.

"I'm sure you've heard about what was found at Rolling Hill," Gladys said.

"Yes, I did," Emma said. "I went to see it with Leo, actually."

"You don't say," Gladys said. "You saw it all?"

"I'm not sure if I saw everything," Emma said, "but I certainly saw quite a lot. The Department of Justice was cataloging it all."

Gladys clicked her tongue. "How awful," she said. "You know, some of the ladies think we could try for historical status on the estate again. Now that things have changed. But it's all too distasteful for me."

It was all too distasteful for Emma, as well, but she didn't say that. In fact, she didn't know quite what to say to Gladys.

Gladys filled the silence: "Oh! But I forgot the other reason I called. Your *friend* called." She said the word *friend* as if it were a dirty word.

"Leo has my contact information," Emma said. "In fact, I was planning to call him later today anyway. But thank you."

"No, not the evil developer," Gladys said, making her voice sound extra dramatic at the mention of the word *developer.* "I mean your girlfriend. The one you planned to come to that first meeting with. Stella."

"Oh, she's not my girlfriend," Emma said. "We're not friends."

"Well, I'm relieved to hear you say that."

"I just met her recently, the first time I went to Rolling

Hill. She was the one who brought me to you. She told me that she was a member of the Glen Cove Historical Society. I'm sure you saw the news?"

"I most certainly did," Gladys said.

"Well, then, I guess she fooled us both. If I never hear from Stella again, it will be too soon."

"But that's why I was calling you, dear. She showed up here, at our meeting last night, trying to find you."

48

Then

Age twenty-two

"We have to go back."

"Back where?" Leo asked.

"Home," Emma said, as if it were the most obvious thing in the world.

"We are home." Leo held his arms out wide, as if to show Emma the New York City apartment he shared with three roommates. "Well, I'm home. You've just been crashing on my couch."

"Rolling Hill," Emma said. "We need to see it again. I can't believe Felix and Agnes sold it. I didn't think they would ever sell it."

"What's your mom planning to do?"

"She wants to move to Europe," Emma said. "Paris. Not a bad place to spend Christmas every year, right?"

"That's so far away."

"What about your parents?"

"My mom's getting a place closer to her school. And my

dad said that he would love to go back to Italy," Leo said. "But he needs to be driving distance from wherever I live, he told me. So he's looking at places in Queens."

Leo rolled his eyes dramatically—*look at how embarrassing my father is!*—but Emma knew he secretly loved it. His words about Mila moving to Paris still stung a bit: *that's so far away.*

"Let's take a drive out there today," Emma said. "It may be our last chance to ever see it again. My mom said they have to be out within two weeks."

"Who cares about seeing it again?" Leo said.

"I do," Emma said. "Obviously."

"I don't really need to see Felix's Nazi house again," Leo said. "Don't you think it's shady how he and Agnes just sold it out of the blue like that?"

"My mother said it was because Henry graduated college," she said.

"Now that the prince has graduated from Columbia," Leo said, sitting down on one of the bar stools next to the kitchen counter, "doesn't he need a castle to return home to?"

"They wanted to downsize."

"Or maybe it's because the Feds got their heads out of their asses and they're going to prosecute Felix for being a Nazi. Maybe he's going on the run."

"I think if you go on the run, you leave immediately," Emma said. "I don't think you put your house on the market first and do all that paperwork."

"It's all a part of his plan," Leo said, tapping his fingers on his leg. "He wants you to *think* he's doing everything by the books."

"Well, I'm going," Emma said. "You don't have to come with me today, but I'm going to go out there. See it one more time."

"Where are you going?" Alison said, walking out of the bathroom with a towel on her head.

Emma loved Leo's girlfriend, Alison. Even though Emma hadn't had many girlfriends growing up, she now treasured her female friends. Alison was the cousin of one of Emma's college friends, and Emma had been the one to set them up. Alison had studied abroad in Florence for a semester in college, so she'd easily won over Leo, and then Enzo, with her fluent Italian.

"Out to Rolling Hill," Emma said.

"I want to go!" Alison said. "Give me ten minutes to get dressed!"

Emma loved the way Alison was just as low-maintenance as she was—a ponytail, jeans, and Converse were all Alison needed to get ready, same as Emma. Alison also loved to cook, though she was starting law school in the fall, not culinary school like Emma. They had endless other things in common. They both thought that Bethesda Fountain in Central Park was the most magical place in the city, they both loved going to Broadway musicals but hated plays, and they both refused to read books that were too long (but they both made an exception for *The Count of Monte Cristo*, which Leo felt made the whole rule a moot point, Emma and Alison agreeing that it was the exception that proved the rule).

"I'm not going," Leo said, and dramatically sat down on the couch.

"Of course you're coming," Emma said. "We need to see it one more time before it's sold."

"We really don't."

"We do."

Emma wouldn't get her way that day. Leo would insist that they all go out for a big Sunday brunch at Balthazar, on him, something that Emma was powerless to say no to, but she'd get her way eventually. Before the house was sold, she'd end up helping both her mother and Enzo move out. Under the guise of being the best daughter in the world, she'd get her chance. She would sneak back into the main house all by herself both times, alone with the beauty of the main house at Rolling Hill and the ghosts of the past.

49

Now

"Friend."

Emma wasn't surprised when Stella appeared at her office a few days later. After all, the call from Gladys had prepared her. She knew it wouldn't be long before Stella tracked her down at work—a simple Google search of her name led directly to the La Vie en Rose website.

"It's so good to see you," Stella said, walking into Emma's office.

Stella reached out to give Emma a hug, but Emma stayed seated at her desk. She didn't move, didn't want to let Stella know how much her presence had rattled her. She stuck with the truth: "We're not friends."

"Aren't we?" Stella asked with a broad smile. She sat down in the chair across from Emma's desk. "I thought we were becoming friends."

"I thought so, too," Emma said. "Until I found out who you really are. I'd like for you to leave."

Stella regarded Emma. "I think we have more in common that you care to admit."

"I have nothing in common with you."

"I know who your father was," Stella said. "So I know who *you* are."

"I am not my father," Emma said.

"Wasn't that what you were trying to tell me? That story about purity?"

"That was a story my father told me as a kid."

"Those earrings you wore with the number eights—I know what that's code for." Stella winked. "I understood what you were telling me."

"The Dior earrings?" Emma asked. "They're not code for anything. I wasn't telling you anything."

"88 is code for Heil Hitler," Stella said. "It's how we identify like-minded individuals. But you know that, of course."

"The number eight was Christian Dior's lucky number."

"Mine, too," Stella said.

"They were a birthday gift from friends," Emma said. "Nothing more. You can go now. We have nothing else to talk about."

"You know, my colleagues and I have been following that house for a long time. Researching it. It was rumored to have been a safe harbor for refugees from the war."

"Nazis, you mean," Emma said. "Not refugees. Nazis."

"Yes," Stella said. "Members of the original Nazi party. There were rumors that some of the men and women who lived at that house brought things with them. Souvenirs."

Emma regarded her. "Well, that's all in the care of the Department of Justice now."

"But those treasures are ours," Stella said, her face brightening. "Mine and yours. They're a part of our history. I was hoping you and I could recover them together."

"You mean the evidence of war crimes?" Emma said. "Yeah, those will be used for the trials of the remaining Nazis they can find and prosecute. Everything else will go to the Holocaust Museum so that people will never forget what happened during the war."

Stella paused before speaking again. Then, quietly: "Don't you ever feel like you're special? I know your father did. *His princess, pure of heart and soul.* Don't you feel like you're different from everyone else?"

Emma didn't respond. Her mind raced, first with the thoughts of the stories her father had told her as a child. Then, with shame when she realized that Stella's words resonated.

"I know you feel it," Stella said, leaning forward toward Emma. "I can see it in your eyes."

Emma steeled herself. "The only thing you should see in my eyes is disgust. You disgust me. You, and everything you stand for."

Stella seemed bewildered. "I thought we were kindred spirits. I came here to ask if you'd join us. If you'd join the movement. If you'd continue the work your father had been doing."

"The answer is no," Emma said, then cleared her throat. "I will not be joining you. I will not have anything to do with you. In fact, I will spend the rest of my life trying to make up for all of the damage my father did in his life."

"Maybe you should research him," Stella said. "Could be interesting to learn more about the man you so revered?"

"I don't need to do that," Emma said, unsure of her own words even as she spoke them aloud.

"If your father was so innocent, then why did Felix kill him?"

Emma didn't respond.

"That's okay," Stella said. "Here you go." She tried to give Emma a stack of papers.

When Emma made no move to take them, Stella placed them on her desk carefully. She gently patted them once, as if for luck.

"Why don't you give those a read and call me when you're ready to fulfill your destiny?"

"Get the hell out of here." Emma took the papers and threw them into the trash bin.

"He was a cook, same as you," Stella said as she stood up to leave. Over her shoulder she quietly asked: "Did you know that?"

50

Now

Emma's hands were shaking. She placed them down on her desk, to try to steady herself, but it was no use. Stella's visit had rattled her. What had she conveyed to Stella that would make Stella think she was like her? Had the lessons her father taught her as a child made her into a monster? Made her into what Stella was? What her father was?

Emma shook her head, as if the mere act of shaking the thoughts would remove them from her mind. She knew who she was.

Didn't she?

Emma took the papers that Stella had given her out of the trash bin. She placed them onto her desk and stared at them for a moment. Slowly, she peeled back the first page.

His father was a baker, and as a child, her father had been trained to take over the family bakery. But then the Nazis occupied Holland. At age fourteen, he had taken a job as a cook at Kamp Amersfoort.

Emma put the papers down for a moment to calm her mind. Her father had lied about being a part of the Dutch Resistance. Emma did a quick Google search on her phone for Kamp Amersfoort.

Amersfoort was now a national monument in Holland. Emma quickly scanned the first page of its website: 47,000 prisoners. Inhumane regime. Starvation. Abuse. Forced labor and executions.

Emma set her phone back down on her desk, realizing that she'd been holding her breath. She closed her eyes and forced herself to take a deep breath in, and counted to four. She held the breath for another count of four, and then exhaled. She felt her heartbeat return to normal.

She slowly picked up the papers Stella had left for her. The files on Hans Jansen. Articles about Kamp Amersfoort. Many members of the Dutch Resistance passed through its gates, but one thing that the articles made clear: Hans Jansen was not a part of the Resistance.

Everything she'd been told as a child was a lie. Overcome by this realization, Emma found she couldn't stay seated at her desk, she felt the need to move. To get out of her office. To get out of her head. She jumped up from her desk and made her way outside. At first, she wasn't sure where she was going. She wanted to walk. She wanted to run. But then, she realized what she needed: she needed to see her mother.

She walked out into the street and hailed a cab.

Once at the cemetery, Emma stood over her mother's grave, willing her to speak. To rise from the dead.

Who was he? Who am I? she thought. *Who were you?*

Emma knew that her mother wouldn't respond, of course she wouldn't, but being there made her feel closer to her. Like she could feel her spirit, still with her.

Did you know who he was when you married him? she thought.

Emma knelt down by the grave and whispered the thing she most wanted to know: "Am I evil?"

She closed her eyes as she began to cry. Armed with the truth about who her father was, Emma no longer knew who *she* was.

Her father was a cook—was that why Emma had always taken to the kitchen, felt at home there? She'd always credited that to Fleur and her influence, but was cooking in her bones? And if so, was cruelty, too?

Emma stood up and took a deep breath. She looked around the cemetery—they were setting up for a funeral a few rows over, but an eerie silence surrounded her. No one was here who could answer her questions. She'd have to figure it all out for herself. She ordered a rideshare to bring her back to the train station.

When she got back to her apartment, Henry was waiting for her outside of her building.

"What are you doing here?"

"Hey," he said. "Your office didn't know where you were."

"I went to the cemetery," Emma said. "To see my mother."

"Why didn't you call me? I would have driven you."

Emma sighed. "Because you're the last person I want to see right now."

"I've been calling you for days," he said.

He followed her down the hallway to the elevator.

She spun around. "How could you know something like this and not tell me?"

"My grandfather wouldn't let me," Henry said. "And your mother… She didn't want you to know."

"Didn't want me to know?" Emma said, her voice getting louder. "Don't you think I had a right to know?"

"Yes," Henry said, reaching out for Emma. "It wasn't my choice."

Emma took a step back. "The moment you found out the truth, you had a choice." Emma barely recognized the sound of her own voice, deep and rough. "You could have told me. You should have told me."

"I'm sorry."

"You're sorry?" Emma said, her voice getting louder, a roar. She felt like she was out of her body, like it was another woman standing there, her voice building with every word she spoke. "That's all you have to say to me? You're sorry?"

"Yes, Emma, I'm sorry," Henry said. "I'm so sorry. It's the secret I held my entire adult life."

"It wasn't your secret to keep!"

"I know that," Henry said. "I know. But your mother—"

"My mother is dead!"

"My grandfather and your mother told me that I was wrong," he said. "That it was selfish and wrong to tell you, to ruin your life like that. Your mother begged me to let you go off to college, start a new life."

"And then you spent the summer ignoring me, when you knew something that could have changed my life. Something I deserved to know."

"I didn't want to hurt you," he said. "They told me that if you found out the truth, it would destroy you."

"I could have had closure with my mother," Emma said. "But now it's too late. It's all too late."

"I thought I was protecting you," he said. "I did it for you. I didn't think that you'd ever need to know."

"But I deserved to know," she said, "and you didn't have the right to make that choice for me. Then or now."

"I'm sorry," Henry said.

The elevator dinged as the doors opened.

"I'm sorry," Henry said. A broken record.

"I need to be alone right now," Emma said. She stepped into the elevator and let the door close behind her, leaving Henry alone in the lobby.

51

Now

Speaking to her mother at her grave didn't help anything—there was still so much that Emma didn't know. But there was one person who did. Before she even knew where her legs were taking her, she found herself at Felix's building the following afternoon.

"I thought I might be seeing you," Felix said. He sat in the living room of his Upper East Side apartment, on a chaise with a blanket covering his legs. He set his book down on the side table and motioned for Emma to come in.

The Upper East Side apartment, though large by Manhattan standards, was small compared to the main house at Rolling Hill. Emma was used to seeing Felix in the imposing study, the door always closed with Mila inside, leaving her on the outside. Always on the outside of that door. How she'd longed to go in. Now she was on the inside, only she didn't want to be anymore.

The decorating style was the same as it had been at Rolling

Hill—intricate millwork, dark wood covering the walls with bookcases and built-ins. It didn't look particularly lived-in. It looked formal, from the Victorian-inspired couches to the fine Oriental rugs to the thick window treatments, covered in heavy draperies. Felix could easily have moved in a week ago, from the look of things. But Emma knew that he'd lived here since leaving Rolling Hill a decade ago.

Emma studied the walls, which displayed major pieces of art. Each one had a gold-plated picture light above it, with low-wattage bulbs that offered the precise amount of light to highlight the painting but not damage it. She didn't recognize any of the works—she figured he must have sold the ones that were most valuable—but there was one that she remembered clearly from her time growing up at Rolling Hill.

The Chagall.

How many times had she stood before that painting, discovering something new every time? She'd first kissed Henry while standing in front of it, and she spent countless nights with Leo sitting cross-legged underneath it, researching Felix, trying to figure out who he was.

Now she knew.

What she should have been trying to discover all along was who her own father was. But she didn't know that then.

"Please, sit down," Felix said, motioning to the couch.

A smartly dressed woman came into the living room with a silver tray, filled with a teapot, teacups, and a plate of sugar cookies.

"Is she the new Mila?" Emma asked.

Felix smiled. "Alice, this is Emma. Emma, this is Alice. She runs the apartment for me."

"Nice to meet you," Alice said as she poured the tea and passed a teacup to Felix.

"So, yes," Emma said. "She's the new Mila."

"No one could ever replace your mother," he said. His eyes looked sad as he mentioned her.

Emma picked up a cookie and took a small bite. It was too buttery, and left a residue on her fingers. "So, your reaction when I told you that I was a chef..."

"Yes," Felix said. He took a small sip of his tea. "I was surprised. That threw me."

"I thought it was because you were embarrassed for me because I'd become the help, like my mother."

"What an awful thing to say," Felix said, furrowing his brow. "Your mother was not *the help*. She was my colleague. She was my friend."

"Did you know that Leo tore down the house at Rolling Hill?" Emma asked.

"I did," Felix said. "I wanted to come to the groundbreaking ceremony, but it's harder for me to get around these days."

Felix's reaction surprised Emma. "That doesn't hurt you?"

"Were you trying to hurt me?"

Emma wasn't sure—was she trying to hurt Felix? She truly didn't know.

"No matter," he said, taking another sip of his tea. "Henry says that you're angry, and I suppose you have every right to be. I'm sorry. I apologize for withholding the truth from you. But your mother and I thought it was best."

"Don't you think I should have been able to make that decision for myself?"

"You were a child," Felix said, not unkindly. "It's the job of the adults to protect the child."

"And is that what you think you did, protected me?"

"Your mother and I tried to protect you the best way we knew how."

"By hiding the truth."

"Yes."

Emma looked down at the floor.

"But that's not what you really want to know, is it?" Felix asked. "You want to know what your mother knew, and when she knew it."

"Yes."

"When your mother married Hans, she had no idea that he'd worked in a concentration camp. She was young, so much younger than him. And here was this handsome man, a man who swept her off her feet. He'd told her that he was part of the Dutch Resistance, and who knows? Maybe he fancied himself that way in order to make himself feel bigger. But that's not important. What's important is that your mother believed that he was a Resistance fighter. One of the good guys. He allowed her to believe it. After all, he was on the run. She didn't learn the truth about your father until much later, when she was already working for me. You were around—"

"Seven," Emma interrupted, answering for him. "I was seven years old. I remember that's when my mother changed. She seemed to no longer love my father anymore and I didn't know why."

"Can you blame her?"

"I can blame her for not telling me the truth. Explaining what was happening," Emma said. "I was a kid. I had no idea why my mother was pulling away from him. From us… From me."

"Well, she couldn't very well have told you the truth when you were seven."

"She could have tried."

"You have to understand what a difficult time this was for your mother. She was still processing it all herself. She didn't know what to do."

Emma's eyes filled with tears. She took one of the linen

napkins and dabbed the sides of her eyes. "But he was my father."

"Can you imagine what this was like for your mother? By the time she found out, they'd been married for years. They had a child together, a life."

"*I* had a life," Emma said.

"We thought it was the right thing to do," Felix said. "Especially since, well…"

"You were going to kill him the following year."

"We didn't kill your father," Felix said, studying her. His voice remained calm, impassive. It made Emma angrier, seeing how tranquil he seemed. Felix continued: "We confronted him in my office. We told him that we knew who he was, and we asked him to turn himself in. He said that he would. But instead, he killed himself in the garage later that night."

Emma bowed her head.

Felix regarded her. "I truly am sorry. She thought the best thing would be to let you live your life without this burden of the awful truth. We didn't think you'd ever have to know. The memory of your father could stay intact, unviolated. We thought it was the right thing to do."

"I need to go," Emma said, and stood up abruptly. Her leg caught on the silver tray that held her teacup and plate, and the whole thing came crashing to the ground.

52

Now

Emma was grateful to find herself alone in the elevator after leaving Felix's apartment. She didn't want to have to put on a polite face for his neighbors, or make small talk. Once the elevator doors opened to the lobby, she would rush out, and avoid eye contact with the doorman. She would go home and process everything that had just happened.

The elevator doors opened, and Emma found Henry waiting for her. He looked so at home, sitting there in the opulent lobby. Like he belonged there. Meanwhile, Emma no longer knew where she belonged, if she belonged anywhere.

"What are you doing here?" she asked roughly. The exchange with Felix had left her feeling raw. Uninhibited.

"Why do you keep asking me that?" Henry said, nervous laughter in his voice. "I'm your boyfriend, aren't I? I thought I could give you a ride home. Maybe get a quiet dinner somewhere? Are you all right?"

"I'd like to be alone."

"That's what you said last night," Henry said, edging closer to where she stood. "Say it again and you'll start to give me a complex."

"I guess I need more alone time." Emma pulled her jacket tight around her body, wrapped her arms around herself.

"Alone time?" Henry asked, furrowing his brow. "Or time without me?"

"Either," Emma said, moving past him. "Both."

Quietly, Henry asked: "How long are you going to punish me for this?"

"Punish you?" Emma stopped walking and turned back to Henry.

"I said I was sorry," Henry said, his voice small. "I promise to spend every day trying to make up for it. Is that not enough?"

Emma didn't respond. She wasn't sure it *was* enough, actually. How could she be with someone when there was a giant secret, a giant lie between them? She'd forgiven him so many times, made the same mistake over and over. Emma continued walking through the lobby and out onto the city street.

Henry followed. "That was a rhetorical question," he said. He ran his hand through his hair to push it back into place after the wind had had its way with it. "Look, why don't we drive downtown, go have a quiet evening together. We can talk things through. I'm parked around the corner."

The wind hit Emma's face, and she took a deep breath in. "There's not much to say, is there?"

"We don't have to talk if you don't want to. I just want to be with you."

There was a time when that was all she'd wanted Henry to say to her. A time when those words would have meant the world to her. But now they seemed empty. Hollow. Henry may have wanted to be with her, but she didn't want to be with Henry. Not anymore.

Even if she accepted the fact that he couldn't tell her the truth when they were seventeen years old, what was his excuse now? How could he have seen her again, as adults, and not said a word? How could he have begun a relationship with her, let her fall in love with him all over again, with this huge secret between them?

"I think we should end this," Emma said, her hair blowing in the wind. She made no move to smooth it back.

"But I love you."

"Too much has happened," Emma said. "There's been too much between us. I don't think I'll ever be able to trust you again."

"We've gotten through worse," Henry said. "Much worse."

Emma laughed. Henry was right—he had done other awful things to her in the past, and she'd forgiven him each time. Acted like it didn't happen, like it was no big deal. But those things did happen. They *were* big deals. And she didn't want to pretend otherwise. Not anymore.

"We got through worse because I allowed myself to be treated like a fool," Emma said. "Like trash. Like the help. But I don't want to do that anymore."

"It wasn't only my grandfather that made the decision," Henry said. "It was your mother, too. Your mother's decision on what was best."

"It may have been your grandfather or my mother back when we were seventeen years old," Emma said. "But what about now?"

"I thought—"

"These months, I've been steeped in the past, trying to get it back somehow, especially when it came to you. But the reality is, I'm not the same girl I was. The past changed me, made me who I am today."

"What does that mean for us?"

"I guess I've realized that I no longer want that past back."

"Then let's not go into the past," he said. "Let's create something different. A new future together."

"Henry, you need to let me go."

Henry's shoulders slumped as Emma's words sank in.

Emma walked away, certain that this time, Henry wouldn't follow.

53

Now

"What's wrong?"

"Who said there's something wrong?" Emma replied. She looked up at Francisco from her prep work. The two-hundred-person wedding they were catering would begin in three hours. Emma had never before booked a job at this vineyard out on the North Fork of Long Island, so it was important to make a good impression.

"You've tenderized the same piece of meat three times."

"I want it to melt in the mouth."

"Is this really about the steak?"

Emma had to admit it—this wasn't about the steak. But Francisco knew that already. He motioned for one of the line cooks to take over Emma's station, and they made their way out of the prep tent together.

They walked out onto the property. Emma was surprised that she'd never before catered a wedding at a vineyard out here before—it was such a spectacular backdrop for a wedding. And the North Fork of Long Island was so ridiculously charming, had its own unique personality. The bride and groom were off in town taking pictures, but Emma knew that the best ones would be snapped here on the property, when the sun set right past the many rows of vines.

"You wanna talk?" Francisco asked. "Or just walk it out?"

"Neither," Emma said, shaking her head. "Both."

"You still thinking about what Felix told you?" After breaking up with Henry, Francisco had been her first phone call. She'd told him everything, from the fight to her accusations to the way she walked away from Henry.

"I'm still so angry," Emma said. "They withheld something from me. My whole life."

"Are you really mad at Felix and your mother? Or even Henry, for that matter?" Francisco asked. "Or is it really just about your father?"

"It's not like I can confront my father now."

"So you confronted Felix instead," Francisco said. "Good. So, it's over. And now you need to process the pain of what you've learned about your father so that you can begin to move on from it."

"I need to make things right," Emma said. "My father did so much damage... So many victims... I can't help but think I need to do something."

"And you will," Francisco said. "But you need to give yourself time first. It's like that airplane thing—you need to put the oxygen mask on yourself first before you can help others."

"Right," Emma said, and looked off into the fields. The rows and rows of grapes seemed to go on endlessly. She had the sudden urge to run down one of those rows and keep on running.

"No one's saying that what you're going through isn't rough," Francisco said. "It is. You basically found out that everything you thought about your life was the exact opposite. It's a lot. But you're tough. You're going to get through this."

"I feel like jumping out of my skin, you know?"

"I know," Francisco said. "Try sitting still the night before you go upstate for a ten-year stint."

Emma hadn't known Francisco before he did time. She wondered what he'd been like, the kind of man he'd been before. She only knew him now—the smart, motivated guy who reveled in hard work and loved his girlfriend. "What was that like?"

"Weird, man," Francisco said, linking his hands together at the back of his head. "I basically went around the neighborhood, saying my goodbyes. I honestly didn't know if I'd survive my time. I wanted to make sure I made peace with everyone before I left, you know?"

Emma looked at her friend. She was surprised to see Francisco recounting the story without emotion. "Well, what you went through is so much worse than what I'm going through."

"And the people who survived the Holocaust, the people whose memory your mom and Felix tried to honor through their work? They had it worse than both of us put together. But that doesn't mean you can't be all in your feelings about what happened. What happened to you is a lot to deal with. You're allowed to let yourself feel it."

"Right." Emma could smell the sweetness coming off the vines. "You're right."

"And once I let myself feel things," he continued, "once I processed what I'd been through, look at what happened to me. I got out, I got a good job, I met Blanca."

"Well, I already have a job." Emma couldn't help but laugh at her own joke.

"Then maybe you'll meet your Blanca."

"You sound like those old biddies from the Glen Cove Historical Society," Emma said. "Do you want to fix me up with your grandson from Columbia, too?"

Francisco laughed. "You can be sure that if I had a grandson who went to Columbia, I'd be telling the world about him, too."

"You'll be bragging about your Ivy League grandson," Emma said, "and I'll still be coming to terms with my Nazi father."

"They taught us this thing in therapy, when I was upstate," Francisco said. "It really helped me. It's that you need to hold two thoughts in your head at once."

"What does that mean?"

"Both of these things are true: I did a terrible thing. But I am not a terrible person."

"Right."

"Both of these things are also true: Hans Jansen was your father, who loved you very much."

"True."

"And Hans Jensen was also a Nazi."

Emma hung her head. Hearing the words come out of Francisco's mouth was hard to hear. Emma couldn't help but think of the countless victims of the Holocaust. What did she owe the families that her father destroyed?

"Before we knew the whole story, when we were still figuring stuff out and thought Felix was the Nazi," Emma said, "I asked Leo if he thought that Agnes was a Nazi, too. He said that even if she wasn't, she was married to a Nazi. She loved a Nazi. And that was worse."

"So?"

"I loved my father. Does that make me evil, too?"

"You didn't know he was a Nazi, Emma," Francisco said. "The decisions of an adult and your world as a child are two completely different things."

"I don't know what having a Nazi father says about me," Emma said. "Who am I?"

"You're Emma Jansen," Francisco said. "Badass cook, kick-ass businesswoman, and one of my best friends in the world. Don't talk shit about her."

Emma laughed.

"Look," he said. "I'm having a kid. My kid's gonna love me, even though I'm an ex-con."

"Ex-con is not exactly on the same level as actual Nazi."

"No," he said, smiling. "It's not. But you can't blame yourself for being a kid and loving your father. Kids are supposed to love their dads. It doesn't make you evil because it turns out that he was."

"Samantha says that accepting what happened doesn't mean that it's okay. It just means that it happened."

"So, what, Samantha's wise now?"

"No," Emma said. "Not wise. In therapy."

Now it was Francisco's turn to laugh.

"It's okay," he said, putting his hands on her shoulders. "It's okay. You're going to be okay. You know that, right?"

Emma wasn't sure.

54

Now

"There's something that doesn't make sense."

Emma had seen Leo's name come up on her phone when he called, but when she picked up, he'd started talking, as if they'd been in the middle of a conversation, even though they hadn't spoken in two weeks.

"Hello to you, too," Emma said. She leaned back in her office chair and put her feet up on the desk.

"I don't have time for *hello*," Leo said, speaking so fast his words jumbled together. "There are too many questions: Why did Felix leave everything there?"

Emma didn't respond. Francisco had been right—she didn't want to dwell on Felix anymore. Didn't want to dwell on the past. What she needed to do now was to process everything that had happened so that she could start to move on. Begin healing so that she could get better. So that she could get on a path of helping others, trying to rectify the horrifying misdeeds of her father.

Leo continued: "I mean, he sold the house in a hurry, all those years ago. He left everything there, the furnishings, the light fixtures, things that other people might have taken with them."

"Leo, I..."

"Doesn't that sound like the actions of a guilty person to you?"

"Not necessarily," Emma said. "I don't know, maybe he sold the house furnished because all of that stuff wouldn't fit in his new place."

"Or maybe he's really a Nazi, like we always thought," Leo said. "Maybe we were right all along."

Emma held her breath. They'd researched it endlessly when they were in high school, but they couldn't find any proof. Leo had even told her, just a month prior, that he'd sent a tip in to the Department of Justice, who'd determined that Felix was clean.

"We've been down this road before," Emma finally said.

"But there's new evidence now," Leo said. "The subbasement changes everything. Why would he flee in the night like a criminal if he wasn't a criminal?"

"I don't think he fled in the night," Emma said. "And anyway, if he was running away, then why would he leave all of that evidence in the subbasement?"

"My question exactly. When my crew found the subbasement, it had been walled off with concrete. I don't think he thought anyone would ever find the subbasement."

"But you found it," Emma said. "And anyway, he needed all of that evidence because he was a Nazi *hunter*, not a Nazi."

"Then why would he leave it all there?" Leo asked. "If it was evidence, evidence he needed to hunt and then arrest all of these Nazis, then why would he leave it all behind like that? Why wouldn't he give it to the authorities before leaving?"

"I have no idea," Emma said. "But I need to move on with my life. Heal so that I can start doing some good in the world."

"I can't think of anything else," Leo said quietly. "For starters, I can't build at Rolling Hill while it's in the midst of a DOJ investigation."

"So, this is about your money?"

"No, Emma," Leo said. "It's about the truth. After all this time, don't you want to know the truth?"

Leo was right; Emma wanted to know the truth. An hour later, he was at her office, ready to pick her up to go to Felix's apartment.

"What are we even going to say?" Emma asked.

"We're going to get answers."

The elevator doors opened directly into Felix's apartment, and Leo led the way. Anne, Felix's aide, greeted them at the elevator and showed them to the living room.

"Lovely to see you again, Emma," Felix said. "And it's good to see you, too, Leo. Please forgive me for not getting up." He motioned toward his wheelchair, which sat in the corner of the room.

"We won't take much of your time," Leo said, his voice businesslike. "We have a few questions."

"Questions?"

"Why did you leave everything behind at Rolling Hill?" Leo asked, still standing.

Emma sat down on the couch, in the same spot she'd been in only a week prior. Leo made no move to sit down. Alice, Felix's house manager, came in with that same silver tea tray, this time filled with pastries.

"Please, have something to eat," Felix said, gesturing to the tray, which Alice had set down on the large leather ottoman.

"I'm not hungry," Leo said. "So tell us. Why did you leave everything behind? When you sold the property?"

"I was moving on to a new period in my life," Felix said. "I left everything behind the same way that I did when my family left the Netherlands. A fresh start after the war. A fresh start after the house."

"But if you were a Nazi hunter, didn't you need to take everything with you?" Leo asked. "Preserve the evidence?"

"I tied up all of my loose ends before leaving."

Felix and Leo stared each other down, as if they were having a duel. Emma didn't dare speak.

"Why did you leave everything in the subbasement?" Leo asked again.

"I didn't know about the subbasement."

Emma could see the edges of Leo's mouth twitch. This was not the response he was looking for. "You didn't?"

"I'm afraid not." Felix took a sip of his tea.

"Did you know about the secret room off the pantry?"

Felix set down his teacup and furrowed his brow. "How did you know about that?"

"We saw the dishes with the Nazi swastikas on them when we were kids," Leo said. "It's why we thought you were a Nazi."

"Ah, I see," Felix said. He glanced down into his teacup, as if the answers were down at the bottom of it, nestled among the tea leaves.

"So, did you?"

"I'm sorry," Felix said, his eyes fixed on Leo again. "Did I what?"

"Did you know about the secret room off the pantry?"

"I did."

"But you didn't know about the subbasement?"

Felix didn't respond. He took a deep breath, and then set his teacup down. "In for a penny, in for a pound, I suppose."

Leo looked at Emma. Emma looked back at Leo.

Felix cleared his throat. "I *did* know about the subbasement."

"I knew it," Leo said, under his breath.

"Let me explain," Felix said. "I knew about everything. We used the subbasement as a place to hide evidence that we'd later be able to use. For years, we were only using the hidden rooms and passageways, but we later determined that we needed someplace safer, once we realized that they'd been compromised."

"Because we found them?" Leo asked.

"I didn't know that it was you," Felix said. "At the time, we thought it was Fleur."

"But then why would you leave everything in the subbasement when you retired from the Department of Justice and left the house?"

"That part is a bit more complicated, I'm afraid," Felix said. "First of all, I didn't retire. I quit. And second, the things you found in the basement were from closed cases, and it was evidence no longer needed by Justice. I didn't leave anything behind that was needed for an active investigation. I figured it would stay buried forever."

"Why did you quit?"

"I'd been tracking an infamous Nazi doctor, one of the men who conducted medical experiments on Jewish prisoners. He was a horrible person, truly evil. It took me over two years, two long years of secret work, but I finally apprehended him. Only, when I brought him in, they told me to set him loose."

"Set him loose?" Leo asked.

"But why?" Emma pressed. She found herself inching to the edge of the couch.

"It was called Operation Paperclip," Felix said. "After the war, the United States had a secret intelligence program to recruit certain Nazi scientists, bring them to America, and employ them within our government."

"What?" Emma whispered, so softly she could barely hear her own voice.

"The idea was that if we didn't recruit them," Felix explained, "the Russians surely would, putting the United States at a distinct disadvantage in both the Cold War and the Space Race."

"I never heard of Operation Paperclip," Leo said.

"It was a top secret intelligence program," Felix said. "Not everyone knows about it. I did, but I was initially told it was something different. I was told that Operation Paperclip only recruited low-level scientists, engineers, and technicians. Not the people in charge. Not the people who were responsible for everything that happened in the camps. But that was a lie. Once I found out the truth, it changed everything for me. It felt like the opposite of what I'd been working for—I'd spent two years tracking down a man who had committed acts of pure evil, and the United States government had invited him here, gave him sanctuary, gave him a job. I could not abide this."

"So, you just left?" Leo asked.

"Yes," Felix said. "I immediately stopped working for the Department of Justice, put Rolling Hill on the market, and made my cover, the art, my full-time life's work. I left everything behind and never turned back."

55

Then

Age twenty-five

"I'm going to ask Alison to marry me."

They sat across from each other, at a booth at the Corner Bistro, one of Emma's favorite restaurants.

"Congratulations!" Emma said, jumping up from her side of the booth and rushing around to Leo. She threw her arms around his neck. "That's great news!"

"Is it?" Leo asked. His face wore an expression Emma couldn't quite decipher.

"Of course it is," Emma said, suddenly uneasy. She made her way back to her side of the booth. "I'm happy for you both. Do I get to be the best man?"

"You're sure I should ask her?"

"I mean, you've certainly been together long enough. Four years," Emma said. "Why not?"

Leo stared back at her. Emma wasn't quite sure what she was missing here.

"So, you're telling me there's no reason why I shouldn't propose?"

"I can't think of anything," Emma said slowly. She looked at her friend. "Is there something you want me to say right now?"

"No," Leo said, staring down at the table. "I just didn't know how you'd react."

"How I'd react? I'm thrilled for you, of course," Emma said. "You're my best friend in the world."

And he was. Emma and Leo had a lifetime of memories together. Good times and bad. From their childhood spent roaming the halls of Rolling Hill, to their young adult life in the city, they were always there for each other. Three years ago, Emma had helped move Leo's father out of Rolling Hill and into his new Queens apartment. Two years ago, they'd rented a Hamptons share with a bunch of friends. The year prior, he'd dropped everything the moment she called to tell him that her mother died. And for the three weeks before that, as Mila's health rapidly deteriorated due to pancreatic cancer, he and Enzo had been there to take Emma out for long dinners at the diner next to the hospital. Even Leo's mother showed up a few times to sit with her and offer warm hugs. Leo had made sure a local florist delivered freshly cut lilacs each week, perfuming the air with sweetness so that Mila's last days would be filled with her favorite scent.

Then, he was by her side as she planned the funeral, got her through the day, and in the lonely months that followed.

"And you're *my* best friend," Leo said. "So, are you sure I should marry Alison?"

"I don't think you need my permission," Emma said, furrowing her brow.

Leo laughed. "Right."

"What? What am I missing here?" Emma asked. "What is it that you want me to say?"

"I think I've been waiting for you to realize that we should be together."

"You're my best friend," Emma said.

"Exactly," Leo said. He looked up at Emma, and their eyes met.

"If we ever tried this and it didn't work out, I would lose you."

"You wouldn't lose me."

"Of course I would."

"So you're not willing to take a chance?" Leo asked. "Take a chance on us?"

"What are you even saying right now?" Emma asked, suddenly uncomfortable in her seat. "You're *with* Alison. You're going to *marry* Alison."

"I don't *have to* marry Alison," Leo said, shaking his head. "Especially if there's a chance that we could be together."

Emma didn't know how to respond.

"When we were kids, I wanted you. But you didn't want me. So, I settled for friends. Best friends," Leo said. "But now I want more."

"But... Alison."

"Why don't you want me?" Leo asked quietly.

Emma didn't know what to say to that. She stared off at a table across the restaurant. It was a young couple with two small children. They looked like such a happy family—the kids quietly coloring in their notebooks as the adults chatted and drank red wine. Emma didn't know what that was like. How that felt, to have two loving parents. To feel that secure.

"I don't know what to say."

"Right," Leo said. He threw a few bills on the table and stood to leave.

"Where are you going?" Emma asked. "Our burgers haven't even come out yet."

"I think I should go," Leo said.

She rose from the booth. "Don't go, Leo. Stay."

"Emma, I love you. I have loved you since we were eleven years old. But you need to choose. If you want me, then I won't propose to Alison, and we can give things a go. If you don't, though, then you have to let me go."

Emma didn't respond. She stared at Leo as he put his jacket on and walked out. Just then, their burgers and fries were brought to the table. Emma knew that she should run after him. She knew that if she let him walk out the door, she might never see him again. He had made himself clear: if she wanted him, she could have him. If she didn't, she would have to let him go.

Emma knew what she should do. Still, her legs refused to move. She sat at the table, staring at the two burgers and large order of fries in front of her. And then, not knowing what else to do, she ate.

56

Now

"You got what you wanted."

Emma and Leo sat in a booth at an Italian restaurant around the corner from Felix's apartment. Emma felt like her heart was still beating outside of her chest from everything Felix had told them. She looked over to Leo, but he seemed calm, as if nothing had happened.

The lights in the restaurant were dim. So dim that Emma could barely make out the words on the menu, but that didn't matter. They weren't there for the food. They were there to talk.

"This isn't how I wanted it," Emma said, glancing up from the menu to face Leo.

"How did you want it, exactly?"

Emma found it hard to meet Leo's gaze. "I guess I wanted you to realize that the place meant something to me, something to us."

"What did it mean?" Leo asked, shrugging. "You and

Henry, sneaking off to the indoor tennis court to humiliate me when we were kids? Or you and Henry now, making a fool of me, still?"

"I never meant to make a fool of you. I had this childish notion that Henry and I were meant to be together or something. Like the bride and the groom in the Chagall." Emma's face flushed with shame. "But that's over now. We broke up."

Leo rubbed his forehead.

"You don't have anything to say about that?" Emma asked.

"I think you know what I'm going to say." Leo looked down and then back up again at Emma. As their eyes met: "I'm not a consolation prize."

"I know that."

"Do you?"

The server came to the table, and they ordered baked clams to start, and then a family-style portion of chicken parm, with pasta on the side. A bottle of house red was on the table almost immediately, and they both drank it down as if it were water.

"So, I guess there won't be a grand opening party, after all," Emma said, tearing a piece of garlic bread from the loaf that had been set down on the table.

"Like I said, you got what you wanted," Leo said. "No party, no development called Hepburn."

"What will you do next, then?"

"I'm going back to Chicago," Leo said. "There's a property that I almost bid on before I bought Rolling Hill. I guess this is a sign that I should buy it, after all."

"So soon?" Emma said.

"Yeah." Their eyes met across the table.

"I was getting used to you being around again. We should do something before you leave."

"We're doing something right now." Leo refilled their glasses of house red.

"You know what I meant," Emma said. She took a big gulp of her wine. "We should make a plan, hit some museums, or spend the day out on the Long Beach boardwalk. Something fun."

The server came to the table with a piping hot platter filled with baked clams, the bread crumbs on top all browned, just the way Emma liked it.

"May I?" Emma asked Leo, scooping a clam onto the serving spoon and holding it up toward Leo's plate.

"Thank you," Leo said. "But I'm afraid I won't have time for a last hurrah with you."

"What if I sweetened the deal with some grapefruit soda?" Emma smiled at her own joke and hoped that it would give Leo a chuckle as well

Leo didn't laugh. "My plane leaves tomorrow."

57

Now

"I don't play games."

"Games are fun," Samantha said, making an exaggerated frowny-face as they stood in Francisco and Blanca's kitchen, getting the remainder of the hors d'oeuvres out and onto the dining room table.

Everything for Francisco and Blanca's baby shower had to be perfect—and they'd been working tirelessly to make it so. The plan was this: Emma, Samantha, and Kendall would oversee the prep for the party, and then, at 11:30 a.m. on the dot, whip off their aprons, let Samantha's crew work the party, and become party guests themselves.

"We didn't say anything about games," Emma said, admiring the plate of deviled eggs. They'd crafted them into tiny baby carriages, with Vienna sausages subbing in the for the little tot.

"That's because I thought you would say no."

"I am saying no."

"Blanca," Samantha called out, "you want games today, right?"

"God, no!" she yelled back from the bedroom. "I don't think games will go with the elegant food." She poked her head out. "The food is gonna be super elegant, right?"

"So elegant," Emma said, eyeing the deviled eggs again. Tiny baby carriages were elegant, right? Emma frantically began pulling the sausages out of the carriages.

Emma looked around at the party: an omelet station with fifteen different types of add-ins; a caviar bar with three different bases and two different types of crème fraîche; and a made-to-order crepe station as well, with savory and sweet add-ins. (Emma could barely wait to get a freshly made banana and Nutella crepe for herself.) Her baker had outdone himself this morning: baskets overflowed with muffins in three flavors: blueberry, carrot ginger, and chocolate chip; and croissants in four: caramelized onion and goat cheese, brie with bacon and honey, almond dusted with powdered sugar, and classic chocolate. He'd also gifted Francisco and Blanca with a large sourdough bread that had their names carved onto the top.

"Games are fun," Samantha said under her breath.

"Tell you what," Emma said. "When we do your shower, we can have games."

"Games are stupid," Kendall said from behind the bar. "Baby showers are all about the nonalcoholic cocktails." She had a line of mocktails set up, ready for the guests. One row was pink, and the other was blue. They also planned a "make your own mimosa" bar, with five different fruit juices, for those guests who would be drinking. Kendall had her carafes lined up neatly, and the prosecco on ice.

"You're stupid," Samantha said, and chucked a tomato from the crudités platter in her direction. Kendall caught it with her left hand and popped it into her mouth.

The bell rang, and Blanca came half running, half walking out of the bedroom, holding her belly, which was beginning to pop. "The party's not supposed to start for a half hour! Who's here?"

Emma motioned for one of the servers to get behind the table that held the omelet station. "We're ready, don't worry!"

"Who's here?" Francisco said, coming out of the baby's room. "They're early."

He and Blanca opened the door, and it wasn't a party guest. Someone had sent an enormous arrangement of flowers.

"Want me to get that into a vase for you?" Emma asked.

"That better not sub in for someone's gift," Samantha said. "Was there a card?"

"They're from me," Francisco said. "But they were supposed to come at the end of the party, as everyone was leaving. Sorry, baby."

"That's so sweet," Blanca said. "I love them."

Blanca went back into the bedroom to finish getting ready, while Emma and Francisco checked the kitchen cabinets for a vase big enough to hold the flowers.

"They were supposed to come in a vase, too," Francisco said.

Emma found a beautiful ceramic pitcher and held it out for Francisco's approval.

"That belonged to my grandmother," he said, his face softening. "It's perfect."

"Let me do that for you," Emma said, glad that she hadn't removed her apron just yet. "You can finish getting ready."

"Blanca already laid out my clothes on the bed," Francisco said. "I'm about three minutes from being ready. How are you doing?"

"Great," Emma said. "I'm so excited for the party."

"Don't think that I didn't see the charger plates."

Emma tried to hold her laugh in. "I know how much you love chargers."

"Chargers are stuffy and pointless and another thing you have to clean at the end of the night. You know this."

"Chargers make a table feel complete," Emma said. "And anyway, what do you care? You're not in charge of cleanup."

Francisco crinkled his eyes and smiled. "You speak to Leo since he left?"

Emma shook her head.

"You feeling any better about things?"

"Yeah."

"That doesn't sound convincing," Francisco said. "Why don't you tell him how you feel?"

"I don't know how I feel."

"I think you do."

Francisco gave Emma a peck on the cheek, and then took the pitcher of flowers out of the kitchen.

Emma felt like home when she was at Francisco and Blanca's. That was why she'd been so upset about Leo tearing down Rolling Hill, wasn't it? Rolling Hill had been her home for as long as she could remember. Since the main house had been torn down, Emma had felt untethered.

"Need help in here?" Blanca asked as she entered the kitchen. She looked radiant in her white maxi-dress—ethereal, bridal, and mother earth, all wrapped into one. "You should come out. Samantha has already gotten started on the mimosa bar without you."

"Sorry. I was thinking about how you and Francisco have created this lovely home here."

"Thank you," Blanca said, running her hand along the countertop. "I hope that all of the improvements we made will help with resale."

"You're selling?"

"At some point," Blanca said. "Yes. This place is big enough for right now, but once baby number two comes, and then baby number three..."

"But *this* is your home."

"I mean, for now it is," Blanca said. "But home is so much more than just some physical place, right?"

"It's a physical place, too."

"Francisco spent ten years upstate. You think he thinks of that place as his home?"

Emma didn't respond.

Blanca passed her a napkin, and as Emma took it, she realized her eyes had teared up. "You need a minute?"

"I'm okay," Emma said, and Blanca linked their arms. They walked back out into the living room like that, arm in arm. Soon the apartment was filled with friends and family, all there to celebrate the next part of Francisco and Blanca's life. Blanca's cousin brought a guitar and conducted an impromptu concert as guests mingled and ate.

After an hour, Samantha carried out the cake. Francisco and Blanca were supposed to cut into it, and the inside would reveal the sex of their baby. Emma handed the cake knife to Francisco, who then gave it to Blanca. He pretended to close his eyes as she cut into it.

It was pink—they were having a girl. Servers immediately began passing out the pink mocktails to guests. Francisco cried, and held on to Blanca tightly, whispering in her ear.

Samantha and Kendall came over to clink their pink mock-tails with Emma's.

"I knew it was a girl all along," Samantha said.

"Because of the way she's carrying?" Kendall asked. "Don't tell her that. A great aunt once told my cousin that she was having a girl because girls steal your beauty, and they haven't spoken since."

"No," Samantha said, adding some prosecco to her mock-tail. "I slept with the baker two nights ago, and he told me."

Kendall stared at Samantha open-mouthed.

"What?" Samantha said. "I don't like surprises."

Emma thought about what Blanca had said about home—how it was not merely a physical place. She couldn't help but remember what Leo had said to her about the meaning of home, at the groundbreaking ceremony, when she'd pleaded for him to leave the house intact: *It's the life you create for yourself, not an actual place.*

She looked around the party and thought about the life she'd created for herself. She'd filled it with work that was fulfilling, friends who felt like family. She was happy, financially stable, and had people to share her life with. As a kid, she'd dreamed that she would one day marry Henry, and live her life at Rolling Hill. But things didn't turn out that way. Emma had to admit, life had turned out much, much better.

Not bad for the maid's daughter.

58

Now

"I didn't expect to hear from you."

Emma immediately regretted calling. She scrunched her face up as she considered what to say next. Perhaps Leo didn't want to hear from her? Was this phone call a mistake? "Checking in on you. How was your flight to Chicago? Are you all settled in?"

"Well, I'm in a temporary sublet," Leo said. "I sold my place in Chicago because I thought I'd be in New York for a couple of years."

"Sorry," Emma said, cringing. She definitely should not have called. This was all her fault.

"You don't have to be sorry," Leo said. "Even if you hadn't weaponized the Glen Cove Historical Society against me and tried to get that injunction, we still would have found the sub-basement, and we'd be in the same place."

"I don't think I *weaponized* the Glen Cove Historical Society," Emma said, laughing despite herself. Even with Leo angry at her, he could still make her laugh.

"Those old biddies are terrifying," Leo said. "Don't underestimate them."

"Oh, I would never," Emma said. "You're right. They can be very intimidating. Though they also make incredible cookies."

"Those women contain multitudes."

"Yes, they do," Emma said, catching the reference to Walt Whitman's famous poem "Song of Myself." "Remember when I used to edit your English essays for you?"

"I do."

Emma cursed her inability to make small talk. "Did we ever study Whitman?"

"I don't think we did," Leo said. "Did you call to discuss the English curriculum at Glen Cove High?"

Of course that wasn't why she'd called. She'd called to tell him that she'd made a mistake. She'd made a mistake when they were kids, when she chose Henry over him. She'd made that same mistake when they were adults, when she did it again. And she made a mistake seven years ago, when she wouldn't give things a try with him, *couldn't* give things a try with him, and she didn't know why.

When Emma didn't respond, he said: "Look, I'm late to meet up with some friends. Can I call you back later?"

"No need to call me back," Emma said. "I was just checking in. Nothing important."

"Okay," Leo said. "Take care, Emma."

"Take care."

Emma stared at her phone for a long time after ending the call. She tried to think about what she should have said, how she could have made the call go better. But perhaps this was how things were meant to end. Perhaps Henry was right all along—Emma needed to let the past go. Perhaps it was time to let Leo go.

59

Now

The office manager said that she did not want to take the leftovers.

Emma and Samantha looked at each other, and then turned toward the massive spread of food remaining from the company retreat they'd catered on Long Island. Usually, customers loved being left with a fridge full of leftovers. And a corporate retreat? They would take those prepacked sandwiches and salads and then, the next workday, brag to their employees about free lunch. But the office manager was firm. The answer was no. Emma wasn't sure if anyone had ever refused leftovers before. She didn't know whether or not she should take it personally. She picked up a grilled chicken sandwich and gingerly took a small bite.

"We can pack the salads and sandwiches into takeaway trays for you," Samantha suggested. "And then you can offer your employees free lunch tomorrow at work."

"I just got fired, so I don't really care what you do with

the leftovers," the office manager replied, and walked off in a hurry.

"Strange way to end a team-building exercise," Samantha said to Emma.

"Remind me to never do a company retreat," Emma said. "Let's pack it all up and figure out what to do with it."

Most of their team was breaking down the food service tents, so Emma and Samantha began packing the food up into coolers.

"Where can we donate all this?" Samantha said. "It would be a shame to let this much go to waste. Do you know of any shelters out here, or should we bring it back to one of the ones we usually donate to in the city?"

"I don't know of any out on Long Island off the top of my head," Emma said, as an idea suddenly came to her. "But I do know some women who probably do."

She took out her phone and found Gladys's number.

"You saved my phone number!" Gladys said in lieu of hello.

Ten minutes later, they were at the Glen Cove Food Pantry, with Gladys greeting them at the door.

"Well, this is a lovely thing you're doing," Gladys said as Emma and Samantha walked in. "Girls, meet Constance. She runs this whole shebang."

"It's nice to meet you," Emma said.

Constance took the tray she'd been carrying. "We're so appreciative," she said as she set it on a table.

They walked out to the truck to get more trays full of food. Emma, Samantha, and Constance each took a tray from the back.

"Now that you've saved my phone number, does this mean you'll be attending the Glen Cove Historical Society meetings more regularly?" Gladys said, meeting them at the front door again to help with the trays.

Emma looked at Gladys like a deer caught in headlights.

"Or were you only interested in the fate of Rolling Hill?" Gladys asked, her eyes narrowing.

"She was only interested in Rolling Hill," Samantha said, nodding.

Emma shot Samantha a look.

"What?" Samantha said. "It's true!"

Gladys laughed. "I appreciate honesty."

Samantha and Constance went back out to the truck to get the remaining trays, but Emma and Gladys stayed inside.

"I'm sorry," Emma said, setting down two trays on a table. "I really did want to help you get historical status for Rolling Hill. But I'm afraid that that's the only property I was really interested in."

"Like your friend, Stella," Gladys said.

"Please don't group me in with a Neo-Nazi," Emma said.

"Do you think she knew what was buried under the house?" Gladys asked. "Is that why she needed the building's blue-prints?"

"She did," Emma said. "She called them *treasures*. Said they were part of her history. That's why she didn't want Leo tearing the place down."

"My word," Gladys said, literally clutching her pearls. "How awful."

"It really was," Emma said.

"Well, come to a meeting, anyway," Gladys said, shrugging. "We could use the fresh blood."

Emma went home that night feeling different. Happier. As if the act of helping others had left her high. She hadn't felt that contented in a while.

She was glad that she'd called Gladys. Glad that she'd finally saved her number in her phone.

And the afternoon, filled with charitable acts, had planted a seed in her mind.

Later that night, Emma researched how she could donate meals to Holocaust survivors. She could never make up for her father's unforgivable acts—nothing could ever make up for the atrocities committed during World War II—but this was something she could do now. A way to give back. A way to acknowledge what had happened, and use her time, money, and resources to help the victims.

Emma was shocked to learn that around thirty thousand Holocaust survivors were living in the New York area. Half of them living in poverty. The numbers seemed overwhelming. She immediately reached out to some organizations about how she could donate food and her time on a regular basis.

Within weeks, Emma would set up an arm of her business dedicated to charity—feeding Holocaust survivors weekly through a traveling pantry and a meal delivery service. Within a year, she would have the charity up and running, with its own staff. Gladys would come to serve on the board, and three years later, once they found themselves again on speaking terms, so would Henry.

Emma knew that she could never make up for what her father had done. Anything she did now would be a small drop in the bucket compared to the massive amounts of damage her father had inflicted on humanity. Not to mention the ripple effect it had on the world, even now, so many decades later. But Emma was also coming to find that because her father was evil, it didn't mean that she was. She could be whatever she wanted to be. And just as her mother had taken what she'd learned about Emma's father and used that knowledge for forces of good, so would Emma.

Leo had once asked her why, after the way they'd grown up, she'd become *the help*. At the time, Emma had been offended. She'd taken the term as an insult. But Emma finally had her answer to Leo's question. It was simple: she wanted to be a person who helped.

She wasn't yet. But soon she would be.

60

Now

They were greeted like long-lost relatives, back from a long and arduous journey. Plied with food and attention and in one case, a giant bear hug, Emma was glad that they'd come.

One week after donating the trays of food to the Glen Cove Food Pantry, Emma and Samantha attended the Glen Cove Historical Society meeting. They were still dressed in their chef's whites, no match for the women in their pretty cashmere sweater sets, silk slacks, and double strands of pearls. But it was either chef's whites or miss the meeting entirely. They came straight from that afternoon's event—a high tea outside on the porch overlooking the golf course at the Glen Cove Country Club. It was an elegant affair, thrown annually to raise money for North Shore Hospital. They'd never been hired for this event before, but Henry had graciously suggested La Vie en Rose after he made a generous donation. He wasn't in attendance, which Emma was grateful for. She wasn't quite ready to see Henry again, even if only as friends.

She made a mental note to recommend him to a client who recently bought a new home and was searching for some artwork for their formal living room.

Emma was exhausted from the day's event, and the truth was, she hadn't planned to attend the Glen Cove Historical Society meeting at all. But Samantha had been convinced by Francisco, who had mentioned Gladys's grandson, Charlie, at Columbia.

"What?" Samantha said when Emma stared at her, slack-jawed. "He sounds cute!"

Edith and Myrtle spotted them first.

"Emma!" Edith cried out. "You brought a friend! A young person!"

The members of the Glen Cove Historical Society all surrounded them, oohing and aahing over their new youthful members.

"Give them some room, ladies!" Gladys cleared a path for Emma and Samantha. She'd saved three seats at the front of the room, and she'd saved them a plate of Edith's delicious cookies to share during the meeting.

The sound of a gavel hitting the table rang out. "Let's call this meeting to order!" Vivian bellowed. All the other women, about fourteen of them total, hurriedly found their seats.

"You didn't save seats for us?" Edith called out loudly from a few rows back.

Gladys turned around and shook her head. Emma didn't dare turn around. She guiltily took a bite of one of Edith's cookies. Just as delicious as the first time she'd tried them.

"Good news first," Vivian said. "By now, we've all heard about the museum they'll be building where the main house at Rolling Hill stood." Vivian looked to Emma as she said it, and Emma nodded in assent. Leo's company had donated the property to the Holocaust Museum and Tolerance Center of

Long Island, also located in Glen Cove. Felix had made a substantial charitable donation in his late wife's honor so that the HMTC could build a learning center on top of the subbasement, the goal of which would be teaching children about the horrors of the Holocaust, with a focus on the Nazi occupation of the Netherlands. The Chagall, also donated by Felix, would welcome guests as they entered.

"That Leo turned out to be such a good boy," Gladys whispered to Emma.

"I know we're all disappointed about Summer Cove," Vivian said, continuing the meeting. The crowd murmured their agreement.

Gladys leaned over to Emma and explained: Summer Cove was a massive estate that was about to go on the market. Built in 1898 by one of Teddy Roosevelt's close advisers, it was a Gilded Age gem. In the Madeline family for four generations, the whole town was shocked when the great-grandchildren collectively decided to sell. The property was fifteen acres, waterfront. The Glen Cove Historical Society did not want this estate to go to commercial developers. It had value, since Teddy Roosevelt had attended many parties there.

"I don't get it," Samantha whispered. "So, what's the historic value?"

"Why, Teddy Roosevelt, dear," Gladys whispered back.

"Didn't Teddy Roosevelt kind of suck?" Samantha asked.

Gladys audibly gasped.

"Decorum, please," Vivian said, banging her gavel.

Samantha raised her hand. "I'm sorry," she said, even though she hadn't yet been called on. "I don't understand what makes Summer Cove have historic value."

"Teddy Roosevelt, dear," Vivian said, same as Gladys.

Gladys nodded, seemingly glad to have Vivian affirm her answer.

"Oh," Samantha said. "So, Teddy Roosevelt was the first owner of the house?"

"No," Vivian said, her mouth arranging itself downward, "the first owner of the house was Michael Madeline, one of Roosevelt's most trusted advisors."

"So what makes that historically relevant?"

Vivian gave a deep exhale, as if she were speaking to a child who had exhausted her. "Teddy Roosevelt."

"But he didn't own the house."

"He visited the house many times. For meetings, for parties. He was a Long Island fixture."

"So, if Teddy Roosevelt stepped foot in your home," Samantha reasoned, "then your property can be granted historical status."

"We believe so, dear," Vivian said. "That's what we argued. Unfortunately, we lost."

Emma raised her hand. Vivian pretended not to see it at first, but Emma waved it wildly.

"Do *you* have a question about Teddy Roosevelt?" Vivian asked.

"No," Emma said. "I was wondering, has the property gone up for sale yet?"

61

Now

"Nice to see you," Emma said.

"Nice to see you, too," Leo said. He leaned over and gave Emma a kiss on the cheek. He wore his usual work uniform of dark jeans, button-down shirt, and dark blazer. Today, he had on work boots to tour Summer Cove.

Emma had come directly from the prep kitchen and forgotten to change her shoes. She wore black clogs—not exactly proper footwear to tour a fifteen-acre estate.

"You're going to walk the property in those?" Leo asked, pointing at her clogs.

"I forgot to change," Emma said. "They're fine. Surprisingly comfortable."

"Here, hold my hand," Leo said, and extended it to Emma.

She waited a beat before taking his hand. She felt silly, holding hands with Leo. So much had happened. So many things were said. So many things hadn't been said.

"I just don't want you to fall," Leo said, reading Emma's

mind. "If I buy the property, we can't have any lawsuits hanging over our heads."

"I'm not going to fall," she said, and as if on cue, stumbled
over some unevenness in the grass.

"Let's get you into the house," Leo said, and led the way
toward the main house on the property.

The house was gorgeous. Of course, it reminded Emma of
Rolling Hill, with its Gilded Age details. Custom millwork,
intricate in the way that things weren't built anymore. The
entryway was enormous, grand, big enough to accommodate
the many people who would attend parties that the owners
threw in the ballroom, which was right off the entryway, almost in view.

"What do you think?" Emma asked. She looked up and
saw the chandelier. It was covered in cloth, so it was hard to
tell what it looked like, but it was humongous. Grand enough
to befit a house of this stature, a home that Teddy Roosevelt
would visit often. She looked around for a switch—at Rolling
Hill, the chandeliers had been operated by a switch. Every few
months, her mother would call her in to watch as they came
down for their cleaning. Emma's mother would dust them and
clean them, and Emma would sit in wonder, thinking about
the stories those chandeliers would tell if they could speak.

"I couldn't possibly tell you what I think," Leo said, his
eyes taking in the space, his fingertips touching every surface,
"because you'll try to torpedo this, too."

Emma sighed. "I deserved that."

"Yeah, you did."

"Think this place has any secret passageways?"

"Definitely," Leo said, his face lighting up. He walked toward the entryway to the ballroom and ran his hands along
the molding. "Right here."

Emma walked over. Leo had discovered two buttons, similar to the ones they'd seen at Rolling Hill when they were kids. "Press it."

Leo pressed the first one, and nothing happened. Then, the bottom button. Still, nothing.

"I'll run into the kitchen," Emma said. "When I call out, press them again."

Emma waited in the kitchen, but heard no sounds. Maybe this place wasn't like Rolling Hill, after all.

"Nothing?" Leo asked, walking into the kitchen.

"Afraid not."

"They must have shorted out and then never got replaced," Leo wondered aloud. He looked up at the ceiling.

"Well, that's good," Emma said. "Now you can bid at least a million dollars less for this place. All you need to tell them is: servant's buttons, busted."

Leo laughed. Then his expression turned serious. "Why am I here?"

"To tour Summer Cove," Emma said, not meeting his eye. "When I heard about this opportunity, I thought of you."

"So, you found this place on the market," Leo said. "And asked me to come back?"

"It's not on the market yet," Emma said. "My friends at the Glen Cove Historical Society told me about it. I called the broker and asked about an off-market deal for you."

"Why?"

"I feel bad about what happened."

"About the house?"

"Yes," Emma said. "The house."

"*Just* the house?"

"No," Emma said. "Not just the house."

She took a few steps toward Leo. They were closer now, but not close enough to touch. Leo stood still. Emma inched another few steps. A little closer.

"If you want me," he said, "you're going to have to come to me this time."

Emma took a big leap, and found herself standing toe-to-toe with Leo. "Here I am."

"Here you are."

Emma thought about all the times she and Leo had almost kissed. That time in the tree when they were kids, her disastrous try to make their movie double feature date romantic, and only a few months prior, in the main house at Rolling Hill. It wasn't that she hadn't wanted to kiss Leo all of those times. It was timing, usually. Her fear about what it would mean if they kissed, mostly.

But Emma wasn't scared anymore. Now, armed with the knowledge of who she really was, and who she wanted to be moving forward, she knew what she wanted. And what she wanted was Leo.

She got up on her tippy toes and leaned in to Leo. Their lips touched, slowly, tentatively at first.

Leo pulled away. "I'm not sure I can do this. You hurt me, Emma. You hurt me so badly."

"I know I did," Emma said. "And I'm sorry. I'm so sorry."

"You never wanted me. When we were kids, you didn't want me. And then, seven years ago? I was all in. But you didn't want me. Seeing you again, I wanted you still. But you didn't want me. You wanted him."

"I'm sorry," Emma said. "I can't change the past. I wish I could, but I can't. I didn't know who I really was, so I held on to some childish notion that Henry was the right one for me, because we were raised side by side. But everything that happened taught me that the things I thought when I was a kid aren't necessarily the same things I think when I'm an adult."

"Like how we thought Felix was a Nazi, but it turned out he was actually a Nazi hunter?"

"Like that."

"And seven years ago?"

"I wasn't ready," Emma said, more sure than she'd ever been. "My mother had just died the year prior, and I felt so lost. I didn't know who I was."

"And now?"

"I think I needed to find out who I was before I could be ready for you. Because I guess I always knew that if I were with you, then it was for good. Forever. Now that I know who I am, for better or for worse, I think I—" Emma was about to say more, about to fill the silence with more nervous rambling, but Leo began to speak.

"I waited for you to come back to me," he said quietly.

"I'm back now," Emma said.

"Well, I came to you, technically," Leo said, a slow smile forming on his face.

"I lured you back," Emma said. "And now here you are."

"Here I am," Leo said, and leaned down to kiss Emma again. This time, his kiss was more powerful, more assured. Emma kissed him back and could see her whole future unfold with him. He'd come back to New York and they'd be together.

Maybe with Leo, she could finally find the meaning of home.

Emma told him this, about the meaning of home, as they shopped for Manhattan apartments a month later. Leo would win the bid on Summer Cove, and would begin construction immediately. He would need to get settled in an apartment in New York as soon as possible, and after a week of touring Manhattan apartments, one worse than the next, Emma would suggest that he stay with her. They'd live in her downtown apartment for a year, where Leo would be surprised to see that

Emma had installed, on her bedroom door, the crystal door-knob that he'd given to her at Rolling Hill.

Once they married and Emma got pregnant, they would move into another home. Specifically, the model home at Summer Cove, which Leo would be turning into a development of chic town houses, inspired by the downtown aesthetic of Emma's apartment. At Emma's coaxing, he would leave the main house standing, and turn it into the community's clubhouse. Emma and Leo would host a lunch at the clubhouse to celebrate their first child's christening, a little girl they named Mila. And he would relieve Summer Cove's main house of its many crystal doorknobs, and gift them to Emma for her birthday.

When Mila turned two, they would move once again. They'd find a four-bedroom house in Glen Cove, which was only a fifteen-minute drive from the colonial that Francisco and Blanca had bought in Syosset. Two days after moving in, they would find out that Emma was pregnant once again, this time with a boy. Enzo would move into the basement apartment so that he could help out with the kids, where he would love chasing after Mila and his namesake, Enzo Junior, all day, and then cooking with Emma in the evenings, when she was home from work. The doorknobs would all be crystal, and the fridge would always be stocked with grapefruit soda.

The Glen Cove house would be the site of many firsts— Enzo Junior's first steps, Mila's first visit from the Tooth Fairy, the first days of school for both kids. It would also be the site of many family celebrations—a big Christmas lunch that lasted all day, an annual Fourth of July barbecue, and Samantha's wedding. (Samantha would marry Gladys's grandson, Charlie, after he graduated with his PhD from Columbia, and Emma and Leo would host the wedding in their backyard.)

Emma and Leo would move a total of three more times in

their lives together. Each place would be home, since, as Leo once told Emma, home isn't a physical place. A true home is the life you create for yourself.

They say lots of things about going home. Home is where the heart is. There's no place like home. You can never go home again.

And so far, Emma had found all of them to be true.

★ ★ ★ ★ ★

AUTHOR'S NOTE

We think of Audrey Hepburn as the glamorous beauty in impossibly chic gowns, but her life wasn't like one of her films.

When I began researching Audrey Hepburn for this novel, I was surprised to learn about her connection to World War II and Nazi Germany. I'd had no idea about this chapter in her life, which had a ripple effect on the rest of it.

In 1935, Audrey's parents were members of the British Union of Fascists, heavily involved in fundraising and recruitment. Her mother wrote an essay for the British Union Fascists publication, *Blackshirt*, called "The Call of Fascism," endorsing the merits of her political views. In May 1935, both of Audrey's parents had lunch with Hitler in Munich, and missed Audrey's birthday.

A few weeks later, Audrey's father, Joseph Ruston, left their family without explanation. Audrey was only six years old. She described it as the most traumatic event of her life, a wound that would never heal. For the rest of her life, she was never able to trust that love could truly last. She lived in fear of abandonment, which informed her relationships and life choices.

When England declared war on Germany in 1939, Audrey's mother, Baroness Ella van Heemstra, felt that London was no longer safe. Since Holland had been neutral in World War I, she took Audrey out of school in Elham, England, and brought her to Arnhem.

But they were not safe for long. German forces invaded the Netherlands in May 1940, and soon thereafter, Holland was under Nazi control. Audrey was only eleven years old. During the five years that followed, life became untenable, and Audrey and her mother barely survived. In 1941, the Nazis began deporting Jews to concentration camps. For the rest of her life, Audrey would have nightmares with the faces of the Jewish people she'd witnessed being taken away in cattle cars. Unbeknownst to Audrey and her mother, her father had become imprisoned in Britain during the war as an enemy of the state, due to his position as director of a Nazi-controlled news agency, known to be a front for the Third Reich.

Though only a child, Audrey became involved with the Dutch Resistance, carrying messages in her shoes to Allied forces. She also danced at underground concerts to raise money to feed and clothe Jews in hiding, and delivered newspapers for the Resistance. After the Battle of Arnhem, Audrey's family hid a British paratrooper in the cellar of their home for a week.

Audrey suffered from severe malnutrition during this time. They ate bread made from tulip bulbs to survive. During the last winter of the war, known as the Hunger Winter, Germans cut off food to the Netherlands, creating a famine. Approximately twenty thousand people died. Audrey developed a number of serious health problems from this malnutrition.

Audrey Hepburn had many connections to another Dutch girl living through the war: Anne Frank. Both born the same year, just weeks apart, both spent their childhoods in the Netherlands, just sixty miles apart. When Audrey read Anne Frank's diary, she was said to have been devastated. The diary even made mention of the execution of Audrey's uncle Otto.

In 1958, George Stevens offered Audrey the role of Anne Frank in the film version of *The Diary of a Young Girl*, but Audrey turned it down. Anne's father, Otto Frank, met with Audrey to ask her to take the role, but she was still too haunted by the war to do it. She said: "I was so destroyed by it again that I said I couldn't deal with it. It's a little bit as if this had happened to my sister. I couldn't play my sister's life. It's too close, and in a way, she was a soul sister."

By 1990, Audrey had changed her mind. She provided the voice-over for a musical composition, inspired by *The Diary of a Young Girl*, by Michael Tilson Thomas, to raise money for UNICEF.

To read more about this time in Audrey's life, I recommend *Dutch Girl: Audrey Hepburn and World War II* by Robert Matzen, with a foreword by Audrey's son, Luca Dotti.

FINDING AUDREY HEPBURN
IN
THE AUDREY HEPBURN ESTATE

Like many of you, I have long been fascinated by Audrey Hepburn. There's just something about her. Her elegance, her grace, her style.

But there was so much more than that to this incredible woman. She was, and still is, an icon. She is one of only seventeen performers, as of August 2022, to have earned an EGOT, winning all four major American entertainment awards (Emmy, Grammy, Oscar, and Tony). She was the fifth person to do it, and the first to have done it posthumously.

Audrey Hepburn was also a humanitarian. The tireless work she did for UNICEF still has an impact on the world today. She testified before Congress on behalf of UNICEF and was awarded with the highest honor a US civilian can receive: the Presidential Medal of Freedom.

This novel was heavily influenced by the film *Sabrina*, in which Audrey Hepburn played the titular role, but I also took inspiration from her life and her other films. I hope you will enjoy this list of Easter Eggs that appear in the text.

Chapter 1

Our protagonist's name, Emma, is a nod to the name that Audrey Hepburn used during World War II.

As detailed in my Author's Note, Audrey lived under German occupation of the Netherlands for five years.

Ella didn't want her daughter to be known by the name Audrey during this time, fearing it was too British-sounding. They doctored Ella's own papers, changing the name from Ella to Edda.

Audrey Hepburn also has a granddaughter named Emma.

Chapter 2

The death of Emma's father is a nod to Audrey Hepburn's relationship with her own father. Audrey's father left their family, without explanation, when Audrey was only six years old, leaving an indelible mark on her life.

Fleur makes freshly baked treats for Emma and her father each afternoon. This mention of baked goods was inspired by the filming of *Breakfast at Tiffany's*. In the iconic opening scene, Audrey's character, Holly Golightly, comes out of a cab with a cup of coffee and a breakfast pastry. Audrey famously hated eating the Danish pastry and asked to substitute an ice cream cone instead, but director Blake Edwards would not allow it.

Fleur and Emma's father tell stories of eating bread made of tulip bulbs. During the winter of 1944 to 1945, known as the Hunger Winter, Audrey and her family survived on bread made from tulip bulbs.

The Japanese maple is meant to invoke images of the tree that Audrey Hepburn's character in *Sabrina* climbs to watch the Larrabee parties from afar.

Leo hails from Italy, like Audrey's second husband, Andrea Dotti. While married to Dotti, she lived in Rome as a typical Italian housewife. She said: "I am a Roman housewife, just what I wanted to be."

The bikes that the kids constantly ride are a reference to a favorite Audrey Hepburn film, *Roman Holiday*. Who could forget Audrey riding around Rome on a scooter with Gregory Peck behind her?! Audrey won her first Oscar for her performance, her first starring film role. Peck famously insisted that Audrey get double billing on the film (and not the sole billing dictated by his contract), even though he was an established star and she was an unknown.

(Fans of my seventh novel, *The Liz Taylor Ring*: before William Wyler cast Audrey Hepburn in *Roman Holiday*, Frank Capra tried to make the film at Paramount with Elizabeth Taylor and Cary Grant.)

Audrey herself loved bicycles. As a child, she rode bikes during the war to help the Dutch Resistance. As she grew older, she continued riding bikes. One of the most famous stills from *Sabrina* features her perched on a bicycle. And in the December 1953 nine-page photo spread about Audrey in *Life* magazine, there's a gleeful photograph of her riding from the makeup department to the set, playfully posing with her legs akimbo.

Chapter 3

Emma and Leo talk about the idea of home. Home was so incredibly important to Audrey Hepburn. In his book, *Audrey at Home*, her son, Luca Dotti, recalls his mother saying: "All my life, what I wanted to earn money for was to have a house of my own. I dreamed of having a house in the country with a garden and fruit trees."

When Luca got his first apartment, she told him: "You will never forget this moment."

Audrey rented a small apartment on Wilshire Boulevard for $120 a month when she was in Los Angeles shooting *Sabrina*.

Chapter 6

When Emma finds out that her mother has forbidden her to date Henry, this is inspired by the fact that Audrey's mother strongly objected to both of her husbands, Mel Ferrer and Andrea Dotti. (Though she was said to have approved of Robbie Wolders, Audrey's companion later in life.)

Emma and Leo discover Nazi memorabilia in a hidden closet at the house. This was inspired by Audrey Hepburn's life during Nazi occupation of Holland, as detailed in my Author's Note.

Chapter 7

Emma and Leo research to find out whether Mr. van der Wraak was a Nazi. As detailed in my Author's Note, Audrey Hepburn was born in the same year as Anne Frank, and felt a strong connection to her.

Chapter 9

Emma is a chef. This is a nod to the importance of food in Audrey Hepburn's life. During World War II, Audrey suffered from severe malnutrition, which affected her through her entire life. Later in life, she stated that she worked with UNICEF because she felt so grateful for receiving international aid after the war.

Chapter 10

Leo refers to Felix as a Nazi. While filming *Sabrina*, anytime Humphrey Bogart got angry at director Billy Wilder, he'd call him "Nazi son of a bitch" or "Kraut bastard." These insults were in especially bad taste, since Billy Wilder was Jewish and his mother was murdered at Auschwitz.

Humphrey Bogart was extremely unhappy on the *Sabrina* set, and it cast a pall over the entire shooting experience. For starters, he did not even want to be in the film. He knew that Cary Grant had been offered the role first but turned it down. (Some say this was due to the age difference between him and Audrey Hepburn—Cary Grant was twenty-five years older than Audrey. Humphrey Bogart was four years older than that—but others say that Grant turned it down because he didn't want to carry an umbrella in the film. If anyone knows why carrying an umbrella on-screen is undesirable, please call me immediately.)

Humphrey Bogart was also upset because he'd wanted his wife, Lauren Bacall, to be cast as Sabrina. On set, he was annoyed that Audrey Hepburn kept flubbing her lines, and he felt that he was miscast as Linus Larrabee. Oh, and he was angry that everyone would meet up for drinks in William Holden's trailer and exclude him. Bogie's constant bad attitude made for a miserable shooting experience for everyone involved in the film.

Chapter 11

When Emma and Leo put on masks, this was inspired by a favorite scene from *Breakfast at Tiffany's*. Holly Golightly (Audrey Hepburn) and Paul Varjack (George Peppard) spend the day together, and steal masks from the Five and Dime. They wear the masks out into the street.

Chapter 12

The van der Wraaks throw a party to raise money for the ballet. Audrey studied ballet as a child, and dance remained an important part of her life, even though the malnutrition she suffered during the war kept her from a professional dance career.

Emma wears a strapless white organza dress with intricate black floral embroidery to the benefit. This is meant to invoke the Givenchy dress Audrey wears in *Sabrina*, when she attends the Larrabee party after her return from Paris. Edith Head famously won an Oscar for the wardrobe she created for *Sabrina*. However, Head did not thank Givenchy in her speech, even though he created this gown, along with many of the other iconic looks from the film.

The white organza gown was almost given to Goodwill when it was discovered in a long-forgotten trunk that belonged to Debbie Reynolds and Carrie Fisher. (Note to self: start shopping at Goodwill more often.)

Chapter 13

Emma caters a wedding at Oheka Castle. Now, the mention of a castle may conjure images of Princess Ann from *Roman Holiday*, but Audrey Hepburn herself was titled. Her mother was a baroness, and when she married Andrea Dotti, Audrey became a countess.

Her father, Joseph Ruston, believed that he was a descendant of James Hepburn, third husband of Mary, Queen of Scots. He later changed his name to Hepburn-Ruston, so as to sound more aristocratic.

Chapter 14

When Emma and Henry hook up secretly, this was inspired by the affair Audrey Hepburn had with William Holden during the filming of *Sabrina*. Audrey fell madly in love with Bill, but the relationship ultimately did not work out. For starters, he was married to another woman. But when Audrey discovered that he'd had a vasectomy, she was devastated. Having a family was all she'd ever wanted in life. They broke up, but would reunite years later for *Paris When It Sizzles*. Holden is said to have tried to woo Audrey once again (even though he was dating one of her best friends at the time), though this time he was unsuccessful.

(Fans of my sixth novel, *The Grace Kelly Dress*: Guess which other Hollywood starlet had an affair with William Holden? That's right—our girl, Grace. That Bill really got around!)

Chapter 15

When Emma takes Henry to a fancy French restaurant, we can't help but think of Audrey's titular role in *Sabrina*, and her time at the culinary school in Paris.

Chapter 18

Henry picks Emma up in a green convertible. This is meant to invoke David Larrabee's Nash Healey Spider, and the scene where he picks Sabrina up from the Glen Cove train station, unaware of who she really is (though David didn't get out of the car in that scene, that cad).

When Henry takes her to the food truck rally, Emma is embarrassed. This was inspired by the filming of *My Fair Lady*. Audrey Hepburn took singing lessons to prepare for the film, but later had her songs dubbed by Marni Nixon. It was especially embarrassing, since many thought Audrey didn't deserve the role, reasoning that Julie Andrews, who originated the role on Broadway, should have been cast instead. The humiliation continued at the Oscars, when Audrey wasn't even nominated for Best Actress. Julie Andrews then won for her work in *Mary Poppins*, the final insult.

Chapter 19

When Emma and Leo choose the picnic baskets for his event, I was inspired by the flirty picnic scene in Audrey's film *Love in the Afternoon*.

Chapter 21

When it starts to rain, this is meant to invoke one of my favorite scenes in *Sabrina*, where Sabrina explains to Linus what he should do on his first day in Paris: get himself some rain, because that's when Paris smells its sweetest. (And yes, I know. This scene takes place in New York City, but is there anything more romantic than a kiss in the rain?!)

Chapter 22

Leo tries to ask Emma to the prom, but she wants to go with Henry. Truman Capote did not want Audrey for the lead role in *Breakfast at Tiffany's*. Instead, he wanted Marilyn Monroe to play Holly Golightly.

Chapter 23

The museum fundraiser takes place in a garden. Nature and gardens, in particular, had a special place in Audrey's heart. She won an Emmy for her PBS series *Gardens of the World with Audrey Hepburn*. It was her last screen appearance before her death, and winning an Emmy made her a posthumous EGOT winner (Emmy for *Gardens of the World with Audrey Hepburn*; Grammy for *Audrey Hepburn's Enchanted Tales*; Oscar for *Roman Holiday*; Tony for *Ondine*).

When Leo punches Henry, we can't help but think of the scenes in *Sabrina* when the brothers fight: first, David punches Linus in the face for scheming to be with Sabrina, and then later, Linus punches David in the face for besmirching Sabrina.

Chapter 25

When Emma discovers who Stella really is, this was inspired by my favorite Audrey Hepburn film, *Charade*. (Finally! A

Cary Grant–Audrey Hepburn film, age difference be damned!) I love the cat-and-mouse aspect of that film, as well as the fact that you never quite know who is good and who is bad right until the very end.

Chapter 27

Emma oversleeps. One of the most interesting tidbits I learned about Audrey was that she always woke up for work early because she had a sort of impostor syndrome. She feared that those who had hired her would realize their mistake and send her home. It only made her work harder.

Chapter 28

When Emma says that the air was tinged with glitter, I was thinking of Audrey's performance on Broadway in *Ondine*. She was unhappy with the wig she had to wear for her role as the water sprite, so she sprinkled gold dust onto her own dark hair and went onstage. The glitter caught the light beautifully, and as she moved, it flew off behind her, creating in a magical effect. Audrey Hepburn would win a Tony for her role.

When Emma tells Leo that she's been in love with Henry for her whole life, this is meant to echo Audrey Hepburn, when her character in *Sabrina* says of David Larrabee: "I've been in love with him all my life."

Chapter 31

When Emma wears the tea-length black dress with ties on the shoulders, this is an homage to the Givenchy black gown Audrey Hepburn, as Sabrina, wears on her pre-theater date at The Colony in the film. Audrey chose that particular dress by Givenchy because she wanted something to hide her collarbone. The dress later became known as "the Sabrina dress," and though it was Givenchy's original design, his name did not appear in the credits of the film (or get mentioned in Edith Head's Oscars speech!).

Chapter 32

When Leo comes to find Emma at the indoor tennis court, it is an homage to the famous scene from *Sabrina*, where Humphrey Bogart's Linus comes to see Audrey Hepburn's Sabrina, even though she is expecting his brother, William Holden's David.

Chapter 39

Emma says "It's too much" when she learns the truth about why Rolling Hill was called the Audrey Hepburn Estate. When Audrey Hepburn accepted the Oscar for *Roman Holiday* at the 1954 Academy Awards, this was the first line of her speech.

Henry tells the story of his grandfather witnessing the brutal murder of his friend's father. On August 15, 1942, Audrey's uncle, Otto Ernst Gelder, Count van Limburg Stirum, was one of six people shot by German soldiers in a forest. These murders were referenced in Anne Frank's diary, since it was the first execution of civilians motivated solely by retaliation against Dutch people who were guilty of resisting the Nazis.

Chapter 44

Leo goes to Chicago for college. In 1990, Mayor Richard Daley presented Audrey with the key to the city. This coincided with her visit to Orchestra Hall, where she'd be headlining "A Concert for Life," her project where she narrated passages of *The Diary of a Young Girl* accompanied by the New World Symphony.

Chapter 45

Kendall's girlfriend Anka's bar is inside a subway station. I was again inspired by one of my favorite Audrey Hepburn films, *Charade*, and the exciting chase sequence that takes place in the Paris Metro.

Chapter 46

Blanca makes her famous brownies for Emma and Samantha. Chocolate was one of Audrey's favorite foods, and she made sure to eat it nearly every day. When soldiers came to liberate the Netherlands at the end of the war, one gave her seven chocolate bars, which she immediately devoured.

Chapter 48

When Emma mentions that Mila wants to move to Paris, it brings to mind the quote that is often attributed to Audrey Hepburn: "Paris is always a good idea." But here's the thing: Audrey never said that. I dug deeper, and people attributed it to her character in *Sabrina*. But guess what? Sabrina doesn't say it, either. It was only on the viewing of the 1995 *Sabrina* remake that I heard the line. Julia Ormond, as Sabrina, says it toward the end of the movie. (But honestly, Paris really *is* always a good idea, so I still love the quote!)

Chapter 51

Emma stands up quickly, bringing the silver tray crashing to the ground. The first time Audrey Hepburn met Cary Grant, she was so nervous at dinner that she accidentally spilled red wine all over his cream suit. (!!)

Chapter 59

Upon learning the truth about her father, Emma feels compelled to give back. Audrey, too, felt it necessary to give back. Holland was liberated on the day of Audrey's sixteenth birthday, May 4, 1945. She never forgot the UNRRA (the United Nations Relief and Rehabilitation Administration, whose work is now continued by UNICEF, the United Nations International Children's Emergency Fund), which provided desperately needed food and medical relief. Audrey felt they had saved her life.

She became a UNICEF Goodwill Ambassador in 1988. She worked tirelessly for UNICEF, traveling extensively, making over fifty trips, and even testifying before the US Congress. In 1992, she received the Presidential Medal of Freedom for her work.

Audrey's charitable legacy continues, with her granddaughter Emma taking the reins.

ADDITIONAL READING

On Audrey Hepburn

Books

Audrey and Bill: A Romantic Biography of Audrey Hepburn and William Holden by Edward Z. Epstein

Audrey at Home by Luca Dotti

Audrey Hepburn by Barry Paris

Audrey Hepburn, An Elegant Spirit by Sean Hepburn Ferrer

Audrey: Her Real Story by Alexander Walker

Charmed by Audrey: Life on the Set of Sabrina by Mark Shaw

Dutch Girl: Audrey Hepburn and World War II by Robert Matzen, foreword by Luca Dotti

Enchantment: The Life of Audrey Hepburn by Donald Spoto

On Sunset Boulevard: The Life and Times of Billy Wilder by Ed Sikov

The Audrey Hepburn Treasures by Ellen Erwin and Jessica Z. Diamond, foreword by Sean Ferrer

Films

Audrey

Audrey Hepburn Magical

Audrey Hepburn: In the Movies

Audrey: More than an Icon

Sabrina Documentary, Parts One and Two

The Audrey Hepburn Story

The Hollywood Collection: Audrey Hepburn: Remembered

The Magic of Audrey Hepburn, Behind the Reel Life

On Nazis And Nazi Hunters

Books

Citizen 865 by Debbie Cenziper

The Nazis Next Door by Eric Lichtblau

ACKNOWLEDGMENTS

Thank you to my incredible agent, Jess Regel, founder of Helm Literary, my biggest cheerleader and advocate.

Thank you to my wonderful editor, Melanie Fried, and her fabulous team at Graydon House Books. They say the third time is the charm, so here's to lucky number three!

Thank you to the awesome HarperCollins sales team. Thank you to my phenomenal publicity and marketing team: Heather Connor, Leah Morse, Diane Lavoie, Pamela Osti, and Randy Chan. Thank you to my amazing copy editor, Jennifer Stimson. Special thanks go to Loriana Sacilotto, Margaret Marbury, Susan Swinwood, Amy Jones, and Heather Foy. Thank you to Lindsey Reeder, Brianna Wodabek, Hodan Ismail, and Ciara Loader for the top-notch digital media support. And for that cover art that is truly spectacular, thank you to Quinn Banting.

Thank you to Kyra Schuster, Curator, The David M. Rubenstein National Institute for Holocaust Documentation at the United States Holocaust Memorial Museum. All mistakes are my own.

Thank you to Rich Green and the incredible team at The Gotham Group.

Thank you to my dear friends who have been reading first drafts of my work since forever: Shawn Morris, Danielle Schmelkin, and JP Habib. Thank you to Jillian Cantor for the reads, the advice, and the friendship.

Book people are the best people. A big giant thank you to: Amy Impellizzeri, Andrea Peskind Katz, Annissa Armstrong, Ashley Hasty, Ashley Spivey, Carilyn Platt, Carol Hoenig, Caroline Leavitt, Cindy Burnett, Courtney Marzilli, Dan Bubbeo, Emily Giffin, Emily Liebert, Eve Rodsky, Gisselle Diaz, Heather Cocks, Heather Gudenkauf, Holly Palker, Jackie Ranaldo, Jamie Rosenblit, Jane Green, Jenna Blum, Jessica Morgan, Jordan Moblo, Kate Olson, Kerri Maher, Kimberly Belle, Kirsten Baritz, Kristin Harmel, Kristy Barrett, Kristy Woodson Harvey, Lauren Margolin, Linda Zagon, Lisa Barr, Lisa Steinke, Liz Fenton, Marion Winik, Mary Kay Andrews, Meg Walker, Pam Jenoff, Patti Callahan Henry, Rachel McRady, Renee Weingarten, Robin Kall, Sabienna Bowman, Ston Tantraporn, Suzy Leopold, Wade Rouse, and Zibby Owens.

When I was a little girl, my mom and dad would take me to bookstores and let me buy all the books I wanted. Thank you for raising me to be a reader.

Thank you to Ben and Davey. You challenge me, you inspire me, and you fill my life with love.

Thank you to my husband, Doug. You are the person I always want to come home to.

THE
AUDREY
HEPBURN
ESTATE

BRENDA JANOWITZ

Reader's Guide

GRAYDON
HOUSE

1. Emma returns to Rolling Hill because it's about to be torn down. Do you have a connection to the house you grew up in? How would you feel if it were to be demolished?

2. How do you feel about the place you grew up? Do you ever go back to visit?

3. Which love interest did you prefer most for Emma? Do you think she made the right choice in the end?

4. Emma describes her work friends as family. Which is more important—friends or family? Do you believe that friends can become family?

5. Discuss the role of food in Emma's story. How is food a source of healing and connection in your own life?

6. Have you ever discovered a family secret? How did it change your perception of your family? Did it change how you felt about yourself?

7. Henry tells Emma that her family secret is the thing he's had to keep hidden his whole life. Are you good at keeping

secrets? Have you ever held a secret for someone else? Is there ever a responsibility to tell someone else's secret? Should parents keep secrets from their children?

8. Have you seen the movie *Sabrina*? Discuss how the author updated that movie plot in *The Audrey Hepburn Estate*. What is your favorite Audrey Hepburn film?

9. What did you learn about Audrey Hepburn from reading this novel? Has your opinion of her changed?

10. Leo tells Emma, "Home isn't a place. A house is a physical space, but a home? Home is the people you want to be with, the ones you come back to at the end of a long day. It's the life you create for yourself, not an actual place." Do you agree with this? What is your definition of *home*?